S0-BEV-116

JUPITER

Edited by Carol and Frederik Pohl

Introduction by Isaac Asimov

BALLANTINE BOOKS • NEW YORK

BALLANTINE BOOKS, INC.
201 East 50th Street, New York, N.Y. 10022

Contents

JUPITER THE GIANT
Introduction

♃

When I was a little boy I read astronomy books. I also read science fiction. Astronomy books told me a few facts about Jupiter, but not many of the intimate details. Few intimate details were known in the prehistoric times in which I was a boy. Besides, I preferred what the science-fiction tales said concerning Jupiter, and in many of them Jupiter was an inhabited world not terribly different from Earth, except that it might be the haunt of space pirates or intelligent insects.

The truth dawned on me not through more careful reading of more up-to-date astronomy books, but through that remarkable phenomenon, John W. Campbell, Jr. Even before he became an editor and single-handedly turned science fiction into a mature and rational branch of literature, he was educating us with a series of astronomical articles for *Astounding Stories*. These taught me, for the first time, that science could be as fascinating as science fiction.

The best article in the series was "Other Eyes Watching" in the February 1937 issue. It was about Jupiter and never again did I think of Jupiter as anything but what it more or less was.

In fact, the second story I wrote (in 1938) dealt with Jupiter's satellite system, and in writing it I used some of the views I had read in Campbell's article a year and a half earlier. I sold that second story to none other than Fred Pohl, the male half of the editorial team of this anthology. He published it under the title of "The Callistan Menace" in the April 1940 issue of *Astonishing Stories*.

I doubt that any self-respecting science-fiction writer would nowadays write any story about Jupiter that didn't take into account what we know (or think we know) about the planet—as this anthology demonstrates. Naturally, then, we are all fascinated by the new knowledge that the space age may be on the point of bringing us.

As I write this, the space-probe Pioneer 11 has taken off from Cape Kennedy in a long-drawn-out flash of blazing orange light. Beyond the atmosphere it reached a speed of nine miles a second, and it passed the Moon after eleven hours of flight. Some time in February 1975, it will pass near Jupiter.

But it will be only the second probe to pass that planet. Ahead of it is Pioneer 10, which took off on March 2, 1972, and has passed safely through the asteroid belt (as I write this) and is still transmitting. It will reach Jupiter on December 3, 1973 (about the time this book is published), and will pass only 85,000 miles from the planet's surface—still transmitting, if all goes well.

Whipping about the giant planet, Pioneer 10 will gain enough speed to break out of the Sun's gravitational grip and go skittering past the orbits of all the outer planets. In 1984 it will pass beyond Pluto, and will continue farther still.

Pioneer 10 will be the first man-made object ever to leave the solar system. It will be moving in the direction of the star Aldebaran and will reach the neighborhood of that star (or the neighborhood where it now is) in about 1,700,000 years.

On Pioneer 10 is a message from Earth, etched into

a 6-by-9-inch gold-covered aluminum slab. It is not an ordinary message, but a mixture of figures and symbols that could be properly interpreted only by sophisticated astronomers of the type we would expect in any society advanced enough to detect the small probe in space and to pluck it out of emptiness— millions of years from now, if ever.

But Pioneer 10 (and Pioneer 11, too if it follows in the tracks of the earlier probe) will have ceased transmitting long before it leaves the solar system. What will happen to it after it passes Jupiter we will never know. But that doesn't matter. All we ask of it is to tell us something of the environment it encounters as it speeds by Jupiter and its twelve satellites.

How strong are the radiation belts around Jupiter? What is the strength of its magnetic field? How many particles does it encounter? How strong are the pulls of Jupiter's satellites? What is the appearance of the satellites' surfaces? What is the appearance of Jupiter's cloud cover at close range? Its colors? Its movement? Its chemistry? Its temperature?

Question mark, question mark, question mark . . .

And why do we want to know?

Because Jupiter is different, enormously different, and we don't know what to make of it.

We live on a planet, and we know its characteristics. There are other planets in the solar system that are essentially like Earth—different in detail, but Earth-like overall. And since we know about the Earth, we automatically know something about them.

We have landed on our sister-world, the Moon. It is smaller than Earth and has neither air nor water, but its soil and rocks are not very different from those of Earth. And the scenery of the Moon could be similar to that in some areas of the Earth if you allow for the lack of air and water.

We have seen Mars close up, and it is different in

detail from the Moon and Earth, but there is a broad similarity, too. We have touched the surface of Venus with several Soviet probes and with radar waves, and it, too, is rough and hard and mountainous.

And Mercury, no doubt, and the asteroids, and the satellites of the various planets— All different in detail, but all members of the same species. That Earth is sufficiently different to support life is the result of the accident that it is the largest of all these bodies and is at a distance from the Sun that allows water to remain liquid.

Among all the bodies circling the Sun, there are only four that do not belong to Earth's species, but to a different species altogether. These four are Jupiter, Saturn, Uranus, and Neptune, and the reason they are of a different species is that they are much larger than Earth—so much larger that they form in a different way and end with a different composition and nature.

Of them all, Jupiter is the largest and therefore the most extreme in its differences. It is the one closest to the Sun, so that it receives more energy from solar radiation and is more violently stormy than the rest, and also the one closest to *us,* so that it is most easily examined.

To study this other species of planet, we must study Jupiter.

Of course, though it is closest to us of any of its kind, it is still not very close. At its closest, Jupiter is nearly 400,000,000 miles from us—sixteen hundred times as far away as the Moon, four times as far away as the Sun. Is it any wonder the probes take nearly two years to reach it?

And it really is a giant.

It has a diameter a little over eleven times that of the Earth. In other words, if you place eleven bodies like the Earth side by side, they won't quite stretch across the width of Jupiter. That's the usual way of comparing planetary sizes, but it doesn't begin to show the difference.

Jupiter's surface area is 125 times that of the Earth. If you imagine the surface of the Earth peeled off and flattened out and pasted on the surface of Jupiter, it would cover about half as much of that planet as the United States does of the Earth.

And if you consider volumes, Jupiter is fourteen hundred times as large as the Earth.

Of course, Jupiter isn't as well packed as Earth is. Although it has fourteen hundred times as much room as Earth has in which to pack away matter, it has only 318 times the mass of Earth. That's enough, to be sure, since it means that Earth is to Jupiter as your weight is to that of two African elephants, of the largest size, put together.

Jupiter's mass is enough to hold a far-flung system of satellites to itself. One of those satellites, Jupiter-VIII, can recede to a distance of 20 million miles from Jupiter—eighty times as far as the Moon is from Earth—without breaking away. Four of the satellites are Moon-sized or larger. The largest, Ganymede, is larger than the planet Mercury.

The nearest of the four large satellites, Io, is exactly as far from the center of Jupiter as the Moon is from the center of Earth (and it is almost exactly the size of the Moon, too). Earth's relatively feeble gravity, however, can only drive the Moon into a motion of five-eighths of a mile per second, so that it does not complete its circle about the Earth for over twenty-seven days. Io, driven by Jupiter's colossal gravity, moves at nearly eleven miles per second and circles Jupiter in less than two days.

Everything about Jupiter is big and lavish.

Well, not everything. Its density is small because, as aforesaid, there is only three hundred times Earth's mass spread out through fourteen hundred times Earth's volume. Jupiter's density is only one-quarter that of Earth.

That alone should tell us that Jupiter does not belong to the same species as Earth. If Jupiter had anything like the chemical composition of Earth, its gigantic gravitational field would pull it together so as to make it considerably denser than Earth.

To be less dense than Earth despite the pull of its gravity, Jupiter must be made up largely of materials less dense than those that make up Earth, materials common enough in the Universe to be found in quantities sufficient to build a giant planet.

This leaves us with one possibility only—hydrogen, together with a few minor impurities such as helium, neon, carbon, nitrogen, and oxygen. Helium and neon don't react with any other substances but exist only as single, standoffish atoms. Anything else must combine with the overwhelming quantities of hydrogen. Carbon, nitrogen, and oxygen must exist as methane (CH_4), ammonia (NH_3), and water (H_2O).

And that's what we find. In the last half century, astronomers have slowly gathered evidence to show that Jupiter's atmosphere is largely hydrogen, with admixtures of helium and probably neon, plus some methane and ammonia. (Water is undoubtedly present also, but is frozen solid somewhere below.)

Yet it is an odd atmosphere, filled with cloud banks through which we cannot see. And the clouds have colors, even though none of the constituents we can detect are colored.

There is a great elliptical spot in Jupiter's atmosphere that never goes away. Its color darkens and fades; and since it seems reddish when it is dark, it is called the Great Red Spot. The Great Red Spot is about thirty thousand miles wide in its long diameter, eight thousand miles wide in the other, and has a surface area just about equal to that of the Earth.

Nor is it fixed to the surface. It doesn't move north or south, but it does move east or west. It sometimes gains or loses a whole lap on the rest of the planet.

Well, what is the Great Red Spot? Why is it red? Why does the color grow darker and lighter? Why does it move about relative to other parts of the planet? Why does it move east and west but not north and south?

No one knows.

For that matter, why are there colors in the rest of the atmosphere? Why do the colors concentrate in certain dark bands with lighter areas between? What are the various light spots that form, and why do they come and go whereas the Great Red Spot is apparently permanent?

No one knows.

For that matter, how deep is the atmosphere of Jupiter? Does its composition remain the same as one penetrates deeper? If it changes, how does it change? Is there a solid surface under the atmosphere? If so, how far under, and what is it made of? What is it like at Jupiter's core?

And how strong are the winds? What kind of storms are there? Is there lightning? What is the temperature in the depths of the atmosphere? Does the atmosphere trap enough solar radiation to make the temperature fairly mild in the depths? Warm enough to allow an ocean of water and ammonia? And if so, can life develop in such an ocean?

No one knows.

Jupiter has an enormous magnetic field. How does that affect the space around it? How did it originate? Why do the radio waves issue in bursts that seem to have a timing related to the position of Io in its orbit?

No one knows.

And no one will ever know if all our data is derived

only from our knowledge of Earth, Moon, Mars, and other members of *our* species of world.

Jupiter is of a different species and probably one that is quite common in the Universe. Delicate wobblings of six small nearby stars seem to be the result of an asymmetric center of gravity imposed on those stars by planets circling them that are as large or even larger than Jupiter. Perhaps any star with a planetary system has one or more Jupiters. Perhaps there are more Jupiters than Earths in the Universe.

Of course, as in almost everything else that calls for speculation, science-fiction writers have been there first. The strange and utterly alien world of Jupiter is a challenge to be met and writers willing to respond are not lacking. The challenge has been met in a variety of ways and in this book a broad sampling is spread out for your delectation.

And if you should want to compare the pictures you see drawn here with what is actually known of Jupiter, I refer you (if I may be permitted an unabashed plug) to my book *Jupiter, the Largest Planet,* published by Lothrop in 1973.

And let me add a personal note about the man-and-wife team (or woman-and-husband, in view of the times) that is editing this anthology. I have known and loved Fred and Carol Pohl for many years and I must tell you that, on the average, they are an extraordinarily good-looking couple. This is true despite the fact that Fred himself drags down that average about two miles.

—ISAAC ASIMOV

JUPITER AT LAST
Preface

♃

In December, 1972, we were part of a strange and delightful odyssey aboard the *S.S. Statendam,* cruising off the shores of Florida to watch the Apollo 17 launch, going on to visit the sin spots of the (how can they say it?) Virgin Islands and the big radio telescope in Puerto Rico. Among the crew were Carl Sagan and his pretty artist-wife Linda. They were only two of a marvelous ship's company—Ted Sturgeon, Bob Heinlein, Marvin Minsky the robot man, Hugh Downs the TV man, Norman Mailer the man's man, and so many others that to list them would be plain name-dropping. But the Sagans were a very special two. Carl is a remarkable person, sort of a volunteering encyclopedia with charm. (I had given a paper on population limits to the nonstop scientific symposium that was part of the cruise's entertainment, and in it quoted some energy-consumption estimates. Carl called me on them after I was through. With some disdain I quoted my source, and Carl said, "I know, he got those figures from me and didn't quite understand them.") In a ship's company that included at least a dozen certifiable geniuses, Carl Sagan was the one to whom difficult questions were referred for final decision.

Carl and Linda had been part of one of the most charming scientific projects I know of: the engraving, on the outer shell of the Pioneer 10 spacecraft, of a message designed to be read and understood by alien creatures native to the planet of some other sun. Pioneer 10 was then only well launched, had not yet reached even the orbit of Mars; it was planned to visit the Jupiter system, take pictures and send back reports, and then go on forever, out of the solar system entirely. In a few million years it may approach another star, or be intercepted en route by some alien interstellar spaceship. If it is, and if the beings who collect it are half as bright as space-faring creatures should be, they will read a message from Earth, put there by Carl and Linda Sagan.

However, the central wonder of Pioneer 10 to me was that, at last, some human eye would get a look at the planet Jupiter and its moons. Maybe only through a TV camera, and even that picture run through a computer to make it make sense—but still, a look from near at hand.

Jupiter was always the great puzzle of the solar system in the science-fiction magazines that formed such a large part of my youthful reading. In those days we had one great hope. We knew one planet very well—the Earth—and as the Earth had breathable air and drinkable lakes and survivable climate ranges, we hoped that all the other planets, or anyway some of them, would be obligingly similar.

Now we know more, and most of what we know about the living conditions elsewhere in our solar system is disappointing: too cold, too hot, too airless, too poisonous, whatever. The early sf writers, who had a tendency to write about Jupiter as though it were a fatter Earth, seem to have been so badly wrong that their stories don't make sense any more.

But there were also a lot of stories, written later and more carefully constructed in line with better astronomical observations.

We wondered how well those other stories would square with what Pioneer 10 would find . . . and so we came off the cruise and began to plunge into blizzards of old magazines. And this book is the result. Betty Ballantine gave us the go-ahead, the authors gave us their blessing—and we give you the book.

To make it complete, we insisted on an introduction from Isaac Asimov (another shipmate on that memorable cruise). You have already read it, no doubt. You may wonder why I, the male member of this team, should encourage an introduction from a person who slanders my good looks. I can explain that—it is simply for old friendship's sake. Isaac and I go back a long way —to when we were both seventeen or so, and the world was new. That is well over a third of a century ago, and we have been friends all that time. In that time, I think, we have gained a good deal in wisdom, charm, maturity, and personality . . . on the average, of course.

FREDERIK POHL
CAROL POHL

Red Bank, April 1973

JUPITER

BRIDGE
James Blish

24

James Blish lives with his artist wife in a handsome old
house near Oxford, England, where he spends his time
writing first-class science fiction. "Bridge" was one of the
first scientifically accurate sf stories ever written about the
"gas giants"—the planets Jupiter, Saturn, Uranus, and
Neptune—and as a matter of fact Blish may have been
responsible for bringing that term into the language of
astronomy; he was the first to use it, in a series of
scientific articles for an sf magazine, a quarter of a
century or so ago.

I

A screeching tornado was rocking the Bridge when
the alarm sounded; it was making the whole structure
shudder and sway. This was normal and Robert Helmuth barely noticed it. There was always a tornado
shaking the Bridge. The whole planet was enswathed
in tornadoes, and worse.

The scanner on the foreman's board had given 114
as the sector of the trouble. That was at the northwest-
ern end of the Bridge, where it broke off, leaving nothing but the raging clouds of ammonia crystals and
methane, and a sheer drop thirty miles to the invisible
surface. There were no ultraphone "eyes" at that end
which gave a general view of the area—in so far as any

1

general view was possible—because both ends of the Bridge were incomplete.

With a sigh Helmuth put the beetle into motion. The little car, as flat-bottomed and thin through as a bedbug, got slowly under way on ball-bearing races, guided and held firmly to the surface of the Bridge by ten close-set flanged rails. Even so, the hydrogen gales made a terrific siren-like shrieking between the edge of the vehicle and the deck, and the impact of the falling drops of ammonia upon the curved roof was as heavy and deafening as a rain of cannon balls. As a matter of fact, they weighed almost as much as cannon balls here, though they were not much bigger than ordinary raindrops. Every so often, too, there was a blast, accompanied by a dull orange glare, which made the car, the deck, and the Bridge itself buck savagely.

These blasts were below, however, on the surface. While they shook the structure of the Bridge heavily, they almost never interfered with its functioning, and could not, in the very nature of things, do Helmuth any harm.

Had any real damage ever been done, it would never have been repaired. There was no one on Jupiter to repair it.

The Bridge, actually, was building itself. Massive, alone, and lifeless, it grew in the black deeps of Jupiter.

The Bridge had been well-planned. From Helmuth's point of view almost nothing could be seen of it, for the beetle tracks ran down the center of the deck, and in the darkness and perpetual storm even ultrawave-assisted vision could not penetrate more than a few hundred yards at the most. The width of the Bridge was eleven miles; its height, thirty miles; its length, deliberately unspecified in the plans, fifty-four miles at the moment—a squat, colossal structure, built with engineering principles, methods, materials, and tools never touched before—

For the very good reason that they would have been impossible anywhere else. Most of the Bridge, for instance, was made of ice: a marvelous structural material under a pressure of a million atmospheres, at a temperature of −94°C. Under such conditions, the best structural steel is a friable, talc-like powder, and aluminum becomes a peculiar, transparent substance that splits at a tap.

Back home, Helmuth remembered, there had been talk of starting another Bridge on Saturn, and perhaps still later, on Uranus, too. But that had been politicians' talk. The Bridge was almost five thousand miles below the visible surface of Jupiter's atmosphere, and its mechanisms were just barely manageable. The bottom of Saturn's atmosphere had been sounded at sixteen thousand eight hundred and seventy-eight miles, and the temperature there was below −150°C. There even pressure-ice would be immovable, and could not be worked with anything except itself. And as for Uranus . . .

As far as Helmuth was concerned, Jupiter was quite bad enough.

The beetle crept within sight of the end of the Bridge and stopped automatically. Helmuth set the vehicle's eyes for highest penetration, and examined the nearby beams.

The great bars were as close-set as screening. They had to be, in order to support even their own weight, let alone the weight of the components of the Bridge. the whole webwork was flexing and fluctuating to the harpist-fingered gale, but it had been designed to do that. Helmuth could never help being alarmed by the movement, but habit assured him that he had nothing to fear from it.

He took the automatics out of the circuit and inched

the beetle forward manually. This was only Sector 113, and the Bridge's own Wheatstone-bridge scanning system—there was no electronic device anywhere on the Bridge, since it was impossible to maintain a vacuum on Jupiter—said that the trouble was in Sector 114. The boundary of Sector 114 was still fully fifty feet away.

It was a bad sign. Helmuth scratched nervously in his red beard. Evidently there was really cause for alarm—real alarm, not just the deep, grinding depression which he always felt while working on the Bridge. Any damage serious enough to halt the beetle a full sector short of the trouble area was bound to be major.

It might even turn out to be the disaster which he had felt lurking ahead of him ever since he had been made foreman of the Bridge—that disaster which the Bridge itself could not repair, sending man reeling home from Jupiter in defeat.

The secondaries cut in and the beetle stopped again. Grimly, Helmuth opened the switch and sent the beetle creeping across the invisible danger line. Almost at once, the car tilted just perceptibly to the left, and the screaming of the winds between its edges and the deck shot up the scale, sirening in and out of the soundless-dogwhistle range with an eeriness that set Helmuth's teeth on edge. The beetle itself fluttered and chattered like an alarm-clock hammer betweeen the surface of the deck and the flanges of the tracks.

Ahead there was still nothing to be seen but the horizontal driving of the clouds and the hail, roaring along the length of the Bridge, out of the blackness into the beetle's fanlights, and onward into blackness again towards the horizon no eye would ever see.

Thirty miles below, the fusillade of hydrogen explosions continued. Evidently something really wild was going on on the surface. Helmuth could not remember having heard so much activity in years.

There was a flat, esecially heavy crash, and a long line of fuming orange fire came pouring down the seething atmosphere into the depths, feathering horizontally like the mane of a Lipizzan horse, directly in front of Helmuth. Instinctively, he winced and drew back from the board, although that stream of flame actually was only a little less cold than the rest of the streaming gases, far too cold to injure the Bridge.

In the momentary glare, however, he saw something —an upward twisting of shadows, patterned but obviously unfinished, fluttering in silhouette against the hydrogen cataract's lurid light.

The end of the Bridge.

Wrecked.

Helmuth grunted involuntarily and backed the beetle away. The flare dimmed; the light poured down the sky and fell away into the raging sea below. The scanner clucked with satisfaction as the beetle recrossed the line into Zone 113.

He turned the body of the vehicle 180°, presenting its back to the dying torrent. There was nothing further that he could do at the moment on the Bridge. He scanned his control board—a ghost image of which was cast across the scene on the Bridge—for the blue button marked *Garage,* punched it savagely, and tore off his helmet.

Obediently, the Bridge vanished.

II

Dillon was looking at him.

"Well?" the civil engineer said. "What's the matter, Bob? Is it bad—?"

Helmuth did not reply for a moment. The abrupt transition from the storm-ravaged deck of the Bridge to the quiet, placid air of the control shack on Jupiter V was always a shock. He had never been able to anticipate it, let alone become accustomed to it; it was worse each time, not better.

He put the helmet down carefully in front of him and got up, moving carefully upon shaky legs; feeling implicit in his own body the enormous pressures and weights his guiding intelligence had just quitted. The fact that the gravity on the foreman's deck was as weak as that of most of the habitable asteroids only made the contrast greater, and his need for caution in walking more extreme.

He went to the big porthole and looked out. The unworn, tumbled, monotonous surface of airless Jupiter V looked almost homey after the perpetual holocaust of Jupiter itself. But there was an overpowering reminder of that holocaust—for through the thick quartz, the face of the giant planet stared at him, across only one hundred and twelve thousand and six hundred miles: a sphere-section occupying almost all of the sky except the near horizon. It was crawling with color, striped and blotched with the eternal, frigid, poisonous storming of its atmosphere, spotted with the deep planet-sized shadows of farther moons.

Somewhere down there, six thousand miles below the clouds that boiled in his face, was the Bridge. The Bridge was thirty miles high and eleven miles wide and fifty-four miles long—but it was only a sliver, an intricate and fragile arrangement of ice-crystals beneath the bulging, racing tornadoes.

On Earth, even in the West, the Bridge would have been the mightiest engineering achievement of all history, could the Earth have borne its weight at all. But on Jupiter, the Bridge was as precarious and perishable as a snowflake.

"Bob?" Dillon's voice asked. "You seem more upset than usual. Is it serious?" Helmuth turned. His superior's worn young face, lantern-jawed and crowned by black hair already beginning to grey at the temples, was alight both with love for the Bridge and the consuming ardor of the responsibility he had to bear. As always, it touched Helmuth, and reminded him that the implacable universe had, after all, provided one warm corner in which human beings might huddle together.

"Serious enough," he said, forming the words with difficulty against the frozen inarticulateness Jupiter forced upon him. "But not fatal, as far as I could see. There's a lot of hydrogen vulcanism on the surface, especially at the northwest end, and it looks like there must have been a big blast under the cliffs. I saw what looked like the last of a series of fireballs."

Dillon's face relaxed while Helmuth was talking, slowly, line by engraved line. "Oh. Just a flying chunk, then."

"I'm almost sure that's what it was. The cross-drafts are heavy now. The Spot and the STD are due to pass each other some time next week, aren't they? I haven't checked, but I can feel the difference in the storms."

"So the chunk got picked up and thrown through the end of the Bridge. A big piece?"

Helmuth shrugged. "That end is all twisted away to the left, and the deck is burst to flinders. The scaffolding is all gone, too, of course. A pretty big piece, all right, Charity—two miles through at a minimum."

Dillon sighed. He, too, went to the window, and looked out. Helmuth did not need to be a mind reader to know what he was looking at. Out there, across the stony waste of Jupiter V plus one hundred and twelve thousand and six hundred miles of space, the South Tropical Disturbance was streaming towards the great Red Spot, and would soon overtake it. When the whirling funnel of the STD—more than big enough to suck three Earths into deep-freeze—passed the planetary island of sodium-tainted ice which was the Red Spot, the Spot would follow it for a few thousand miles, at the same time rising closer to the surface of the atmosphere.

Then the Spot would sink again, drifting back towards the incredible jet of stress-fluid which kept it in being —a jet fed by no one knew what forces at Jupiter's hot, rocky, twenty-two-thousand-mile core, under sixteen thousand miles of eternal ice. During the entire passage, the storms all over Jupiter became especially violent; and the Bridge had been forced to locate in anything but the calmest spot on the planet, thanks to the uneven distribution of the few permanent landmasses.

Helmuth watched Dillon with a certain compassion, tempered with mild envy. Charity Dillon's unfortunate given name betrayed him as the son of a hangover, the only male child of a Witness family which dated back to the great Witness Revival of 2003. He was one of the hundreds of government-drafted experts who had planned the Bridge, and he was as obsessed by the Bridge as Helmuth was—but for different reasons.

Helmuth moved back to the port, dropping his hand gently upon Dillon's shoulder. Together they looked at the screaming straw yellows, brick reds, pinks, oranges, browns, even blues and greens that Jupiter threw across the ruined stone of its innermost satellite. On Jupiter V, even the shadows had color.

Dillon did not move. He said at last: "Are you pleased, Bob?"

"Pleased?" Helmuth said in astonishment. "No. It scares me white; you know that. I'm just glad that the whole Bridge didn't go."

"You're quite sure?" Dillon said quietly.

Helmuth took his hand from Dillon's shoulder and returned to his seat at the central desk. "You've no right to needle me for something I can't help," he said, his voice even lower than Dillon's. "I work on Jupiter four hours a day—not actually, because we can't keep a man alive for more than a split second down there—

but my eyes and my ears and my mind are there, on the Bridge, four hours a day. Jupiter is not a nice place. I don't like it. I won't pretend I do.

"Spending four hours a day in an environment like that over a period of years—well, the human mind instinctively tries to adapt, even to the unthinkable. Sometimes I wonder how I'll behave when I'm put back in Chicago again. Sometimes I can't remember anything about Chicago except vague generalities, sometimes I can't even believe there is such a place as Earth—how could there be, when the rest of the universe is like Jupiter, or worse?"

"I know," Dillon said. "I've tried several times to show you that isn't a very reasonable frame of mind."

"I know it isn't. But I can't help how I feel. No, I don't think the Bridge will last. It can't last; it's all wrong. But I don't *want* to see it go. I've just got sense enough to know that one of these days Jupiter is going to sweep it away."

He wiped an open palm across the control boards, snapping all the toggles "Off" with a sound like the fall of a double-handful of marbles on a pane of glass. "Like that, Charity! And I work four hours a day, every day, on the Bridge. One of these days, Jupiter is going to destroy the Bridge. It'll go flying away in little flinders into the storms. My mind will be there, supervising some puny job, and my mind will go flying away along with my mechanical eyes and ears—still trying to adapt to the unthinkable, tumbling away into the winds and the flames and the rains and the darkness and the pressure and the cold."

"Bob, you're deliberately running away with yourself. Cut it out. Cut it out, I say!"

Helmuth shrugged, putting a trembling hand on the edge of the board to steady himself. "All right. I'm all right, Charity. I'm here, aren't I? Right here on Jupiter V, in no danger, in no danger at all. The bridge is one hundred and twelve thousand and six hundred miles away from here. But when the day comes that the Bridge is swept away—

"Charity, sometimes I imagine you ferrying my body back to the cosy nook it came from, while my soul goes tumbling and tumbling through millions of cubic miles of poison. All right, Charity, I'll be good. I won't think about it out loud; but you can't expect me to forget it. It's on my mind; I can't help it, and you should know that."

"I do," Dillon said, with a kind of eagerness. "I do, Bob. I'm only trying to help, to make you see the problem as it is. The Bridge isn't really that awful, it isn't worth a single nightmare."

"Oh, it isn't the Bridge that makes me yell out when I'm sleeping," Helmuth said, smiling bitterly. "I'm not that ridden by it yet. It's while I'm awake that I'm afraid the Bridge will be swept away. What I sleep with is a fear of myself."

"That's a sane fear. You're as sane as any of us," Dillon insisted, fiercely solemn. "Look, Bob. The Bridge isn't a monster. It's a way we've developed for studying the behavior of materials under specific conditions of temperament, pressure, and gravity. Jupiter isn't Hell, either; it's a set of conditions. The Bridge is the laboratory we set up to work with those conditions."

"It isn't going anywhere. It's a bridge to no place."

"There aren't many *places* on Jupiter," Dillon said, missing Helmuth's meaning entirely. "We put the bridge on an island in the local sea because we needed solid ice we could sink the caissons in. Otherwise, it wouldn't have mattered where we put it. We could have floated it on the sea itself, if we hadn't wanted to fix it in order to measure storm velocities and such things."

"I know that," Helmuth said.

"But, Bob, you don't show any signs of understanding it. Why, for instance, should the Bridge *go* any place?

It isn't even, properly speaking, a bridge at all. We only call it that because we used some bridge engineering principles in building it. Actually, it's much more like a travelling crane—an extremely heavy-duty overhead rail line. It isn't going anywhere because it hasn't any place interesting to go, that's all. We're extending it to cover as much territory as possible, and to increase its stability, not to span the distance between places. There's no point to reproaching it because it doesn't span a real gap—between, say, Dover and Calais. It's a bridge to knowledge, and that's far more important. Why can't you see that?"

"I can see that; that's what I was talking about," Helmuth said, trying to control his impatience. "I have as much common sense as the average child. What I was trying to point out is that meeting colossalness with colossalness—out here—is a mug's game. It's a game Jupiter will always win, without the slightest effort. What if the engineers who built the Dover-Calais bridge had been limited to broomstraws for their structural members? They could have got the bridge up somehow, sure, and made it strong enough to carry light traffic on a fair day. But what would you have had left of it after the first winter storm came down the Channel from the North Sea? The whole approach is idiotic!"

"All right," Dillon said reasonably. "You have a point. Now you're being reasonable. What better approach have you to suggest? Should we abandon Jupiter entirely because it's too big for us?"

"No," Helmuth said. "Or maybe, yes. I don't know. I don't have any easy answer. I just know that this one is no answer at all—it's just a cumbersome evasion."

Dillon smiled. "You're depressed, and no wonder. Sleep it off, Bob, if you can—you might even come up with that answer. In the meantime—well, when you stop to think about it, the surface of Jupiter isn't any more hostile, inherently, than the surface of Jupiter V, except in degree. If you stepped out of this building naked, you'd die just as fast as you would on Jupiter. Try to look at it that way."

Helmuth, looking forward into another night of dreams, said: "That's the way I look at it now."

III

There were three yellow "Critical" signals lit on the long gang board when Helmuth passed through the gang deck on the way back to duty. All of them, as usual, were concentrated on Panel 9, where Eva Chavez worked.

Eva, despite her Latin name—such once-valid tickets no longer meant anything among Earth's uniformly mixed-race population—was a big girl, vaguely blonde, who cherished a passion for the Bridge. Unfortunately, she was apt to become enthralled by the sheer Cosmicness of it all, precisely at the moments when cold analysis and split-second decisions were most crucial.

Helmuth reached over her shoulder, cut her out of the circuit except as an observer, and donned the co-operator's helmet. The incomplete new shoals caisson sprang into being around him. Breakers of boiling hydrogen seethed seven hundred feet up along its slanted sides—breakers that never subsided, but simply were torn away into flying spray.

There was a spot of dull orange near the top of the north face of the caisson, crawling slowly towards the pediment of the nearest truss. Catalysis—

Or cancer, as Helmuth could not help but think of it. On this bitter, violent monster of a planet, even the tiny specks of calcium carbide were deadly. At these wind velocities, such specks imbedded themselves in everything; and at fifteen million pounds per square inch, pressure ice catalyzed by sodium took up ammonia and carbon dioxide, building protein-like compounds in a rapid, deadly chain of decay:

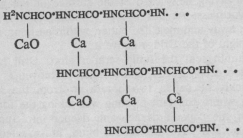

For a second, Helmuth watched it grow. It was, after all, one of the incredible possibilities the Bridge had been built to study. On Earth, such a compound, had it occurred at all, might have grown porous, bony, and quite strong. Here, under nearly eight times the gravity, the molecules were forced to assemble in strict aliphatic order, but in cross section their arrangement was hexagonal, as if the stuff would become an aromatic compound if it only could. Even here it was moderately strong in cross section—but along the long axis it smeared like graphite, the calcium atoms readily surrendering their valence hold on one carbon atom to grab hopefully for the next one in line—

No stuff to hold up the piers of humanity's greatest engineering project. Perhaps it was suitable for the ribs of some Jovian jellyfish, but in a Bridge-caisson, it was cancer.

There was a scraper mechanism working on the edge of the lesion, flaking away the shearing aminos and laying down new ice. In the meantime, the decay of the caisson-face was working deeper. The scraper could not possibly get at the core of the trouble—which was not the calcium carbide dust, with which the atmosphere was charged beyond redemption, but was instead one imbedded sodium speck which was taking no part in the reaction—fast enough to extirpate it. It could barely keep pace with the surface spread of the disease.

And laying new ice over the surface of the wound was worthless. At this rate, the whole caisson would slough away and melt like butter, within an hour, under the weight of the Bridge above it.

Helmuth sent the futile scraper aloft. Drill for it? No—too deep already, and location unknown.

Quickly he called two borers up from the shoals below, where constant blasting was taking the foundation of the caisson deeper and deeper into Jupiter's dubious "soil". He drove both blind, fire-snouted machines down into the lesion.

The bottom of that sore turned out to be forty-five metres within the immense block. Helmuth pushed the red button all the same.

The borers blew up, with a heavy, quite invisible blast, as they had been designed to do. A pit appeared on the face of the caisson.

The nearest truss bent upward in the wind. It fluttered for a moment, trying to resist. It bent farther.

Deprived of its major attachment, it tore free suddenly, and went whirling away into the blackness. A sudden flash of lightning picked it out for a moment, and Helmuth saw it dwindling like a bat with torn wings being borne away by a cyclone.

The scraper scuttled down into the pit and began to fill it with ice from the bottom. Helmuth ordered down a new truss and a squad of scaffolders. Damage of this order took time to repair. He watched the tornado tearing ragged chunks from the edges of the pit until he was sure that the catalysis had stopped. Then, suddenly, prematurely, dismally tired, he took off the helmet.

He was astounded by the white fury that masked Eva's big-boned, mildly pretty face.

"You'll blow the Bridge up yet, won't you?" she said, evenly, without preamble. "Any pretext will do!"

Baffled, Helmuth turned his head helplessly away; but that was no better. The suffused face of Jupiter peered swollenly through the picture-port, just as it did on the foreman's desk.

He and Eva and Charity and the gang and the whole of satellite V were falling forward towards Jupiter; their uneventful cooped-up lives on Jupiter V were utterly unreal compared to the four hours of each changeless day spent on Jupiter's ever-changing surface. Every new day brought their minds, like ships out of control, closer and closer to that gaudy inferno.

There was no other way for a man—or a woman— on Jupiter V to look at the giant planet. It was simple experience, shared by all of them, that planets do not occupy four-fifths of the whole sky, unless the observer is himself up there in that planet's sky, falling, falling faster and faster—

"I have no intention," he said tiredly, "of blowing up the Bridge. I wish you could get it through your head that I want the Bridge to stay up—even though I'm not starry-eyed to the point of incompetence about the project. Did you think that rotten spot was going to go away by itself when you'd painted it over? Didn't you know that—"

Several helmeted, masked heads nearby turned blindly towards the sound of his voice. Helmuth shut up. Any distracting conversation or activity was taboo, down here in the gang room. He motioned Eva back to duty.

The girl donned her helmet obediently enough, but it was plain from the way her normally full lips were thinned that she thought Helmuth had ended the argument only in order to have the last word.

Helmuth strode to the thick pillar which ran down the central axis of the shack, and mounted the spiraling cleats towards his own foreman's cubicle. Already he felt in anticipation the weight of the helmet upon his own head.

Charity Dillon, however, was already wearing the helmet; he was sitting in Helmuth's chair.

Charity was characteristically oblivious of Helmuth's entrance. The Bridge operator must learn to ignore, to be utterly unconscious of anything happening around his body except the inhuman sounds of signals; must learn to heed only those senses which report something going on thousands of miles away.

Helmuth knew better than to interrupt him. Instead, he watched Dillon's white, blade-like fingers roving with blind sureness over the controls.

Dillon, evidently, was making a complete tour of the Bridge—not only from end to end, but up and down, too. The tally board showed that he had already activated nearly two-thirds of the ultraphone eyes. That meant that he had been up all night at the job; had begun it immediately after last talking to Helmuth.

Why?

With a thrill of unfocused apprehension, Helmuth looked at the foreman's jack, which allowed the operator here in the cubicle to communicate with the gang when necessary, and which kept him aware of anything said or done at gang boards.

It was plugged in.

Dillon sighed suddenly, took the helmet off, and turned.

"Hello, Bob," he said. "Funny about this job. You can't see, you can't hear, but when somebody's watching you, you feel a sort of pressure on the back of your neck. ESP, maybe. Ever felt it?"

"Pretty often, lately. Why the grand tour, Charity?"

"There's to be an inspection," Dillon said. His eyes

met Helmuth's. They were frank and transparent. "A mob of Western officials, coming to see that their eight billion dollars isn't being wasted. Naturally, I'm a little anxious to see that they find everything in order."

"I see," Helmuth said. "First time in five years, isn't it?"

"Just about. What was that dust-up down below just now? Somebody—you, I'm sure, from the drastic handiwork involved—bailed Eva out of a mess, and then I heard her talk about your wanting to blow up the Bridge. I checked the area when I heard the fracas start, and it did seem as if she had let things go rather far, but— What was it all about?"

Dillon ordinarily hadn't the guile for cat-and-mouse games, and he had never looked less guileful than now. Helmuth said carefully, "Eva was upset, I suppose. On the subject of Jupiter we're all of us cracked by now, in our different ways. The way she was dealing with the catalysis didn't look to me to be suitable—a difference of opinion, resolved in my favor because I had the authority, Eva didn't. That's all."

"Kind of an expensive difference, Bob. I'm not niggling by nature, you know that. But an incident like that while the commission is here—"

"The point is," Helmuth said, "are we to spend an extra ten thousand, or whatever it costs to replace a truss and reinforce a caisson, or are we to lose the whole caisson—and as much as a third of the whole Bridge along with it?"

"Yes, you're right there, of course. That could be explained, even to a pack of senators. But—it would be difficult to have to explain it very often. Well, the board's yours, Bob. You could continue my spot-check, if you've time."

Dillon got up. Then he added suddenly, as if it were forced out of him:

"Bob, I'm trying to understand your state of mind.

From what Eva said, I gather that you've made it fairly public. I . . . I don't think it's a good idea to infect your fellow workers with your own pessimism. It leads to sloppy work. I know that regardless of your own feelings you won't countenance sloppy work, but one foreman can do only so much. And you're making extra work for yourself—not for me, but for yourself—by being openly gloomy about the Bridge.

"You're the best man on the Bridge, Bob, for all your grousing about the job, and your assorted misgivings. I'd hate to see you replaced."

"A threat, Charity?" Helmuth said softly.

"*No.* I wouldn't replace you unless you actually went nuts, and I firmly believe that your fears in that respect are groundless. It's a commonplace that only sane men suspect their own sanity, isn't it?"

"It's a common misconception. Most psychopathic obsessions begin with a mild worry."

Dillon made as if to brush that subject away. "Anyhow, I'm not threatening; I'd fight to keep you here. But my say-so only covers Jupiter V; there are people higher up on Ganymede, and people higher yet back in Washington—and in this inspecting commission.

"Why don't you try to look on the bright side for a change? Obviously the Bridge isn't ever going to inspire you. But you might at least try thinking about all those dollars piling up in your account every hour you're on this job, and about the bridges and ships and who knows what-all that you'll be building, at any fee you ask, when you get back down to Earth. All under the magic words, 'One of the men who built the Bridge on Jupiter'!"

Charity was bright red with embarrassment and enthusiasm. Helmuth smiled.

"I'll try to bear it in mind, Charity," he said. "When is this gaggle of senators due to arrive?"

"They're on Ganymede now, taking a breather. They

came directly from Washington without any routing. I suppose they'll make a stop at Callisto before they come here. They've something new on their ship, I'm told, that lets them flit about more freely than the usual uphill transport can."

An icy lizard suddenly was nesting in Helmuth's stomach, coiling and coiling but never settling itself. The room blurred. The persistent nightmare was suddenly almost upon him—already.

"Something . . . new?" he echoed, his voice as flat and noncommittal as he could make it. "Do you know what it is?"

"Well, yes. But I think I'd better keep quiet about it until—"

"Charity, nobody on this deserted rock-heap could possibly be a Soviet spy. The whole habit of 'security' is idiotic out here. Tell me now and save me the trouble of dealing with senators; or tell me at least that you know I know. *They have antigravity!* Isn't that it?"

One word from Dillon, and the nightmare would be real.

"Yes," Dillon said. "How did you know? Of course, it couldn't be a complete gravity screen by any means. But it seems to be a good long step towards it. We've waited a long time to see that dream come true— But you're the last man in the world to take pride in the achievement, so there's no sense exulting about it to you. I'll let you know when I get a definite arrival date. In the meantime, will you think about what I said before?"

"Yes, I will." Helmuth took the seat before the board.

"Good. With you, I have to be grateful for small victories. Good trick, Bob."

"Good trick, Charity."

IV

Instead of sleeping—for now he knew that he was really afraid—he sat up in the reading chair in his cabin. The illuminated microfilm pages of a book flipped by across the surface of the wall opposite him, timed precisely to the reading rate most comfortable for him, and he had several weeks' worry-conserved alcohol and smoke rations for ready consumption.

But Helmuth let his mix go flat, and did not notice the book, which had turned itself on, at the page where he had abandoned it last, when he had fitted himself into the chair. Instead, he listened to the radio.

There was always a great deal of ham radio activity in the Jovian system. The conditions were good for it, since there was plenty of power available, few impeding atmosphere layers, and those thin, no Heaviside layers, and few official and no commercial channels with which the hams could interfere.

And there were plenty of people scattered about the satellites who needed the sound of a voice.

". . . anybody know whether the senators are coming here? Doc Barth put in a report a while back on a fossil plant he found here, at least he thinks it was a plant. Maybe they'd like a look at it."

"They're supposed to hit the Bridge team next." A strong voice, and the impression of a strong transmitter wavering in and out; that would be Sweeney, on Ganymede. "Sorry to throw the wet blanket, boys, but I don't think the senators are interested in our rock-balls for their own lumpy selves. We could only hold them here three days."

Helmuth thought greyly: *Then they've already left Callisto.*

"Is that you, Sweeney? Where's the Bridge tonight?"

"Dillon's on duty," a very distant transmitter said. "Try to raise Helmuth, Sweeney."

"Helmuth, Helmuth, you gloomy beetle-gooser! Come in, Helmuth!"

"Sure, Bob, come in and dampen us."

Sluggishly, Helmuth reached out to take the mike, where it lay clipped to one arm of the chair. But the door to his room opened before he had completed the gesture.

Eva came in.

She said, "Bob, I want to tell you something."

"His voice is changing!" the voice of the Callisto operator said. "Ask him what he's drinking, Sweeney!"

Helmuth cut the radio out. The girl was freshly dressed—in so far as anybody dressed in anything on Jupiter V—and Helmuth wondered why she was prowling the decks at this hour, halfway between her sleep period and her trick. Her hair was hazy against the light from the corridor, and she looked less mannish than usual. She reminded him a little of the way she had looked when they first met.

"All right," he said. "I owe you a mix, I guess. Citric, sugar and the other stuff is in the locker . . . you know where it is. Shot-cans are there, too."

The girl shut the door and sat down on the bunk, with a free litheness that was almost grace, but with a determination which Helmuth knew meant that she had just decided to do something silly for all the right reasons.

"I don't need a drink," she said. "As a matter of fact, lately I've been turning my lux-R's back to the common pool. I suppose you did that for me—by showing me what a mind looked like that is hiding from itself."

"Eva, stop sounding like a tract. Obviously, you've advanced to a higher, more Jovian plane of existence, but won't you still need your metabolism? Or have you decided that vitamins are all-in-the-mind?"

"Now you're being superior. Anyhow, alcohol isn't a vitamin. And I didn't come to talk about that. I came to tell you something I think you ought to know."

"Which is?"

She said, "Bob, I mean to have a child here."

A bark of laughter, part sheer hysteria and part exasperation, jack-knifed Helmuth into a sitting position. A red arrow bloomed on the far wall, obediently marking the paragraph which, supposedly, he had reached in his reading, and the page vanished.

"*Women!*" he said, when he could get his breath back. "Really, Evita, you make me feel much better. No environment can change a human being much, after all."

"Why should it?" she said suspiciously. "I don't see the joke. Shouldn't a woman want to have a child?"

"Of course she should," he said, settling back. The flipping pages began again. "It's quite ordinary. All women want to have children. All women dream of the day they can turn a child out to play in an airless rock-garden, to pluck fossils and get quaintly star-burned. How cosy to tuck the little blue body back into its corner that night, promptly at the sound of the trick-change bell! Why, it's as natural as Jupiter-light—as Earthian as vacuum-frozen apple pie."

He turned his head casually away. "As for me, though, Eva, I'd much prefer that you take your ghostly little pretext out of here."

Eva surged to her feet in one furious motion. Her fingers grasped him by the beard and jerked his head painfully around again.

"You reedy male platitude!" she said, in a low grinding voice. "How you could see almost the whole point and make so little of it—*Women*, is it? So you think I came creeping in here, full of humbleness, to settle our technical differences."

He closed his hand on her wrist and twisted it away. "What else?" he demanded, trying to imagine how it would feel to stay reasonable for five minutes at a time with these Bridge-robots. "None of us need bother with games and excuses. We're here, we're isolated, we were all chosen because, among other things, we were judged incapable of forming permanent emotional attachments, and capable of such alliances as we found attractive without going unbalanced when the attraction diminished and the alliance came unstuck. None of us have to pretend that our living arrangements would keep us out of jail in Boston, or that they have to involve any Earth-normal excuses."

She said nothing. After a while he asked, gently, "Isn't that so?"

"Of course it's so. Also it has nothing to do with the matter."

"It doesn't? How stupid do you think I am? *I* don't care whether or not you've decided to have a child here, if you really mean what you say."

She was trembling with rage. "You really don't, too. The decision means nothing to you."

"Well, if I liked children, I'd be sorry for the child. But as it happens, I can't stand children. In short, Eva, as far as I'm concerned you can have as many as you want, and to me you'll *still* be the worst operator on the Bridge."

"I'll bear that in mind," she said. At this moment she seemed to have been cut from pressure-ice. "I'll leave you something to charge your mind with, too, Robert Helmuth. I'll leave you sprawled here under your precious book . . . what is Madame Bovary to you, anyhow, you unadventurous turtle? . . . to think about a man who believes that children must always be born into warm cradles—a man who thinks that men have to huddle on warm worlds, or they won't survive. A man with no ears, no eyes, scarcely any head. A man in terror, a man crying Mamma! *Mamma!* all the stellar days and nights long!"

"Parlor diagnosis!"

"Parlor labeling. Good trick, Bob. Draw your warm wooly blanket in tight about your brains, or some little sneeze of sense might creep in, and impair your—efficiency!"

The door closed sharply after her.

A million pounds of fatigue crashed down without warning on Helmuth's brain, and he fell back into the reading chair with a gasp. The roots of his beard ached, and Jupiters bloomed and wavered away before his closed eyes.

He struggled once, and fell asleep.

Instantly he was in the grip of the dream.

It started, as always, with commonplaces, almost realistic enough to be a documentary film-strip—except for the appalling sense of pressure, and the distorted emotional significance with which the least word, the smallest movement was invested.

It was the sinking of the first caisson of the Bridge. The actual event had been bad enough. The job demanded enough exactness of placement to require that manned ships enter Jupiter's atmosphere itself: a squadron of twenty of the most powerful ships ever built, with the five-million-ton asteroid, trimmed and shaped in space, slung beneath them in an immense cat's cradle.

Four times that squadron had disappeared beneath the clouds; four times the tense voices of pilots and engineers had muttered in Helmuth's ears; four times there were shouts and futile orders and the snapping of cables and someone screaming endlessly against the eternal howl of the Jovian sky.

It had cost, altogether, nine ships and two hundred

and thirty-one men, to get one of five laboriously shaped asteroids planted in the shifting slush that was Jupiter's surface. Helmuth had helped to supervise all five operations, counting the successful one, from his desk on Jupiter V; but in the dream he was not in the control shack, but instead on shipboard, in one of the ships that was never to come back—

Then, without transition, but without any sense of discontinuity either, he was on the Bridge itself. Not *in absentia,* as the remote guiding intelligence of a beetle, but in person, in an ovular, tank-like suit the details of which would never come clear. The high brass had discovered antigravity, and had asked for volunteers to man the Bridge. Helmuth had volunteered.

Looking back on it in the dream, he did not understand why he had volunteered. It had simply seemed expected of him, and he had not been able to help it, even though he had known what it would be like. He belonged on the Bridge, though he hated it—he had been doomed to go there, from the first.

And there was . . . something wrong . . . with the antigravity. The high brass had asked for its volunteers before the scientific work had been completed. The present antigravity fields were weak, and there was some basic flaw in the theory. Generators broke down after only short periods of use, burned out, unpredictably, sometimes only moments after testing up without a flaw—like vacuum tubes in waking life.

That was what Helmuth's set was about to do. He crouched inside his personal womb, above the boiling sea, the clouds raging about him, lit by a plume of hydrogen flame, and waited to feel his weight suddenly become eight times greater than normal. He knew what would happen to him then.

It happened.

Helmuth greeted morning on Jupiter V with his customary scream.

V

The ship that landed as he was going on duty did nothing to lighten the load on his heart. In shape it was not distinguishable from any of the long-range cruisers which ran the legs of the Moon-Mars-Belt-Ganymede trip. But it grounded its huge bulk with less visible expenditures of power than one of the little intersatellary boats.

That landing told Helmuth that his dream was well on its way to coming true. If the high brass had had a real antigravity, there would have been no reason why the main jets should have been necessary at all. Obviously, what had been discovered was some sort of partial screen, which allowed a ship to operate with far less jet action than was normal, but which still left it subject to a sizeable fraction of the universal stress of space.

Nothing less than complete and completely controllable antigravity would do on Jupiter.

He worked mechanically, noting that Charity was not in evidence. Probably he was conferring with the senators, receiving what would be for him the glad news.

Helmuth realized suddenly that there was nothing left for him to do now but to cut and run.

There could certainly be no reason why he should have to reenact the entire dream, helplessly, event for event, like an actor committed to a play. He was awake now, in full control of his own senses, and still at least partially sane. The man in the dream had volunteered—but that man would not be Robert Helmuth. Not any longer.

While the senators were here, he would turn in his resignation. Direct, over Charity's head.

"Wake up, Helmuth," a voice from the gang deck snapped suddenly. "If it hadn't been for me, you'd have run yourself off the end of the Bridge. You had all the automatic stops on that beetle cut out."

Helmuth reached guiltily and more than a little too late for the controls. Eva had already run his beetle back beyond the danger line.

"Sorry," he mumbled. "Thanks, Eva."

"Don't thank me. If you'd actually been in it, I'd have let it go. Less reading and more sleep is what I recommend for you, Helmuth."

"Keep your recommendations to yourself," he snapped.

The incident started a new and even more disturbing chain of thought. If he were to resign now, it would be nearly a year before he could get back to Chicago. Antigravity or no antigravity, the senators' ship would have no room for unexpected passengers. Shipping a man back home had to be arranged far in advance. Space had to be provided, and a cargo equivalent of the weight and space requirements he would take up on the return trip had to be deadheaded out to Jupiter.

A year of living in the station on Jupiter V without any function—as a man whose drain on the station's supplies no longer could be justified in terms of what he did. A year of living under the eyes of Eva Chavez and Charity Dillon and the other men and women who still remained Bridge operators, men and women who would not hesitate to let him know what they thought of his quitting.

A year of living as a bystander in the feverish excitement of direct, personal exploration of Jupiter. A year of watching and hearing the inevitable deaths—while he alone stood aloof, privileged and useless. A year during which Robert Helmuth would become the most hated living entity in the Jovian system.

And, when he got back to Chicago and went looking for a job—for his resignation from the Bridge gang would automatically take him out of government service

—he would be asked why he left the Bridge at the moment when work on the Bridge was just reaching its culmination.

He began to understand why the man in the dream had volunteered.

When the trick-change bell rang, he was still determined to resign, but he had already concluded bitterly that there were, after all, other kinds of hells besides the one on Jupiter.

He was returning the board to neutral as Charity came up the cleats. Charity's eyes were snapping like a skyful of comets. Helmuth had known that they would be.

"Senator Wagoner wants to speak to you, if you're not too tired, Bob," he said. "Go ahead; I'll finish up there."

"He does?" Helmuth frowned. The dream surged back upon him. *NO*. They would not rush him any faster than he wanted to go. "What about, Charity? Am I suspected of unWestern activities? I suppose you've told them how I feel."

"I have," Dillon said, unruffled. "But we're agreed that you may not feel the same after you've talked to Wagoner. He's in the ship, of course. I've put out a suit for you at the lock."

Charity put the helmet over his head, effectively cutting himself off from further conversation, or from any further consciousness of Helmuth at all.

Helmuth stood looking at him a moment. Then, with a convulsive shrug, he went down the cleats.

Three minutes later, he was plodding in a spacesuit across the surface of Jupiter V, with the vivid bulk of Jupiter splashing his shoulders with color.

A courteous Marine let him through the ship's air lock and deftly peeled him out of the suit. Despite a grim determination to be uninterested in the new anti-gravity and any possible consequence of it, he looked curiously about as he was conducted up towards the bow.

But the ship was like the ones that had brought him from Chicago to Jupiter V—it was like any spaceship: there was nothing in it to see but corridor walls and stairwells, until you arrived at the cabin where you were needed.

Senator Wagoner was a surprise. He was a young man, no more than sixty-five at most, not at all portly, and he had the keenest pair of blue eyes that Helmuth had ever seen. He received Helmuth alone, in his own cabin—a comfortable cabin as spaceship accommodations go, but neither roomy nor luxurious. He was hard to match up with the stories Helmuth had been hearing about the current Senate, which had been involved in scandal after scandal of more than Roman proportions.

Helmuth looked around. "I thought there were several of you," he said.

"There are, but I didn't want to give you the idea that you were facing a panel," Wagoner said, smiling. "I've been forced to sit in on most of these endless loyalty investigations back home, but I can't see any point in exporting such religious ceremonies to deep space. Do sit down, Mr. Helmuth. There are drinks coming. We have a lot to talk about."

Stiffly, Helmuth sat down.

"Dillon tells me," Wagoner said, leaning back comfortably in his own chair, "that your usefulness to the Bridge is about at an end. In a way, I'm sorry to hear that, for you've been one of the best men we've had on any of our planetary projects. But, in another way, I'm glad. It makes you available for something much bigger, where we need you much more."

"What do you mean by that?"

"I'll explain in a moment. First, I'd like to talk a little

about the Bridge. Please don't feel that I'm quizzing you, by the way. You're at perfect liberty to say that any given question is none of my business, and I'll take no offense and hold no grudge. Also, 'I hereby disavow the authenticity of any tape or other tapping of which this statement may be a part.' In short, our conversation is unofficial, highly so."

"Thank you."

"It's to my interest; I'm hoping that you'll talk freely to me. Of course my disavowal means nothing, since such formal statements can always be exercised from a tape; but later on I'm going to tell you some things you're not supposed to know, and you'll be able to judge by what I say then that anything you say to me is privileged. Okay?"

A steward came in silently with drinks, and left again. Helmuth tasted his. As far as he could tell, it was exactly like many he had mixed for himself back in the control shack, from standard space rations. The only difference was that it was cold, which Helmuth found startling, but not unpleasant after the first sip. He tried to relax. "I'll do my best," he said.

"Good enough. Now: Dillon says that you regard the Bridge as a monster. I've examined your dossier pretty closely, and I think perhaps Dillon hasn't quite the gist of your meaning. I'd like to hear it straight from you."

"I don't think the Bridge is a monster," Helmuth said slowly. "You see, Charity is on the defensive. He takes the Bridge to be conclusive evidence that no possible set of adverse conditions ever will stop man for long, and there I'm in agreement with him. But he also thinks of it as Progress, personified. He can't admit—you asked me to speak my mind, senator—that the West is a decadent and drying culture. All the other evidence that's available shows that it is. Charity likes to think of the Bridge as giving the lie to that evidence."

"The West hasn't many more years," Wagoner agreed, astonishingly. "Still and all, the West has been responsible for some really towering achievements in its time. Perhaps the Bridge could be considered as the last and the mightiest of them all."

"Not by me," Helmuth said. "The building of gigantic projects for ritual purposes—doing a thing for the sake of doing it—is the last act of an already dead culture. Look at the pyramids in Egypt for an example. Or an even more idiotic and more enormous example, bigger than anything human beings have accomplished yet, the laying out of the 'Diagram of Power' over the whole face of Mars. If the Martians had put all that energy into survival instead, they'd probably be alive yet."

"Agreed," Wagoner said.

"All right. Then maybe you'll also agree that the essence of a vital culture is its ability to defend itself. The West has beaten off the Soviets for a century now—but as far as I can see, the Bridge is the West's 'Diagram of Power', its pyramids, or what have you. All the money and the resources that went into the Bridge are going to be badly needed, *and won't be there,* when the next Soviet attack comes."

"Which will be very shortly, I'm told," Wagoner said, with complete calm. "Furthermore, it will be successful, and in part it will be successful for the very reasons you've outlined. For a man who's been cut off from the Earth for years, Helmuth, you seem to know more about what's going on down there than most of the general populace does."

"Nothing promotes an interest in Earth like being off it," Helmuth said. "And there's plenty of time to read out here." Either the drink was stronger than he had expected, or the senator's calm concurrence in the collapse of Helmuth's entire world had given him another shove towards nothingness; his head was spinning.

Wagoner saw it. He leaned forward suddenly, catching Helmuth flat-footed. *"However,"* he said, "it's difficult for me to agree that the Bridge serves, or ever did serve, a ritual purpose. The Bridge served a huge practical purpose which is now fulfilled—the Bridge, as such, is now a defunct project."

"Defunct?" Helmuth repeated faintly.

"Quite. Of course we'll continue to operate it for a while, simply because you can't stop a process of that size on a dime, and that's just as well for people like Dillon who are emotionally tied up in it. You're the one person with any authority in the whole station who has already lost enough interest in the Bridge to make it safe for me to tell you that it's being abandoned."

"But why?"

"Because," Wagoner went on quietly, "the Bridge has now given us confirmation of a theory of stupendous importance—so important, in my opinion, that the imminent fall of the West seems like a puny event in comparison. A confirmation, incidentally, which contains in it the seeds of ultimate destruction for the Soviets, whatever they may win for themselves in the next fifty years or so."

"I suppose," Helmuth said, puzzled, "that you mean antigravity?"

For the first time, it was Wagoner's turn to be taken aback. "Man," he said at last, "do you know *everything* I want to tell you? I hope not, or my conclusions will be mighty suspicious. Surely Charity didn't tell you we had antigravity; I strictly enjoined him not to mention it."

"No, the subject's been on my mind," Helmuth said. "But I certainly don't see why it should be so worldshaking, any more than I see how the Bridge helped to bring it about. I thought it had been developed independently, for the further exploitation of the Bridge, and would step up Bridge operation, not discontinue it."

"Not at all. Of course, the Bridge has given us information in thousands of different categories, much of it very valuable indeed. But the one job that *only* the Bridge could do was that of confirming, or throwing out, the Blackett-Dirac equations."

"Which are—?"

"A relationship between magnetism and the spinning of a massive body—that much is the Dirac part of it. The Blackett Equation seemed to show that the same formula also applied to gravity. If the figures we collected on the magnetic field strength of Jupiter forced us to retire the Dirac equations, then none of the rest of the information we've gotten from the Bridge would have been worth the money we spent to get it. On the other hand, Jupiter was the only body in the solar system available to us which was big enough in all relevant respects to make it possible for us to test those equations at all. They involve quantities of enormous orders of magnitudes.

"And the figures show that Dirac was right. *They also show that Blackett was right*. Both magnetism *and* gravity are phenomena of rotation.

"I won't bother to trace the succeeding steps, because I think you can work them out for yourself. It's enough to say that there's a drive-generator on board this ship which is the complete and final justification of all the hell you people on the Bridge gang have been put through. The gadget has a long technical name, but the technies who tend it have already nicknamed it the spindizzy, because of what it does to the magnetic moment of any atom—*any* atom—within its field.

"While it's in operation, it absolutely refuses to notice any atom outside its own influence. Furthermore, it will notice no other strain or influence which holds good beyond the borders of that field. It's so snooty that it has to be stopped down to almost nothing when it's brought close to a planet, or it won't let you land. But in deep space . . . well, it's impervious to meteors and

such trash, of course; it's impervious to gravity; and—
it hasn't the faintest interest in any legislation about top
speed limits."

"You're kidding," Helmuth said.

"Am I, now? The ship came to Ganymede directly
from Earth. It did it in a little under two hours, counting maneuvering time."

Helmuth took a defiant pull at his drink. "This thing
really has no top speed at all?" he said. "How can you
be sure of that?"

"Well, we can't," Wagoner admitted. "After all, one
of the unfortunate things about general mathematical
formulas is that they don't contain cut-off points to
warn you of areas where they don't apply. Even quantum
mechanics is somewhat subject to that criticism. However, we expect to know pretty soon just how fast the
spindizzy can drive an object, if there is any limit. We
expect you to tell us."

"I?"

"Yes, Helmuth, you. The coming debacle on Earth
makes it absolutely imperative for us—the West—to
get interstellar expeditions started at once. Richardson
Observatory, on the Moon, has two likely-looking systems picked out already—one at Wolf 359, another at
61 Cygni—and there are sure to be hundreds of others
where Earth-like planets are highly probable. We want
to scatter adventurous people, people with a thoroughly
indoctrinated love of being free, all over this part of
the galaxy, if it can be done.

"Once they're out there, they'll be free to flourish,
with no interference from Earth. The Soviets haven't
the spindizzy yet, and even after they steal it from
us, they won't dare allow it to be used. It's too good
and too final an escape route.

"What we want you to do . . . now I'm getting to
the point, you see . . . is to direct this exodus. You've
the intelligence and the cast of mind for it. Your analysis

of the situation on Earth confirms that, if any more confirmation were needed. And—there's no future for you on Earth now."

"You'll have to excuse me," Helmuth said, firmly. "I'm in no condition to be reasonable now; it's been more than I could digest in a few moments. And the decision doesn't entirely rest with me, either. If I could give you an answer in . . . let me see . . . about three hours. Will that be soon enough?"

"That'll be fine," the senator said.

"And so, that's the story," Helmuth said.

Eva remained silent in her chair for a long time.

"One thing I don't understand," she said at last. "Why did you come to me? I'd have thought that you'd find the whole thing terrifying."

"Oh, it's terrifying, all right," Helmuth said, with quiet exultation. "But terror and fright are two different things, as I've just discovered. We were both wrong, Evita. I was wrong in thinking that the Bridge was a dead end. You were wrong in thinking of it as an end in itself."

"I don't understand you."

"All right, let's put it this way: The work the Bridge was doing was worth-while, as I know now—so I was wrong in being frightened of it, in calling it a bridge to nowhere.

"But you no more saw where it was going than I, and you made the Bridge the be-all and end-all of your existence.

"Now, there's a place to go to; in fact there are places—hundreds of places. They'll be Earth-like places. Since the Soviets are about to win Earth, those places will be more Earth-like than Earth itself, for the next century or so at least!"

She said, "Why are you telling me this? Just to make peace between us?"

"I'm going to take on this job, Evita, if you'll go along?"

She turned swiftly, rising out of the chair with a marvellous fluidity of motion. At the same instant, all the alarm bells in the station went off at once, filling every metal cranny with a jangle of pure horror.

"Posts!" the speaker above Eva's bed roared, in a distorted, gigantic version of Charity Dillon's voice. *"Peak storm overload! The STD is now passing the Spot. Wind velocity has already topped all previous records, and part of the land mass has begun to settle. This is an A-1 overload emergency."*

Behind Charity's bellow, the winds of Jupiter made a spectrum of continuous, insane shrieking. The Bridge was responding with monstrous groans of agony. There was another sound, too, an almost musical cacophony of sharp, percussive tones, such as a dinosaur might make pushing its way through a forest of huge steel tuning-forks. Helmuth had never heard that sound before, but he knew what it was.

The deck of the Bridge was splitting up the middle.

After a moment more, the uproar dimmed, and the speaker said, in Charity's normal voice, "Eva, you too, please. Acknowledge, please. This is it—unless everybody comes on duty at once, the Bridge may go down within the next hour."

"Let it," Eva responded quietly.

There was a brief, startled silence, and then a ghost of a human sound. The voice was Senator Wagoner's, and the sound just might have been a chuckle.

Charity's circuit clicked out.

The mighty death of the Bridge continued to resound in the little room.

After a while, the man and the woman went to

the window, and looked past the discarded bulk of Jupiter at the near horizon, where there had always been visible a few stars.

1952

VICTORY UNINTENTIONAL
Isaac Asimov

2

As in "Bridge" and several of the other stories in this volume, in "Victory Unintentional" Isaac Asimov decided to use a proxy to explore Jupiter, on the grounds that it is not an environment congenial to frail, air-breathing human beings. Unlike the other authors, Isaac had a proxy ready at hand, in the form of his "positronic robots." What is a positronic robot? Why, just your average run-of-the-mill robot, actually; the "positronic" part came about because the positron had just been discovered about the time Asimov began writing the series, and it seemed like a good buzz-word kind of name that would seem to answer the hard questions of "how" and "what" without overly committing anyone. But the positronic element of the robots in Asimov's stories is not important; what is important is that here, for perhaps the first time anywhere, someone seriously considered what the inventors of the robots that would ultimately exist would want to do to keep them from taking over. (And when such intelligent machines came to be built, in the labs of MIT and elsewhere, graduate students were assigned the reading of the Asimov robot stories to help them in their programing.)

The spaceship leaked, as the saying goes, like a sieve.

It was supposed to. In fact, that was the whole idea.

The result, of course, was that during the journey from Ganymede to Jupiter, the ship was crammed just as full as it could be with the very hardest space vacuum. And since the ship also lacked heating devices, this space vacuum was at normal temperature, which is a fraction of a degree above absolute zero.

This, also, was according to plan. Little things like the absence of heat and air didn't annoy anyone at all on that particular spaceship.

The first near vacuum wisps of Jovian atmosphere began percolating into the ship several thousand miles above the Jovian surface. It was practically all hydrogen, though perhaps a careful gas analysis might have located a trace of helium as well. The pressure gauges began creeping skyward.

That creep continued at an accelerating pace as the ship dropped downward in a Jupiter-circling spiral. The pointers of successive gauges, each designed for progressively higher pressures, began to move until they reached the neighborhood of a million or so atmospheres, where figures lost most of their meaning. The temperature, as recorded by thermocouples, rose slowly and erratically, and finally steadied at about seventy below zero, Centigrade.

The ship moved slowly toward the end, plowing its way heavily through a maze of gas molecules that crowded together so closely that hydrogen itself was squeezed to the density of a liquid. Ammonia vapor, drawn from the incredibly vast oceans of that liquid, saturated the horrible atmosphere. The wind, which had begun a thousand miles higher, had risen to a pitch inadequately described as a hurricane.

It was quite plain long before the ship landed on a fairly large Jovian island, perhaps seven times the size of Asia, that Jupiter was not a very pleasant world.

And yet the three members of the crew thought it was. They were quite convinced it was. But then, the three members of the crew were not exactly human. And neither were they exactly Jovian.

They were simply robots, designed on Earth for Jupiter.

ZZ Three said, "It appears to be a rather desolate place."

ZZ Two joined him and regarded the wind-blasted landscape somberly. "There are structures of some sort in the distance," he said, "which are obviously artificial. I suggest we wait for the inhabitants to come to us."

Across the room ZZ One listened, but made no reply. He was the first constructed of the three, and half experimental. Consquently he spoke a little less frequently than his two companions.

The wait was not long. An air vessel of queer design swooped overhead. More followed. And then a line of ground vehicles approached, took position, and disgorged organisms. Along with these organisms came various inanimate accessories that might have been weapons. Some of these were borne by a single Jovian, some by several, and some advanced under their own power, with Jovians perhaps inside.

The robots couldn't tell.

ZZ Three said, "They're all around us now. The logical peaceful gesture would be to come out in the open. Agreed?"

It was, and ZZ One shoved open the heavy door, which was not double or, for that matter, particularly airtight.

Their appearance through the door was the signal for an excited stir among the surrounding Jovians. Things were done to several of the very largest of the inanimate accessories, and ZZ Three became aware of a temperature rise on the outer rind of his beryllium-iridium-bronze body.

He glanced at ZZ Two. "Do you feel it? They're aiming heat energy at us, I believe."

ZZ Two indicated his surprise. "I wonder why?"

"Definitely a heat ray of some sort. Look at that!"

One of the rays had been jarred out of alignment for some undiscernible cause, and its line of radiation intersected a brook of sparkling pure ammonia—which promptly boiled furiously.

Three turned to ZZ One, "Make a note of this, One, will you?"

"Sure." It was to ZZ One that the routine secretarial work fell, and his method of taking a note was to make a mental addition to the accurate memory scroll within him. He had already gathered the hour-by-hour record of every important instrument on board ship during the trip to Jupiter. He added agreeably, "What reason shall I put for the reaction? The human masters would probably enjoy knowing."

"No reason. Or better," Three corrected himself, "no apparent reason. You might say the maximum temperature of the ray was about plus thirty, Centigrade."

Two interrupted, "Shall we try communicating?"

"It would be a waste of time," said Three. "There can't be more than a very few Jovians who know the radio-click code that's been developed between Jupiter and Ganymede. They'll have to send for one, and when he comes, he'll establish contact soon enough. Meanwhile let's watch them. I don't understand their actions, I tell you frankly."

Nor did understanding come immediately. Heat radiation ceased, and other instruments were brought to the forefront and put into play. Several capsules fell at the feet of the watching robots, dropping rapidly and forcefully under Jupiter's gravity. They popped open and a blue liquid exuded, forming pools which proceeded to shrink rapidly by evaporation.

The nightmare wind whipped the vapors away and where those vapors went, Jovians scrambled out of the way. One was too slow, threshed about wildly, and became very limp and still.

ZZ Two bent, dabbed a finger in one of the pools and stared at the dripping liquid. "I think this is oxygen," he said.

"Oxygen, all right," agreed Three. "This becomes stranger and stranger. It must certainly be a dangerous practice, for I would say that oxygen is poisonous to the creatures. One of them died!"

There was a pause, and then ZZ One, whose greater simplicity led at times to an increased directness of thought, said heavily, "It might be that these strange creatures in a rather childish way are attempting to destroy us."

And Two, struck by the suggestion, answered, "You know, One, I think you're right!"

There had been a slight lull in Jovian activity and now a new structure was brought up. It possessed a slender rod that pointed skyward through the impenetrable Jovian murk. It stood in that starkly incredible wind with a rigidity that plainly indicated remarkable structural strength. From its tip came a cracking and then a flash that lit up the depths of the atmosphere into a gray fog.

For a moment the robots were bathed in clinging radiance and then Three said thoughtfully, "High-tension electricity! Quite respectable power, too. One, I think you're right. After all, the human masters have told us that these creatures seek to destroy all humanity, and organisms possessing such insane viciousness as to harbor a thought of harm against a human being"—his voice trembled at the thought—"would scarcely scruple at attempting to destroy us."

"It's a shame to have such distorted minds," said ZZ One. "Poor fellows!"

"I find it a very saddening thought," admitted Two.

"Let's go back to the ship. We've seen enough for now."

They did so, and settled down to wait. As ZZ Three said, Jupiter was a roomy planet, and it might take time for Jovian transportation to bring a radio code expert to the ship. However, patience is a cheap commodity to robots.

As a matter of fact, Jupiter turned on its axis three times, according to chronometer, before the expert arrived. The rising and setting of the sun made no difference, of course, to the dead darkness at the bottom of three thousand miles of liquid-dense gas, so that one could not speak of day and night. But then, neither Jovian nor robot saw by visible light radiation and that didn't matter.

Through this thirty-hour interval the surrounding Jovians continued their attack with a patience and persevering relentlessness concerning which robot ZZ One made a good many mental notes. The ship was assaulted by as many varieties of forces as there were hours, and the robots observed every attack attentively, analyzing such weapons as they recognized. They by no means recognized all.

But the human masters had built well. It had taken fifteen years to construct the ship and the robots, and their essentials could be expressed in a single phrase—raw strength. The attack spent itself uselessly and neither ship nor robot seemed the worse for it.

Three said, "This atmosphere handicaps them, I think. They can't use atomic disruptors, since they would only tear a hole in that soupy air and blow themselves up."

"They haven't used high explosives either," said Two, "which is well. They couldn't have hurt us, naturally, but it would have thrown us about a bit."

"High explosives are out of the question. You can't have an explosive without gas expansion and gas just can't expand in this atmosphere."

"It's a very good atmosphere," muttered One. "I like it."

Which was natural, because he was built for it. The ZZ robots were the first robots ever turned out by the United States Robots and Mechanical Men Corporation that were not even faintly human in appearance. They were low and squat, with a center of gravity less than a foot above ground level. They had six legs apiece, stumpy and thick, designed to lift tons against two and a half times normal Earth gravity. Their reflexes were that many times Earth-normal speed, to make up for the gravity. And they were composed of a beryllium-iridium-bronze alloy that was proof against any known corrosive agent, also any known destructive agent short of a thousand-megaton atomic disruptor, under any conditions whatsoever.

To dispense with further description, they were indestructible, and so impressively powerful that they were the only robots ever built on whom the roboticists of the corporation had never quite had the nerve to pin a serial-number nickname. One bright young fellow had suggested Sissy One, Two, and Three—but not in a very loud voice, and the suggestion was never repeated.

The last hours of the wait were spent in a puzzled discussion to find a possible description of a Jovian's appearance. ZZ One had made a note of their possession of tentacles and of their radial symmetry—and there he had stuck. Two and Three did their best, but couldn't help.

"You can't very well describe anything," Three declared finally, "without a standard of reference. These creatures are like nothing I know of—completely outside the positronic paths of my brain. It's like trying to describe gamma light to a robot unequipped for gamma-ray reception."

It was just at that time that the weapon barrage

ceased once more. The robots turned their attention
to outside the ship.

A group of Jovians were advancing in curiously
uneven fashion, but no amount of careful watching
could determine the exact method of their locomotion.
How they used their tentacles was uncertain. At times
the organisms took on a remarkable slithering motion,
and then they moved at great speed, perhaps with the
wind's help, for they were moving downwind.

The robots stepped out to meet the Jovians, who
halted ten feet away. Both sides remained silent and
motionless.

ZZ Two said, "They must be watching us, but I
don't know how. Do either of you see any photosensitive
organs?"

"I can't say," grunted Three in response. "I don't see
anything about them that makes sense at all."

There was a sudden metallic clicking from among
the Jovian group and ZZ One said delightedly, "It's the
radio code. They've got the communications expert
here."

It was, and they had. The complicated dot-dash
system that over a period of twenty-five years had been
laboriously developed by the beings of Jupiter and the
Earthmen of Ganymede into a remarkably flexible
means of communication was finally being put into
practice at close range.

One Jovian remained in the forefront now, the others
having fallen back. It was he that was speaking. The
clicking said, "Where are you from?"

ZZ Three, as the most mentally advanced, naturally
assumed spokesmanship for the robot group. "We are
from Jupiter's satellite, Ganymede."

The Jovian continued, "What do you want?"

"Information. We have come to study your world
and to bring back our findings. If we could have your
cooperation—"

The Jovian clicking interrupted. "You must be destroyed!"

ZZ Three paused and said in a thoughtful aside to his two companions, "Exactly the attitude the human masters said they would take. They are very unusual."

Returning to his clicking, he asked simply, "Why?"

The Jovian evidently considered certain questions too obnoxious to be answered. He said, "If you leave within a single period of revolution, we will spare you—until such time as we emerge from our world to destroy the unJovian vermin of Ganymede."

"I would like to point out," said Three, "that we of Ganymede and the inner planets—"

The Jovian interrupted, "Our astronomy knows of the Sun and of our four satellites. There are no inner planets."

Three conceded the point wearily, "We of Ganymede, then. We have no designs on Jupiter. We're prepared to offer friendship. For twenty-five years your people communicated freely with the human beings of Ganymede. Is there any reason to make sudden war upon the humans?"

"For twenty-five years," was the cold response, "we assumed the inhabitants of Ganymede to be Jovians. When we found out they were not, and that we had been treating lower animals on the scale of Jovian intelligences, we were bound to take steps to wipe out the dishonor."

Slowly and forcefully he finished, "We of Jupiter will suffer the existence of no vermin!"

The Jovian was backing away in some fashion, tacking against the wind, and the interview was evidently over.

The robots retreated inside the ship.

ZZ Two said, "It looks bad, doesn't it?" He continued thoughtfully, "It is as the human masters said. They possess an ultimately developed superiority complex, combined with an extreme intolerance for anyone or anything that disturbs that complex."

"The intolerance," observed Three, "is the natural consequence of the complex. The trouble is that their intolerance has teeth in it. They have weapons—and their science is great."

"I am not surprised now," burst out ZZ One, "that we were specifically instructed to disregard Jovian orders. They are horrible, intolerant, pseudo-superior beings!" He added emphatically, with robotical loyalty and faith, "No human master could ever be like that."

"That, though true, is beside the point," said Three. The fact remains that the human masters are in terrible danger. This is a gigantic world and these Jovians are greater in numbers and resources by a hundred times or more than the humans of the entire Terrestrial Empire. If they can ever develop the force field to the point where they can use it as a spaceship hull— as the human masters have already done—they will overrun the system at will. The question remains as to how far they have advanced in that direction, what other weapons they have, what preparations they are making, and so on. To return with that information is our function, of course, and we had better decide on our next step."

"It may be difficult," said Two. "The Jovians won't help us." Which, at the moment, was rather an understatement.

Three thought awhile. "It seems to me that we need only wait," he observed. "They have tried to destroy us for thirty hours now and haven't succeeded. Certainly they have done their best. Now a superiority complex always involves the eternal necessity of saving face, and the ultimatum given us proves it in this case. They would never allow us to leave if they could destroy us. But if we don't leave, then rather than admit they cannot force us away, they will surely pretend that they are willing, for their own purposes, to have us stay."

Once again they waited. The day passed. The weapon barrage did not resume. The robots did not leave. The bluff was called. And now the robots faced the Jovian radio-code expert once again.

If the ZZ models had been equipped with a sense of humor, they would have enjoyed themselves immensely. As it was, they felt merely a solemn sense of satisfaction.

The Jovian said, "It has been our decision that you will be allowed to remain for a very short time, so that you see our power for yourself. You shall then return to Ganymede to inform your companion vermin of the disastrous end to which they will unfailingly come within a solar revolution."

ZZ One made a mental note that a Jovian revolution took twelve earthly years.

Three replied casually, "Thank you. May we accompany you to the nearest town? There are many things we would like to learn." He added as an afterthought, "Our ship is not to be touched, of course."

He said this as a request, not as a threat, for no ZZ model was ever pugnacious. All capacity for even the slightest annoyance had been carefully barred in their construction. With robots as vastly powerful as the ZZ's, unfailing good temper was essential for safety during the years of testing on Earth.

The Jovian said, "We are not interested in your verminous ship. No Jovian will pollute himself by approaching it. You may accompany us, but you must on no account approach closer than ten feet to any Jovian, or you will be instantly destroyed."

"Stuck up, aren't they?" observed Two in a genial whisper, as they plowed into the wind.

The town was a port on the shores of an incredible ammonia lake. The external wind whipped furious, frothy waves that shot across the liquid surface at the hectic rate enforced by the gravity. The port itself was neither large nor impressive and it seemed fairly evident that most of the construction was underground.

"What is the population of this place?" asked Three.

The Jovian replied, "It is a small town of ten million."

"I see. Make a note of that, One."

ZZ One did so mechanically, and then turned once more to the lake, at which he had been staring in fascination. He pulled at Three's elbow. "Say, do you suppose they have fish here?"

"What difference does it make?"

"I think we ought to know. The human masters ordered us to find out everything we could." Of the robots, One was the simplest and, consequently, the one who took orders in the most literal fashion.

Two said, "Let One go and look if he likes. It won't do any harm if we let the kid have his fun."

"All right. There's no real objection if he doesn't waste his time. Fish aren't what we came for—but go ahead, One."

ZZ One made off in great excitement and slogged rapidly down the beach, plunging into the ammonia with a splash. The Jovians watched attentively. They had understood none of the previous conversation, of course.

The radio code expert clicked out, "It is apparent that your companion has decided to abandon life in despair at our greatness."

Three said in surprise, "Nothing of the sort. He wants to investigate the living organisms, if any, that live in the ammonia." He added apologetically, "Our friend is very curious at times, and he isn't quite as bright as we are, though that is his misfortune. We understand that and try to humor him whenever we can."

There was a long pause, and the Jovian observed, "He will drown."

Three replied casually, "No danger of that. We don't drown. May we enter the town as soon as he returns?"

At that moment there was a spurt of liquid several hundred feet out in the lake. It sprayed upward wildly and then hurtled down in a wind-driven mist. Another spurt and another, then a wild white foaming that formed a trail toward shore, gradually quieting as it approached.

The two robots watched this in amazement, and the utter lack of motion on the part of the Jovians indicated that they were watching as well.

Then the head of ZZ One broke the surface and he made his slow way out on to dry land. But something followed him! Some organism of gigantic size that seemed nothing but fangs, claws, and spines. Then they saw that it wasn't following him under its own power, but was being dragged across the beach by ZZ One. There was a significant flabbiness about it.

ZZ One approached rather timidly and took communication into his own hands. He tapped out a message for the Jovian in agitated fashion. "I am very sorry this happened, but the thing attacked me. I was merely taking notes on it. It is not a valuable creature, I hope."

He was not answered immediately, for at the first appearance of the monster there had been a wild break in the Jovian ranks. These re-formed slowly, and cautious observation having proven the creature to be indeed dead, order was restored. Some of the bolder were curiously prodding the body.

ZZ Three said humbly, "I hope you will pardon our friend. He is sometimes clumsy. We have absolutely no intention of harming any Jovian creature."

"He attacked me," explained One. "He bit at me without provocation. See!" And he displayed a two-foot fang that ended in a jagged break. "He broke it on my shoulder and almost left a scratch. I just slapped it a bit to send it away—and it died. I'm sorry!"

The Jovian finally spoke, and his code clicking was a rather stuttery affair. "It is a wild creature, rarely found so close to shore, but the lake is deep just here."

Three said, still anxiously, "If you can use it for food, we are only too glad—"

"No. We can get food for ourselves without the help of verm—without the help of others. Eat it yourselves."

At that ZZ One heaved the creature up and back into the sea, with an easy motion of one arm. Three said casually, "Thank you for your kind offer, but we have no use for food. We don't eat, of course."

Escorted by two hundred or so armed Jovians, the robots passed down a series of ramps into the underground city. If, above the surface, the city had looked small and unimpressive, then from beneath it took on the appearance of a vast megalopolis.

They were ushered into ground cars that were operated by remote control—for no honest, self-respecting Jovian would risk his superiority by placing himself in the same car with vermin—and driven at frightful speed to the center of the town. They saw enough to decide that it extended fifty miles from end to end and reached downward into Jupiter's crust at least eight miles.

ZZ Two did not sound happy as he said, "If this is a sample of Jovian development then we shall not have a hopeful report to bring back to the human masters. After all, we landed on the vast surface of Jupiter at random, with the chances a thousand to one against coming near any really concentrated center of population. This must be, as the code expert says, a mere town."

"Ten million Jovians," said Three abstractedly. "Total population must be in the trillions, which is high, very high, even for Jupiter. They probably have a completely urban civilization, which means that their scientific development must be tremendous. If they have force fields—"

Three had no neck, for in the interest of strength the heads of the ZZ models were riveted firmly onto the torso, with the delicate positronic brains protected by three separate layers in inch-thick iridium alloy. But if he had had one, he would have shaken his head dolefully.

They had stopped now in a cleared space. Everywhere about them they could see avenues and structures crowded with Jovians, as curious as any terrestrial crowd would have been in similar circumstances.

The code expert approached. "It is time now for me to retire until the next period of activity. We have gone so far as to arrange quarters for you at great inconvenience to ourselves for, of course, the structure will have to be pulled down and rebuilt afterward. Nevertheless, you will be allowed to sleep for a space."

ZZ Three waved an arm in deprecation and tapped out, "We thank you but you must not trouble yourself. We don't mind remaining right here. If you want to sleep and rest, by all means do. We'll wait for you. As for us," casually, "we don't sleep."

The Jovian said nothing, though if it had had a face, the expression upon it might have been interesting. It left, and the robots remained in the car, with squads of well-armed Jovians, frequently replaced, surrounding them as guards.

It was hours before the ranks of those guards parted to allow the code expert to return. Along with him were other Jovians, whom he introduced.

"There are with me two officials of the central government who have graciously consented to speak with you."

One of the officials evidently knew the code, for this

clicking interrupted the code expert sharply. He addressed the robots, "Vermin! Emerge from the ground car that we may look at you."

The robots were only too willing to comply, so while Three and Two vaulted over the right side of the car, ZZ One dashed through the left side. The word through is used advisedly, for since he neglected to work the mechanism that lowered a section of side so that one might exit, he carried that side, plus two wheels and an axle, along with him. The car collapsed, and ZZ One stood staring at the ruins in embarrassed silence.

At last he clicked out gently, "I'm very sorry. I hope it wasn't an expensive car."

ZZ Two added apologetically, "Our companion is often clumsy. You must excuse him," and ZZ Three made a halfhearted attempt to put the car back together again.

ZZ One made another effort to excuse himself. "The material of the car was rather flimsy. You see?" He lifted a square-yard sheet of three-inch-thick, metal-hard plastic in both hands and exerted a bit of pressure. The sheet promptly snapped in two. "I should have made allowances," he admitted.

The Jovian government official said in slightly less sharp fashion, "The car would have had to be destroyed anyway, after being polluted by your presence." He paused, then, "Creatures! We Jovians lack vulgar curiosity concerning lower animals, but our scientists seek facts."

"We're right with you," replied Three cheerfully. "So do we."

The Jovian ignored him. "You lack the mass-sensitive organ, apparently. How is it that you are aware of distant objects?"

Three grew interested. "Do you mean your people are directly sensitive to mass?"

"I am not here to answer your questions—your impudent questions—about us."

"I take it then that objects of low specific mass would be transparent to you, even in the absence of radiation." He turned to Two, "That's how they see. Their atmosphere is as transparent as space to them."

The Jovian clicking began once more, "You will answer my first question immediately or my patience will end and I will order you destroyed."

Three said at once, "We are energy-sensitive. We can adjust ourselves to the entire electromagnetic scale at will. At present, our long-distance sight is due to radiowave radiation that we emit ourselves, and at close range we see by—" He paused, and said to Two, "There isn't any code word for gamma ray, is there?"

"Not that I know of," Two answered.

Three continued to the Jovian, "At close range we see by other radiation for which there is no code word."

"Of what is your body composed?" demanded the Jovian.

Two whispered, "He probably asks that because his mass sensitivity can't penetrate past our skin. High density, you know. Ought we to tell him?"

Three replied uncertainly, "Our human masters didn't particularly say we were to keep anything secret." In radio code, to the Jovian he said, "We are mostly iridium. For the rest, copper, tin, a little beryllium, and a scattering of other substances."

The Jovians fell back and by the obscure writhing of various portions of their thoroughly indescribable bodies gave the impression that they were in animated conversation, although they made no sound.

And then the official returned. "Beings of Ganymede! It has been decided to show you through some of our factories that we may exhibit a tiny part of our great achievements. We will then allow you to return so that you may spread despair among the other verm—the other beings of the outer world."

Three said to Two, "Note the effect of their psychology. They must hammer home their superiority. It's still a matter of saving face." And in radio code, "We thank you for the opportunity."

But the face-saving was efficient, as the robots realized soon enough. The demonstration became a tour, and the tour a Grand Exhibition. The Jovians displayed everything, explained everything, answered all questions eagerly, and ZZ One made hundreds of despairing notes.

The war potential of that single so-called unimportant town was greater by several times than that of all Ganymede. Ten more such towns would outproduce all the Terrestrial Empire. Yet ten more such towns would not be the fingernail fragment of the strength all Jupiter must be able to exert.

Three turned as One nudged him. "What is it?"

ZZ One said seriously, "If they have force fields, the human masters are lost, aren't they?"

"I'm afraid so. Why do you ask?"

"Because the Jovians aren't showing us through the right wing of this factory. It might be that force fields are being developed there. They would be wanting to keep it secret if they were. We'd better find out. It's the main point, you know."

Three regarded One somberly. "Perhaps you're right. It's no use ignoring anything."

They were in a huge steel mill now, watching hundred-foot beams of ammonia-resistant silicon-steel alloy being turned out twenty to the second. Three asked quietly, "What does that wing contain?"

The government official inquired of those in charge of the factory and explained, "That is the section of great heat. Various processes require huge temperatures which life cannot bear, and they must all be handled indirectly."

He led the way to a partition from which heat could be felt to radiate and indicated a small, round area of transparent material. It was one of a row of such, through which the foggy red light of lines of glowing forges could be made out through the soupy atmosphere.

ZZ One fastened a look of suspicion on the Jovian and clicked out, "Would it be all right if I went in and looked around? I am very interested in this."

Three said, "You're being childish, One. They're telling the truth. Oh well, nose around if you must. But don't take too long; we've got to move on."

The Jovian said, "You have no understanding of the heat involved. You will die."

"Oh, no," explained One casually. "Heat doesn't bother us."

There was a Jovian conference, and then a scene of scurrying confusion as the life of the factory was geared to this unusual emergency. Screens of heat-absorbent material were set up, and then a door dropped open, a door that had never before budged while the forges were working. ZZ One entered and the door closed behind him. Jovian officials crowed to the transparent areas to watch.

ZZ One walked to the nearest forge and tapped the outside. Since he was too short to see into it comfortably, he tipped the forge until the molten metal licked at the lip of the container. He peered at it curiously, then dipped his hand in and stirred it awhile to test the consistency. Having done this, he withdrew his hand, shook off some of the fiery metallic droplets and wiped the rest on one of his six thighs. Slowly he went down the line of forges, then signified his desire to leave.

The Jovians retired to a great distance when he came out of the door and played a stream of ammonia on him, which hissed, bubbled and steamed until he was brought to bearable temperature once more.

ZZ One ignored the ammonia shower and said, "They were telling the truth. No force fields."

Three began, "You see——" but One interrupted impatiently, "But there's no use delaying. The human masters instructed us to find out everything and that's that."

He turned to the Jovian and clicked out, without the slightest hesitation, "Listen, has Jovian science developed force fields?"

Bluntness was, of course, one of the natural consequences of One's less well developed mental powers. Two and Three knew that, so they refrained from expressing disapproval of the remark.

The Jovian official relaxed slowly from his strangely stiffened attitude, which had somehow given the impression that he had been staring stupidly at One's hand—the one he had dipped into the molten metal. The Jovian said slowly, "Force fields? That, then, is your main object of curiosity?"

"Yes," said One with emphasis.

There was a sudden and patent gain in confidence on the Jovian's part, for the clicking grew sharper. "Then come, vermin!"

Whereupon Three said to Two, "We're vermin again, I see—which sounds as if there's bad news ahead." And Two gloomily agreed.

It was to the very edge of the city that they were now led—to the portion which on Earth would have been termed the suburbs—and into one of a series of closely integrated structures, which might have corresponded vaguely to a terrestrial university.

There were no explantions, however, and none was asked for. The Jovian official led the way rapidly, and the robots followed with the grim conviction that the worst was just about to happen.

It was ZZ One who stopped before an opened wall section after the rest had passed on. "What's this?" he wanted to know.

The room was equipped with narrow, low benches, along which Jovians manipulated rows of strange devices, of which strong, inch-long electromagnets formed the principal feature.

"What's this?" asked One again.

The Jovian turned back and exhibited impatience. "This is a students' biological laboratory. There's nothing there to interest you."

"But what are they doing?"

"They are studing microscopic life. Haven't you ever seen a microscope before?"

Three interrupted in explanation, "He has, but not that type. Our microscopes are meant for energy-sensitive organs and work by refraction of radiant energy. Your microscopes evidently work on a mass-expansion basis. Rather ingenious."

ZZ One said, "Would it be all right if I inspected some of your specimens?"

"Of what use will that be? You cannot use our microscopes because of your sensory limitations and it will simply force us to discard such specimens as you approach for no decent reason."

"But I don't need a microscope," explained One, with surprise. "I can easily adjust myself for microscopic vision."

He strode to the nearest bench, while the students in the room crowded to the corner in an attempt to avoid contamination. ZZ One shoved a microscope aside and inspected the slide carefully. He backed away, puzzled, then tried another . . . a third . . . a fourth.

He came back and addressed the Jovian. "Those are supposed to be alive, aren't they? I mean those little worm things."

The Jovian said, "Certainly."

"That's strange—when I look at them, they die!"

Three exclaimed sharply and said to his two companions, "We've forgotten our gamma-ray radiation. Let's get out of here, One, or we'll kill every bit of microscopic life in the room."

He turned to the Jovian, "I'm afraid that our presence is fatal to weaker forms of life. We had better leave. We hope the specimens are not too difficult to replace. And, while we're about it, you had better not stay too near us, or our radiation may affect you adversely. You feel all right so far, don't you?" he asked.

The Jovian led the way onward in proud silence, but it was to be noticed that thereafter he doubled the distance he had hitherto kept between himself and them.

Nothing more was said until the robots found themselves in a vast room. In the very center of it huge ingots of metal rested unsupported in mid-air—or, rather, supported by nothing visible—against mighty Jovian gravity.

The Jovian clicked, "There is your force field in ultimate form, as recently perfected. Within that bubble is a vacuum, so that it is supporting the full weight of our atmosphere plus an amount of metal equivalent to two large spaceships. What do you say to that?"

"That space travel now becomes a possibility for you," said Three.

"Definitely. No metal or plastic has the strength to hold our atmosphere against a vacuum, but a force field can—and a force-field bubble will be our spaceship. Within the year we will be turning them out by the hundreds of thousands. Then we will swarm down upon Ganymede to destroy the verminous so-called intelligences that attempt to dispute our dominion of the Universe."

"The human beings of Ganymede have never attempted—" began Three, in mild expostulation.

"Silence!" snapped the Jovian. "Return now and tell them what you've seen. Their own feeble force fields— such as the one your ship is equipped with—will not stand against us, for our smallest ship will be a hundred times the size and power of yours."

Three said, "Then there's nothing more to do and we will return, as you say, with the information. If you could lead us back to our ship, we'll say good-by. But by the way, just as a matter for the record, there's something you don't understand. The humans of Ganymede have force fields, of course, but our particular ship isn't equipped with one. We don't need any."

The robot turned away and motioned his companions to follow. For a moment they did not speak, then ZZ One muttered dejectedly, "Can't we try to destroy this place?"

"It won't help," said Three. "They'd get us by weight of numbers. It's no use. In an earthly decade the human masters will be finished. It is impossible to stand against Jupiter. There's just too much of it. As long as Jovians were tied to the surface, the humans were safe. But now that they have force fields— All we can do is to bring the news. By the preparation of hiding places, some few may survive for a short while."

The city was behind them. They were out on the open plain by the lake, with their ship a dark spot on the horizon, when the Jovian spoke suddenly:

"Creatures, you say you have no force field?"

Three replied without interest, "We don't need one."

"How then does your ship stand the vacuum of space without exploding because of the atmospheric pressure within?" And he moved a tentacle as if in mute gesture at the Jovian atmosphere that was weighing down upon them with a force of twenty million pounds to the square inch.

"Well," explained Three, "that's simple. Our ship isn't airtight. Pressures equalize within and without."

"Even in space? A vacuum in your ship? You lie!"

"You're welcome to inspect our ship. It has no force field and it isn't airtight. What's marvelous about that? We don't breathe. Our energy is obtained through direct atomic power. The presence or absence of air pressure makes little difference to us and we're quite at home in a vacuum."

"But absolute zero!"

"It doesn't matter. We regulate our own heat. We're not interested in outside temperatures." He paused. "Well, we can make our own way back to the ship. Good-by. We'll give the humans of Ganymede your message—war to the end!"

But the Jovian said. "Wait! I'll be back." He turned and went toward the city.

The robots stared, and then waited in silence.

It was three hours before he returned and when he did, it was in breathless haste. He stopped within the usual ten feet of the robots, but then began inching his way forward in a curious groveling fashion. He did not speak until his rubbery gray skin was almost touching them, and then the radio code sounded, subdued and respectful.

"Honored sirs, I have been in communication with the head of our central government, who is now aware of all the facts, and I can assure you that Jupiter desires only peace."

"I beg your pardon?" asked Three blankly.

The Jovian drove on hastily. "We are ready to resume communication with Ganymede and will gladly promise to make no attempt to venture into space. Our force field will be used only on the Jovian surface."

"But—" Three began.

"Our government will be glad to receive any other

representatives our honorable human brothers of Ganymede would care to send. If your honors will now condescend to swear peace—" a scaly tentacle swung out toward them and Three, quite dazed, grasped it. Two and One did likewise as two more were extended to them.

The Jovian said solemnly: "There is then eternal peace between Jupiter and Ganymede."

The spaceship which leaked like a sieve was out in space again. The pressure and temperature were once more at zero, and the robots watched the huge but steadily shrinking globe that was Jupiter.

"They're definitely sincere," said ZZ Two, "and it's very gratifying, this complete about-face, but I don't get it."

"It is my idea," observed ZZ One, "that the Jovians came to their senses just in time and realized the incredible evil involved in the thought of harm to a human master. That would be only natural."

ZZ Three sighed and said, "Look, it's all a matter of psychology. Those Jovians had a superiority complex a mile thick and when they couldn't destroy us, they were bound to save face. All their exhibitions, all their explanations, were simply a form of braggadocio, designed to impress us into the proper state of humiliation before their power and superiority."

"I see all that," interrupted Two, "but—"

Three went on, "But it worked the wrong way. All they did was to prove to themselves that we were stronger, that we didn't drown, that we didn't eat or sleep, that molten metal didn't hurt us. Even our very presence was fatal to Jovian life. Their last trump was the force field. And when they found out that *we* didn't need them at all, and could live in a vacuum at absolute zero, they broke." He paused and added philo-sophically, "When a superiority complex like that breaks, it breaks all the way."

The other two considered that, and then Two said, "But it still doesn't make sense. Why should they care what we can or can't do? We're only robots. We're not the ones they have to fight."

"And that's the whole point, Two," said Three softly. "It's only after we left Jupiter that I thought of it. Do you know that through an oversight, quite uninten-tionally, we neglected to tell them we were only robots."

"They never asked us," said One.

"Exactly. So they thought we were human beings and that all other human beings were like us!"

He looked once more at Jupiter, thoughtfully. "No wonder they decided to quit!"

1942

DESERTION
Clifford D. Simak

2

Clifford Simak looks like a small-town newspaper editor, and in a sense he is—that is, he lives in a small town outside of Minneapolis, Minnesota, and he was for a considerable time city editor for one of the leading metropolitan papers. He doesn't look a bit like most readers' idea of an sf writer (no starey eyes, no needle tracks in the arm). He looks rather like the sort of man who would spend his vacation taking a troop of Boy Scouts on a tour of New York City (which he also is), but he happens to be the sort of man who for forty years has written some of the finest sf around, including the memorable story that follows.

Four men, two by two, had gone into the howling maelstrom that was Jupiter and had not returned. They had walked into the keening gale—or rather, they had loped, bellies low against the ground, wet sides gleaming in the rain.

For they did not go in the shape of men.

Now the fifth man stood before the desk of Kent Fowler, head of Dome No. 3, Jovian Survey Commission.

Under Fowler's desk, old Towser scratched a flea, then settled down to sleep again.

Harold Allen, Fowler saw with a sudden pang, was young—too young. He had the easy confidence of youth, the face of one who never had known fear. And that was strange. For men in the domes of Jupiter did know fear—fear and humility. It was hard for Man to reconcile his puny self with the mighty forces of the monstrous planet.

"You understand," said Fowler, "that you need not do this. You understand that you need not go."

It was formula, of course. The other four had been told the same thing, but they had gone. This fifth one, Fowler knew, would go as well. But suddenly he felt a dull hope stir within him that Allen wouldn't go.

"When do I start?" asked Allen.

There had been a time when Fowler might have taken quiet pride in that answer, but not now. He frowned briefly.

"Within the hour," he said.

Allen stood waiting, quietly.

"Four other men have gone out and have not returned," said Fowler. "You know that, of course. We want you to return. We don't want you going off on any heroic rescue expedition. The main thing, the only thing, is that you come back, that you prove man can live in a Jovian form. Go to the first survey stake, no farther, then come back. Don't take any chances. Don't investigate anything. Just come back."

Allen nodded. "I understand all that."

"Miss Stanley will operate the converter," Fowler went on. "You need have no fear on that particular score. The other men were converted without mishap. They left the converter in apparently perfect condition. You will be in thoroughly competent hands. Miss Stanley is the best qualified conversion operator in the Solar System. She has had experience on most of the other planets. That is why she's here."

Allen grinned at the woman and Fowler saw something flicker across Miss Stanley's face—something that might have been pity, or rage—or just plain fear. But it was gone again and she was smiling back at the youth who stood before the desk. Smiling in that prim, school-teacherish way she had of smiling, almost as if she hated herself for doing it.

"I shall be looking forward," said Allen, "to my conversion."

And the way he said it, he made it all a joke, a vast, ironic joke.

But it was no joke.

It was serious business, deadly serious. Upon these tests, Fowler knew, depended the fate of men on Jupiter. If the tests succeeded, the resources of the giant planet would be thrown open. Man would take over Jupiter as he already had taken over the other smaller planets. And if they failed—

If they failed, Man would continue to be chained and hampered by the terrific pressure, the greater force of gravity, the weird chemistry of the planet. He would continue to be shut within the domes, unable to set actual foot upon the planet, unable to see it with direct, unaided vision, forced to rely upon the awkward tractors and the televisor, forced to work with clumsy tools and mechanisms or through the medium of robots that themselves were clumsy.

For Man, unprotected and in his natural form, would be blotted out by Jupiter's terrific pressure of fifteeen thousand pounds per square inch, pressure that made terrestrial sea bottoms seem a vacuum by comparison.

Even the strongest metal Earthmen could devise couldn't exist under pressure such as that, under the pressure and the alkaline rains that forever swept the planet. It grew brittle and flaky, crumbling like clay, or it ran away in little streams and puddles of ammonia salts. Only by stepping up the toughness and strength of that metal, by increasing its electronic tension, could it be made to withstand the weight of thousands of miles of swirling, choking gases that made up the atmosphere.

And even when that was done, everything had to be coated with tough quartz to keep away the rain—the liquid ammonia that fell as bitter rain.

Fowler sat listening to the engines in the sub-floor of the dome—engines that ran on endlessly, the dome never quiet of them. They had to run and keep on running, for if they stopped, the power flowing into the metal walls of the dome would stop, the electronic tension would ease up and that would be the end of everything.

Towser roused himself under Fowler's desk and scratched another flea, his leg thumping hard against the floor.

"Is there anything else?" asked Allen.

Fowler shook his head. "Perhaps there's something you want to do," he said. "Perhaps you—"

He had meant to say write a letter and he was glad he caught himself quick enough so he didn't say it.

Allen looked at his watch. "I'll be there on time," he said. He swung around and headed for the door.

Fowler knew Miss Stanley was watching him and he didn't want to turn and meet her eyes. He fumbled with a sheaf of papers on the desk before him.

"How long are you going to keep this up?" asked Miss Stanley and she bit off each word with a vicious snap.

He swung around in his chair and faced her then. Her lips were drawn into a straight, thin line, her hair seemed skinned back from her forehead tighter than ever, giving her face that queer, almost startling death-mask quality.

He tried to make his voice cool and level. "As long as there's any need of it," he said. "As long as there's any hope."

"You're going to keep on sentencing them to death,"

she said. "You're going to keep marching them out face to face with Jupiter. You're going to sit in here safe and comfortable and send them out to die."

"There is no room for sentimentality, Miss Stanley," Fowler said, trying to keep the note of anger from his voice. "You know as well as I do why we're doing this. You realize that Man in his own form simply cannot cope with Jupiter. The only answer is to turn men into the sort of things that can cope with it. We've done it on the other planets.

"If a few men die, but we finally succeed, the price is small. Through the ages men have thrown away their lives on foolish things, for foolish reasons. Why should we hesitate, then, at a little death in a thing as great as this?"

Miss Stanley sat stiff and straight, hands folded in her lap, the lights shining on her graying hair; and Fowler, watching her, tried to imagine what she might feel, what she might be thinking. He wasn't exactly afraid of her, but he didn't feel quite comfortable when she was around. Those sharp blue eyes saw too much, her hands looked far too competent. She should be somebody's Aunt sitting in a rocking chair with her knitting needles. But she wasn't. She was the top-notch conversion unit operator in the Solar System and she didn't like the way he was doing things.

"There is something wrong, Mr. Fowler," she declared.

"Precisely," agreed Fowler. "That's why I'm sending young Allen out alone. He may find out what it is."

"And if he doesn't?"

"I'll send someone else."

She rose slowly from her chair, started toward the door, then stopped before his desk.

"Some day," she said, "you will be a great man. You never let a chance go by. This is your chance. You knew it was when this dome was picked for the tests.

If you put it through, you'll go up a notch or two. No matter how many men may die, you'll go up a notch or two."

"Miss Stanley," he said and his voice was curt, "young Allen is going out soon. Please be sure that your machine—"

"My machine," she told him, icily, "is not to blame. It operates along the co-ordinates the biologists set up."

He sat hunched at his desk, listening to her footsteps go down the corridor.

What she said was true, of course. The biologists had set up the co-ordinates. But the biologists could be wrong. Just a hair-breadth of difference, one iota of digression and the converter would be sending out something that wasn't the thing they meant to send. A mutant that might crack up, go haywire, come unstuck under some condition or stress of circumstance wholly unsuspected.

For Man didn't know much about what was going on outside. Only what his instruments told him was going on. And the samplings of those happenings furnished by those instruments and mechanisms had been no more than samplings, for Jupiter was unbelievably large and the domes were very few.

Even the work of the biologists in getting the data on the Lopers, apparently the highest form of Jovian life, had involved more than three years of intensive study and after that two years of checking to make sure. Work that could have been done on Earth in a week or two. But work that, in this case, couldn't be done on Earth at all, for one couldn't take a Jovian life form to Earth. The pressure here on Jupiter couldn't be duplicated outside of Jupiter and at Earth pressure and temperature the Lopers would simply have disappeared in a puff of gas.

Yet it was work that had to be done if Man ever

hoped to go about Jupiter in the life form of the Lopers. For before the converter could change a man to another life form, every detailed physical characteristic of that life form must be known—surely and positively, with no chance of mistake.

Allen did not come back.

The tractors, combing the nearby terrain, found no trace of him, unless the skulking thing reported by one of the drives had been the missing Earthman in Loper form.

The biologists sneered their most accomplished academic sneers when Fowler suggested the co-ordinates might be wrong. Carefully they pointed out, the co-ordinates worked. When a man was put into the converter and the switch was thrown, the man became a Loper. He left the machine and moved away, out of sight, into the soupy atmosphere.

Some quirk, Fowler had suggested; some tiny deviation from the thing a Loper should be, some minor defect. If there were, the biologists said, it would take years to find it.

And Fowler knew that they were right.

So there were five men now instead of four and Harold Allen had walked out into Jupiter for nothing at all. It was as if he'd never gone, so far as knowledge was concerned.

Fowler reached across his desk and picked up the personnel file, a thin sheaf of paper neatly clipped together. It was a thing he dreaded but a thing he had to do. Somehow the reason for these strange disappearances must be found. And there was no other way than to send out more men.

He sat for a moment listening to the howling of the wind above the dome, the everlasting thundering gale that swept across the planet in boiling, twisting wrath.

Was there some threat out there, he asked himself? Some danger they did not know about? Something that lay in wait and gobbled up the Lopers, making no distinction between Lopers that were *bona fide* and Lopers that were men? To the gobblers, of course, it would make no difference.

Or had there been a basic fault in selecting the Lopers as the type of life best fitted for existence on the surface of the planet? The evident intelligence of the Lopers, he knew, had been one factor in that determination. For if the thing Man became did not have capacity for intelligence, Man could not for long retain his own intelligence in such a guise.

Had the biologists let that one factor weigh too heavily, using it to offset some other factor that might be unsatisfactory, even disastrous? It didn't seem likely. Stiffnecked as they might be, the biologists knew their business.

Or was the whole thing impossible, doomed from the very start? Conversion to other life forms had worked on other planets, but that did not necessarily mean it would work on Jupiter. Perhaps Man's intelligence could not function correctly through the sensory apparatus provided Jovian life. Perhaps the Lopers were so alien there was no common ground for human knowledge and the Jovian conception of existence to meet and work together.

Or the fault might lie with Man, be inherent with the race. Some mental aberration which, coupled with what they found outside, wouldn't let them come back. Although it might not be an aberration, not in the human sense. Perhaps just one ordinary human mental trait, accepted as commonplace on Earth, would be so violently at odds with Jovian existence that it would blast human sanity.

Claws rattled and clicked down the corridor. Listening to them, Fowler smiled wanly. It was Towser coming back from the kitchen, where he had gone to see his friend, the cook.

Towser came into the room, carrying a bone. He wagged his tail at Fowler and flopped down beside the desk, bone between his paws. For a long moment his rheumy old eyes regarded his master and Fowler reached down a hand to ruffle a ragged ear.

"You still like me, Towser?" Fowler asked and Towser thumped his tail.

"You're the only one," said Fowler.

He straightened and swung back to the desk. His hand reached out and picked up the file.

Bennett? Bennett had a girl waiting for him back on Earth.

Andrews? Andrews was planning on going back to Mars Tech just as soon as he earned enough to see him through a year.

Olson? Olson was nearing pension age. All the time telling the boys how he was going to settle down and grow roses.

Carefully, Fowler laid the file back on the desk.

Sentencing men to death. Miss Stanley had said that, her pale lips scarcely moving in her parchment face. Marching men out to die while he, Fowler, sat here safe and comfortable.

They were saying it all through the dome, no doubt, especially since Allen had failed to return. They wouldn't say it to his face, of course. Even the man or men he called before this desk and told they were the next to go, wouldn't say it to him.

But he would see it in their eyes.

He picked up the file again. Bennett, Andrews, Olson. There were others, but there was no use in going on.

Ken Fowler knew that he couldn't do it, couldn't face them, couldn't send more men out to die.

He leaned forward and flipped up the toggle on the intercommunicator.

"Yes, Mr. Fowler."

"Miss Stanley, please."

He waited for Miss Stanley, listening to Towser chewing half-heartedly on the bone. Towser's teeth were getting bad.

"Miss Stanley," said Miss Stanley's voice.

"Just wanted to tell you, Miss Stanley, to get ready for two more."

"Aren't you afraid," asked Miss Stanley, "that you'll run out of them? Sending out one at a time, they'd last longer, give you twice the satisfaction."

"One of them," said Fowler, "will be a dog."

"A dog!"

"Yes, Towser."

He heard the quick, cold rage that iced her voice. "Your own dog! He's been with you all these years—"

"That's the point," said Fowler. "Towser would be unhappy if I left him behind."

It was not the Jupiter he had known through the televisor. He had expected it to be different, but not like this. He had expected a hell of ammonia rain and stinking fumes and the deafening, thundering tumult of the storm. He had expected swirling clouds and fog and the snarling flicker of monstrous thunderbolts.

He had not expected the lashing downpour would be reduced to drifting purple mist that moved like fleeing shadows over a red and purple sward. He had not even guessed the snaking bolts of lightning would be flares of pure ecstasy across a painted sky.

Waiting for Towser, Fowler flexed the muscles of his body, amazed at the smooth, sleek strength he found. Not a bad body, he decided, and grimaced at remembering how he had pitied the Lopers when he glimpsed them through the television screen.

For it had been hard to imagine a living organism based upon ammonia and hydrogen rather than upon water and oxygen, hard to believe that such a form of life could know the same quick thrill of life that human-kind could know. Hard to conceive of life out in the soupy maelstrom that was Jupiter, not knowing, of course, that through Jovian eyes it was no soupy maelstrom at all.

The wind brushed against him with what seemed gentle fingers and he remembered with a start that by Earth standards the wind was a roaring gale, a two-hundred-mile-an-hour howler laden with deadly gases.

Pleasant scents seeped into his body. And yet scarcely scents, for it was not the sense of smell as he remem-bered it. It was as if his whole being was soaking up the sensation of lavender—and yet not lavender. It was something, he knew, for which he had no word, un-doubtedly the first of many enigmas in terminology. For the words he knew, the thought symbols that served him as an Earthman, would not serve him as a Jovian.

The lock in the side of the dome opened and Towser came tumbling out—at least he thought it must be Towser.

He started to call to the dog, his mind shaping the words he meant to say. But he couldn't say them. There was no way to say them. He had nothing to say them with.

For a moment his mind swirled in muddy terror, a blind fear that eddied in little puffs of panic through his brain.

How did Jovians talk? How—

Suddenly he was aware of Towser, intensely aware of the bumbling, eager friendliness of the shaggy animal that had followed him from Earth to many planets. As if the thing that was Towser had reached out and for a moment sat within his brain.

And out of the bubbling welcome that he sensed, came words.

"Hiya, pal."

Not words really, better than words. Thought symbols in his brain, communicated thought symbols that had shades of meaning words could never have.

"Hiya, Towser," he said.

"I feel good," said Towser. "Like I was a pup. Lately I've been feeling pretty punk. Legs stiffening up on me and teeth wearing down to almost nothing. Hard to mumble a bone with teeth like that. Besides, the fleas give me hell. Used to be I never paid much attention to them. A couple of fleas more or less never meant much in my early days."

"But . . . but—" Fowler's thoughts tumbled awkwardly. "You're talking to me!"

"Sure thing," said Towser. "I always talked to you, but you couldn't hear me. I tried to say things to you, but I couldn't make the grade."

"I understood you sometimes," Fowler said.

"Not very well," said Towser. "You knew when I wanted food and when I wanted a drink and when I wanted out, but that's about all you ever managed."

"I'm sorry," Fowler said.

"Forget it," Towser told him. "I'll race you to the cliff."

For the first time, Fowler saw the cliff, apparently many miles away, but with a strange crystalline beauty that sparkled in the shadow of the many-colored clouds.

Fowler hesitated. "It's a long way—"

"Ah, come on," said Towser and even as he said it he started for the cliff.

Fowler followed, testing his legs, testing the strength in that new body of his, a bit doubtful at first, amazed a moment later, then running with a sheer joyousness that was one with the red and purple sward, with the drifting smoke of the rain across the land.

As he ran the consciousness of music came to him, a music that beat into his body, that surged throughout his being, that lifted him on wings of silver speed. Music like bells might make from some steeple on a sunny, springtime hill.

As the cliff drew nearer the music deepened and filled the universe with a spray of magic sound. And he knew the music came from the tumbling waterfall that feathered down the face of the shining cliff.

Only, he knew, it was no waterfall, but an ammonia-fall and the cliff was white because it was oxygen, solidified.

He skidded to a stop beside Towser where the water-fall broke into a glittering rainbow of many hundred colors. Literally many hundred, for here, he saw, was no shading of one primary to another as human beings saw, but a clearcut selectivity that broke the prism down to its last ultimate classification.

"The music," said Towser.

"Yes, what about it?"

"The music," said Towser, "is vibrations. Vibrations of water falling."

"But Towser, you don't know about vibrations."

"Yes, I do," contended Towser. "It just popped into my head."

Fowler gulped mentally. "Just popped!"

And suddenly, within his own head, he held a formula—the formula for a process that would make metal to withstand the pressure of Jupiter.

He stared, astounded, at the waterfall and swiftly his mind took the many colors and placed them in their exact sequence in the spectrum. Just like that. Just out of blue sky. Out of nothing, for he knew nothing either of metals or of colors.

"Towser," he cried. "Towser, something's happening to us!"

"Yeah, I know," said Towser.

"It's our brains," said Fowler. "We're using them, all of them, down to the last hidden corner. Using them to figure out things we should have known all the time. Maybe the brains of Earth things naturally are slow and foggy. Maybe we are the morons of the universe. Maybe we are fixed so we have to do things the hard way."

And, in the new sharp clarity of thought that seemed to grip him, he knew that it would not only be the matter of colors in a waterfall, or metals that would resist the pressure of Jupiter. He sensed other things, things not quite clear. A vague whispering that hinted of greater things, of mysteries beyond the pale of human thought, beyond even the pale of human imagination. Mysteries, fact, logic built on reasoning. Things that any brain should know if it used all its reasoning power.

"We're still mostly Earth," he said. "We're just beginning to learn a few of the things we are to know—a few of the things that were kept from us as human beings, perhaps because we were human beings. Because our human bodies were poor bodies. Poorly equipped for thinking, poorly equipped in certain senses that one has to have to know. Perhaps even lacking in certain senses that are necessary to true knowledge."

He stared back at the dome, a tiny black thing dwarfed by the distance.

Back there were men who couldn't see the beauty that was Jupiter. Men who thought that swirling clouds and lashing rain obscured the planet's face. Unseeing human eyes. Poor eyes. Eyes that could not see the beauty in the clouds, that could not see through the storm. Bodies that could not feel the thrill of trilling music stemming from the rush of broken water.

Men who walked alone, in terrible loneliness, talking with their tongue like Boy Scouts wigwagging out their messages, unable to reach out and touch one another's mind as he could reach out and touch Towser's mind. Shut off forever from that personal, intimate contact with other living things.

He, Fowler, had expected terror inspired by alien things out here on the surface, had expected to cower before the threat of unknown things, had steeled himself against disgust of a situation that was not of Earth.

But instead he had found something greater than Man had ever known. A swifter, surer body. A sense of exhilaration, a deeper sense of life. A sharper mind. A world of beauty that even the dreamers of the Earth had not yet imagined.

"Let's get going," Towser urged.

"Where do you want to go?"

"Anywhere," said Towser. "Just start going and see where we end up. I have a feeling . . . well, a feeling—"

"Yes, I know," said Fowler.

For he had the feeling, too. The feeling of high destiny. A certain sense of greatness. A knowledge that somewhere off beyond the horizons lay adventure and things greater than adventure.

Those other five had felt it, too. Had felt the urge to go and see, the compelling sense that here lay a life of fullness and of knowledge.

That, he knew, was why they had not returned.

"I won't go back," said Towser.

"We can't let them down," said Fowler.

Fowler took a step or two, back toward the dome, then stopped.

Back to the dome. Back to that aching, poison-laden body he had left. It hadn't seemed aching before, but now he knew it was.

Back to the fuzzy brain. Back to muddled thinking. Back to the flapping mouths that formed signals others understood. Back to eyes that now would be worse than no sight at all. Back to squalor, back to crawling, back to ignorance.

"Perhaps some day," he said, muttering to himself.

"We got a lot to do and a lot to see," said Towser. "We got a lot to learn. We'll find things—"

Yes, they could find things. Civilizations, perhaps. Civilizations that would make the civilization of Man seem puny by comparison. Beauty and, more important, an understanding of that beauty. And a comradeship no one had ever known before—that no man, no dog had ever known before.

And life. The quickness of life after what seemed a drugged existence.

"I can't go back," said Towser.

"Nor I," said Fowler.

"They would turn me back into a dog," said Towser.

"And me," said Fowler, "back into a man."

1944

THE MAD MOON
Stanley G. Weinbaum

21

One of the best things that ever happened to science fiction was when Stanley Weinbaum began to write it, as a young man in his twenties some forty years ago. One of the worst things that ever happened was his sudden and premature death, after less than three full years of writing. Weinbaum all by himself changed the concept of the "alien being" from the sort of mindless monster of Wells's **War of the Worlds** to the fanciful and delightful creatures—Tweel, in "A Martian Odyssey," was the first of them—that populate his stories. It is tempting, and poignant, to speculate on what he might have done if he had survived to a normal writing age, but even in his short career he opened up new worlds for all of us.

I

"Idiots!" howled Grant Calthorpe. "Fools—nitwits—imbeciles!" He sought wildly for some more expressive terms, failed, and vented his exasperation in a vicious kick at the pile of rubbish on the ground.

Too vicious a kick, in fact; he had again forgotten the one-third normal gravitation of Io, and his whole body followed his kick in a long, twelve-foot arc.

As he struck the ground the four loonies giggled. Their great, idiotic heads, looking like nothing so much as the comic faces painted on Sunday balloons for children, swayed in unison on their five-foot necks, as thin as Grant's wrist.

"Get out!" he blazed, scrambling erect. "Beat it, skiddoo, scram! No chocolate. No candy. Not until you learn that I want ferva leaves, and not any junk you happen to grab. Clear out!"

The loonie—*Lunae Jovis Magnicapites,* or literally, Bigheads of Jupiter's Moon—backed away, giggling plaintively. Beyond doubt, they considered Grant fully as idiotic as he considered them, and were quite unable to understand the reasons for his anger. But they certainly realized that no candy was to be forthcoming, and their giggles took on a note of keen disappointment.

So keen, indeed, that the leader, after twisting his ridiculous blue face in an imbecilic grin at Grant, voiced a last wild giggle and dashed his head against a glittering stone-bark tree. His companions casually picked up his body and moved off, with his head dragging behind them on its neck like a prisoner's ball on a chain.

Grant brushed his hand across his forehead and turned wearily toward his stone-bark log shack. A pair of tiny, glittering red eyes caught his attention, and a slinker—*Mus Sapiens*—skipped his six-inch form across the threshold, bearing under his tiny, skinny arm what looked very much like Grant's clinical thermometer.

Grant yelled angrily at the creature, seized a stone, and flung it vainly. At the edge of the brush, the slinker turned its ratlike, semihuman face toward him, squeaked its thin gibberish, shook a microscopic fist in manlike wrath, and vanished, its batlike cowl of skin fluttering like a cape. It looked, indeed, very much like a black rat wearing a cape.

It had been a mistake, Grant knew, to throw the stone at it. Now the tiny fiends would never permit him any peace, and their diminutive size and pseudo-human intelligence made them infernally troublesome as enemies. Yet, neither that reflection nor the loony's suicide troubled him particularly; he had witnessed instances like the latter too often, and besides, his head felt as if he were in for another siege of white fever.

He entered the shack, closed the door, and stared down at his pet parcat. "Oliver," he growled, "you're a fine one. Why the devil don't you watch out for slinkers? What are you here for?"

The parcat rose on its single, powerful hind leg, clawing at his knees with its two forelegs. "The red jack on the black queen," it observed placidly. "Ten loonies make one half-wit."

Grant placed both statements easily. The first was, of course, an echo of his preceding evening's solitaire game, and the second of yesterday's session with the loonies. He grunted abstractedly and rubbed his aching head. White fever again, beyond doubt.

He swallowed two ferverin tablets, and sank listlessly to the edge of his bunk, wondering whether this attack of *blancha* would culminate in delirium.

He cursed himself for a fool for ever taking this job on Jupiter's third habitable moon, Io. The tiny world was a planet of madness, good for nothing except the production of ferva leaves, out of which Earthly chemists made as many potent alkaloids as they once made from opium.

Invaluable to medical science, of course, but what difference did that make to him? What difference, even, did the munificent salary make, if he got back to Earth a raving maniac after a year in the equatorial regions of Io? He swore bitterly that when the plane from Junopolis landed next month for his ferva, he'd go back to the polar city with it, even though his contract with Neilan Drug called for a full year, and he'd get no pay if he broke it. What good was money to a lunatic?

II

The whole little planet was mad—loonies, parcats, slinkers and Grant Calthorpe—all crazy. At least, anybody who ever ventured outside either of the two polar cities, Junopolis on the north and Herapolis on the south, was crazy. One could live there in safety from white fever, but anywhere below the twentieth parallel it was worse than the Cambodian jungles on Earth.

He amused himself by dreaming of Earth. Just two years ago he had been happy there, known as a wealthy, popular sportsman. He had been just that, too; before he was twenty-one he had hunted knife-kite and threadworm on Titan, and triops and uniped on Venus.

That had been before the gold crisis of 2110 had wiped out his fortune. And—well, if he had to work, it had seemed logical to use his interplanetary experience as a means of livelihood. He had really been enthusiastic at the chance to associate himself with Neilan Drug.

He had never been on Io before. This wild little world was no sportsman's paradise with its idiotic loonies and wicked, intelligent, tiny slinkers. There wasn't anything worth hunting on the feverish little moon, bathed in warmth by the giant Jupiter only a quarter million miles away.

If he *had* happened to visit it, he told himself ruefully, he'd never have taken the job; he had visualized Io as something like Titan, cold but clean.

Instead it was as hot as the Venus Hotlands because of its glowing primary, and subject to half a dozen different forms of steamy daylight—sun day, Jovian day, Jovian and sun day, Europa light, and occasionally actual and dismal night. And most of these came in the course of Io's forty-two-hour revolution, too—a mad succession of changing lights. He hated the dizzy days, the jungle, and Idiots' Hills stretching behind his shack.

It was Jovian and solar day at the present moment, and that was the worst of all, because the distant sun added its modicum of heat to that of Jupiter. And to complete Grant's discomfort now was the prospect of a white fever attack. He swore as his head gave an additional twinge, and then swallowed another ferverin tablet. His supply of these was diminishing, he noticed; he'd have to remember to ask for some when the plane called—no, he was going back with it.

Oliver rubbed against his leg. "Idiots, fools, nitwits, imbeciles," remarked the parcat affectionately. "Why did I have to go to that damn dance?"

"Huh?" said Grant. He couldn't remember having said anything about a dance. It must, he decided, have been said during his last fever madness.

Oliver creaked like the door, then giggled like a loony. "It'll be all right," he assured Grant. "Father is bound to come soon."

"Father!" echoed the man. His father had died fifteen years before. "Where'd you get that from, Oliver?"

"It must be the fever," observed Oliver placidly. "You're a nice kitty, but I wish you had sense enough to know what you're saying. And I wish father would come." He finished with a suppressed gurgle that might have been a sob.

Grant stared dizzily at him. He hadn't said any of those things; he was positive. The parcat must have heard them from somebody else— Somebody else? Where within five hundred miles was there anybody else?

"Oliver!" he bellowed. "Where'd you hear that? Where'd you hear it?"

The parcat backed away, startled. "Father is idiots, fools, nitwits, imbeciles," he said anxiously. "The red jack on the nice kitty."

"Come here!" roared Grant. "Whose father? Where have you— Come here, you imp!"

He lunged at the creature. Oliver flexed his single
hind leg and flung himself frantically to the cowl of
the wood stove. "It must be the fever!" he squalled.
"No chocolate!"

He leaped like a three-legged flash for the flue opening. There came a sound of claws grating on metal, and
then he had scrambled through.

Grant followed him. His head ached from the effort,
and with the still sane part of his mind he knew that the
whole episode was doubtless white fever delirium, but
he plowed on.

His progress was a nightmare. Loonies kept bobbing
their long necks above the tall bleeding-grass, their
idiotic giggles and imbecilic faces adding to the general
atmosphere of madness.

Wisps of fetid fever-bearing vapors spouted up at
every step on the spongy soil. Somewhere to his right
a slinker squeaked and gibbered; he knew that a tiny
slinker village was over in that direction, for once he
had glimpsed the neat little buildings, constructed of
small, perfectly fitted stones like a miniature medieval
town, complete to towers and battlements. It was said
that there were even slinker wars.

His head buzzed and whirled from the combined
effects of ferverin and fever. It was an attack of *blancha*,
right enough, and he realized that he was an imbecile,
a loony, to wander thus away from his shack. He should
be lying on his bunk; the fever was not serious, but
more than one man had died on Io in the delirium, with
its attendant hallucinations.

He was delirious now. He knew it as soon as he saw
Oliver, for Oliver was placidly regarding an attractive
young lady in perfect evening dress of the style of the
second decade of the twenty-second century. Very obviously that was a hallucination, since girls had no busi-

ness in the Ionian tropics, and if by some wild chance one should appear there, she would certainly not choose formal garb.

The hallucination had fever, apparently, for her face was pale with the whiteness that gave *blancha* its name. Her gray eyes regarded him without surprise as he wound his way through the bleeding-grass to her.

"Good afternoon, evening, or morning," he remarked, giving a puzzled glance at Jupiter, which was rising, and the sun, which was setting. "Or perhaps merely good day, Miss Lee Neilan."

She gazed seriously at him. "Do you know," she said, "you're the first one of the illusions that I haven't recognized? All my friends have been around, but you're the first stranger. Or are you a stranger? You know my name—but you ought to, of course, being my own hallucination."

"We won't argue about which of us is the hallucination," he suggested. "Let's do it this way. The one of us that disappears first is the illusion. Bet you five dollars you do."

"How could I collect?" she said. "I can't very well collect from my own dream."

"That is a problem." He frowned. "My problem, of course, not yours. I know I'm real."

"How do you know my name?" she demanded.

"Ah!" he said. "From intensive reading of the society sections of the newspapers brought by my supply plane. As a matter of fact, I have one of your pictures cut out and pasted next to my bunk. That probably accounts for my seeing you now. I'd like to really meet you some time."

"What a gallant remark for an apparition!" she exclaimed. "And who are you supposed to be?"

"Why, I'm Grant Calthorpe. In fact, I work for your father, trading with the loonies for ferva."

"Grant Calthorpe," she echoed. She narrowed her

fever-dulled eyes as if to bring him into better focus. "Why, you are!"

Her voice wavered for a moment, and she brushed her hand across her pale brow. "Why should you pop up out of my memories? It's strange. Three or four years ago, when I was a romantic schoolgirl and you the famous sportsman, I was madly in love with you. I had a whole book filled with your pictures—Grant Calthorpe dressed in parka for hunting threadworn on Titan—Grant Calthorpe beside the giant uniped he killed near the Mountains of Eternity. You're—you're really the pleasantest hallucination I've had so far. Delirium would be—fun"—she pressed her hand to her brow again—"if one's head—didn't ache so!"

"Gee!" thought Grant, "I wish that were true, that about the book. This is what psychology calls a wish-fulfillment dream." A drop of warm rain plopped on his neck. "Got to get to bed," he said aloud. "Rain's bad for *blancha*. Hope to see you next time I'm feverish."

"Thank you," said Lee Neilan with dignity. "It's quite mutual."

He nodded, sending a twinge through his head. "Here, Oliver," he said to the drowsing parcat. "Come on."

"That isn't Oliver," said Lee. "It's Polly. It's kept me company for two days, and I've named it Polly."

"Wrong gender," muttered Grant. "Anyway, it's my parcat, Oliver. Aren't you, Oliver?"

"Hope to see you," said Oliver sleepily.

"It's Polly. Aren't you, Polly?"

"Bet you five dollars," said the parcat. He rose, stretched and loped off into the underbrush. "It must be the fever," he observed as he vanished.

"It must be," agreed Grant. He turned away. "Good-by, Miss—or I might as well call you Lee, since you're not real. Good-by, Lee."

"Good-by, Grant. But don't go that way. There's a slinker village over in the grass."

"No. It's over there."

"It's *there*," she insisted. "I've been watching them build it. But they can't hurt you anyway, can they? Not even a slinker could hurt an apparition. Goodby, Grant." She closed her eyes wearily.

III

It was raining harder now. Grant pushed his way through the bleeding-grass, whose red sap collected in bloody drops on his boots. He had to get back to his shack quickly, before the white fever and its attendant delirium set him wandering utterly astray. He needed ferverin.

Suddenly he stopped short. Directly before him the grass had been cleared away, and in the little clearing were the shoulder-high towers and battlements of a slinker village—a new one, for half-finished houses stood among the others, and hooded six-inch forms toiled over the stones.

There was an outcry of squeaks and gibberish. He backed away but a dozen tiny darts whizzed about him. One stuck like a toothpick in his boot, but none, luckily, scratched his skin, for they were undoubtedly poisoned. He moved more quickly, but all around in the thick, fleshy grasses were rustlings, squeakings, and incomprehensible imprecations.

He circled away. Loonies kept popping their balloon heads over the vegetation, and now and again one giggled in pain as a slinker bit or stabbed it. Grant cut toward a group of the creatures, hoping to distract the tiny fiends in the grass, and a tall, purple-faced loony curved its long neck above him, giggling and gesturing with its skinny fingers at a bundle under its arm.

He ignored the thing, and veered toward his shack. He seemed to have eluded the slinkers, so he trudged doggedly on, for he needed a ferverin tablet badly. Yet, suddenly he came to a frowning halt, turned, and began to retrace his steps.

"It can't be so," he muttered. "But she told me the truth about the slinker village. I didn't know it was there. Yet how could a hallucination tell me something I didn't know?"

Lee Neilan was sitting on the stone-bark log exactly as he had left her, with Oliver again at her side. Her eyes were closed, and two slinkers were cutting at the long skirt of her gown with tiny, glittering knives.

Grant knew that they were always attracted by Terrestrial textiles; apparently they were unable to duplicate the fascinating sheen of satin, though the fiends were infernally clever with their tiny hands. As he approached, they tore a strip from thigh to ankle, but the girl made no move. Grant shouted, and the vicious little creatures mouthed unutterable curses at him as they skittered away with their silken plunder.

Lee Neilan opened his eyes. "You again," she murmured vaguely. "A moment ago it was father. Now it's you." Her pallor had increased; the white fever was running its course in her body.

"Your father! Then that's where Oliver heard— Listen, Lee. I found the slinker village. I didn't know it was there, but I found it just as you said. Do you see what that means? We're both real!"

"Real?" she said dully. "There's a purple loony grinning over your shoulder. Make him go away. He makes me feel—sick."

He glanced around; true enough, the purple-faced loony was behind him. "Look here," he said, seizing her arm. The feel of her smooth skin was added proof. "You're coming to the shack for ferverin." He pulled her to her feet. "Don't you understand? I'm *real!*"

"No, you're not," she said dazedly.

"Listen, Lee. I don't know how in the devil you got here or why, but I know Io hasn't driven me that crazy yet. You're real and I'm real." He shook her violently. "I'm *real!*" he shouted.

Faint comprehension showed in her dazed eyes. "Real?" she whispered. "Real! Oh, Lord! Then take— me out of—this mad place!" She swayed, made a stubborn effort to control herself, then pitched forward against him.

Of course on Io her weight was negligible, less than a third Earth normal. He swung her into his arms and set off toward the shack, keeping well away from both slinker settlements. Around him bobbed excited loonies, and now and again the purple-faced one, or another exactly like him, giggled and pointed and gestured.

The rain had increased, and warm rivulets flowed down his neck, and to add to the madness, he blundered near a copse of stinging palms, and their barbed lashes stung painfully through his shirt. Those stings were virulent too, if one failed to disinfect them; indeed, it was largely the stinging palms that kept traders from gathering their own ferva instead of depending on the loonies.

Behind the low rain clouds, the sun had set, and it was ruddy Jupiter daylight, which lent a false flush to the cheeks of the unconscious Lee Neilan, making her still features very lovely.

Perhaps he kept his eyes too steadily on her face, for suddenly Grant was among slinkers again; they were squeaking and sputtering, and the purple loony leaped in pain as teeth and darts pricked his legs. But, of course, loonies were immune to the poison.

The tiny devils were around his feet now. He swore in a low voice and kicked vigorously, sending a ratlike form spinning fifty feet in the air. He had both automatic and flame pistol at his hip, but he could not use them for several reasons.

First, using an automatic against the tiny hordes was much like firing into a swarm of mosquitoes; if the bullet killed one or two or a dozen, it made no appreciable impression on the remaining thousands. And as for the flame pistol, that was like using a Big Bertha to swat a fly. Its vast belch of fire would certainly incinerate all the slinkers in its immediate path, along with grass, trees, and loonies, but that again would make but little impress on the surviving hordes, and it meant laboriously recharging the pistol with another black diamond and another barrel.

He had gas bulbs in the shack, but they were not available at the moment, and besides, he had no spare mask, and no chemist has yet succeeded in devising a gas that would kill slinkers without being also deadly to humans. And, finally, he couldn't use any weapon whatsoever right now, because he dared not drop Lee Neilan to free his hands.

Ahead was the clearing around the shack. The space was full of slinkers, but the shack itself was supposed to be slinkerproof, at least for reasonable lengths of time, since stone-bark logs were very resistant to their tiny tools.

But Grant perceived that a group of the diminutive devils were around the door, and suddenly he realized their intent. They had looped a cord of some sort over the knob, and were engaged now in twisting it!

Grant yelled and broke into a run. While he was yet half a hundred feet distant, the door swung inward and the rabble of slinkers flowed into the shack.

He dashed through the entrance. Within was turmoil. Little hooded shapes were cutting at the blankets on his bunk, his extra clothing, the sacks he hoped to fill with ferva leaves, and were pulling at the cooking utensils, or at any and all loose objects.

He bellowed and kicked at the swarm. A wild chorus of squeaks and gibberish arose as the creatures skipped and dodged about him. The fiends were intelligent enough to realize that he could do nothing with his arms occupied by Lee Neilan. They skittered out of the way of his kicks, and while he threatened a group at the stove, another rabble tore at his blankets.

In desperation he charged at the bunk. He swept the girl's body across it to clear it, dropped her on it, and seized a grass broom he had made to facilitate his housekeeping. With wide strokes of its handle he attacked the slinkers, and the squeals were checkered by cries and whimpers of pain.

A few broke for the door, dragging whatever loot they had. He spun around in time to see half a dozen swarming around Lee Neilan, tearing at her clothing, at the wrist watch on her arm, at the satin evening pumps on her small feet. He roared a curse at them and battered them away, hoping that none had pricked her skin with virulent dagger or poisonous tooth.

He began to win the skirmish. More of the creatures drew their black capes close about them and scurried over the threshold with their plunder. At last, with a burst of squeaks, the remainder, laden and empty-handed alike, broke and ran for safety, leaving a dozen furry, impish bodies slain or wounded.

Grant swept these after the others with his erstwhile weapon, closed the door in the face of a loony that bobbed in the opening, latched it against any repetition of the slinkers' tricks, and stared in dismay about the plundered dwelling.

Cans had been rolled or dragged away. Every loose object had been pawed by the slinkers' foul little hands, and Grant's clothes hung in ruins on their hooks against the wall. But the tiny robbers had not succeeded in opening the cabinet nor the table drawer, and there was food left.

Six months of Ionian life had left him philosophical; he swore heartily, shrugged resignedly, and pulled his bottle of ferverin from the cabinet.

His own spell of fever had vanished as suddenly and completely as *blancha* always does when treated, but the girl, lacking ferverin, was paper-white and still. Grant glanced at the bottle; eight tablets remained.

"Well, I can always chew ferva leaves," he muttered. That was less effective than the alkaloid itself, but it would serve, and Lee Neilan needed the tablets. He dissolved two of them in a glass of water, and lifted her head.

She was not too inert to swallow, and he poured the solution between her pale lips, then arranged her as comfortably as he could. Her dress was a tattered silken ruin, and he covered her with a blanket that was no less a ruin. Then he disinfected his palm stings, pulled two chairs together, and sprawled across them to sleep.

He started up at the sound of claws on the roof, but it was only Oliver, gingerly testing the flue to see if it were hot. In a moment the parcat scrambled through, stretched himself, and remarked, "I'm real and you're real."

"Imagine that!" grunted Grant sleepily.

IV

When he awoke it was Jupiter and Europa light, which meant he had slept about seven hours, since the brilliant little third moon was just rising. He rose and gazed at Lee Neilan, who was sleeping soundly with a tinge of color in her face that was not entirely due to the ruddy daylight. The *blancha* was passing.

He dissolved two more tablets in water, then shook the girl's shoulder. Instantly her grey eyes opened, quite clear now, and she looked up at him without surprise.

"Hello, Grant," she murmured. "So it's you again. Fever isn't so bad, after all."

"Maybe I ought to let you stay feverish," he grinned. "You say such nice things. Wake up and drink this, Lee."

She became suddenly aware of the shack's interior. "Why— Where is this? It looks—real!"

"It is. Drink this ferverin."

She obeyed, then lay back and stared at him perplexedly. "Real?" she said. "And you're real?"

"I think I am."

A rush of tears clouded her eyes. "Then—I'm out of that place? That horrible place?"

"You certainly are." He saw signs of her relief becoming hysteria, and hastened to distract her. "Would you mind telling me how you happened to be there— and dressed for a party, too?"

She controlled herself. "I was dressed for a party. A party in Herapolis. But I was in Junopolis, you see."

"I don't see. In the first place, what are you doing on Io, anyway? Every time I ever heard of you, it was in connection with New York or Paris society."

She smiled. "Then it wasn't all delirium, was it? You did say that you had one of my pictures— Oh, that one!" She frowned at the print on the wall. "Next time a news photographer wants to snap my picture, I'll remember not to grin—like a loony. But as to how I happen to be on Io, I came with father, who's looking over the possibilities of raising ferva on plantations instead of having to depend on traders and loonies. We've been here three months, and I've been terribly bored. I thought Io would be exciting, but it wasn't— until recently."

"But what about that dance? How'd you manage to get here, a thousand miles from Junopolis?"

"Well," she said slowly, "it was terribly tiresome in Junopolis. No shows, no sport, nothing but an occasional dance. I got restless. When there were dances in Herapolis, I formed the habit of flying over there. It's only four or five hours in a fast plane, you know. And last week—or whenever it was—I'd planned on flying down, and Harvey—that's father's secretary—was to take me. But at the last minute father needed him, and forbade my flying alone."

Grant felt a strong dislike for Harvey. "Well?" he asked.

"So I flew alone," she finished demurely.

"And cracked up, eh?"

"I can fly as well as anybody," she retorted. "It was just that I followed a different route, and suddenly there were mountains ahead."

He nodded. "The Idiots' Hills," he said. "My supply plane detours five hundred miles to avoid them. They're not high, but they stick right out above the atmosphere of this crazy planet. The air here is dense but shallow."

"I know that. I knew I couldn't fly above them, but I thought I could hurdle them. Work up full speed, you know, and then throw the plane upward. I had a closed plane, and gravitation is so weak here. And besides, I've seen it done several times, especially with rocket-driven craft. The jets help to support the plane even after the wings are useless for lack of air."

"What a damn fool stunt!" exclaimed Grant. "Sure it can be done, but you have to be an expert to pull out of it when you hit the air on the other side. You hit fast, and there isn't much falling room."

"So I found out," said Lee ruefully. "I almost pulled out, but not quite, and I hit in the middle of some stinging palms. I guess the crash dazed them, because I managed to get out before they started lashing around.

But I couldn't reach my plane again, and it was—I only remember two day of it—but it was horrible!"

"It must have been," he said gently.

"I knew that if I didn't eat or drink, I had a chance of avoiding white fever. The not eating wasn't so bad, but the not drinking—well, I finally gave up and drank out of a brook. I didn't care what happened if I could have a few moments that weren't thirst-tortured. And after that it's all confused and vague."

"You should have chewed ferva leaves."

"I didn't know that. I wouldn't have even known what they looked like, and besides, I kept expecting father to appear. He must be having a search made by now."

"He probably is," rejoined Grant ironically. "Has it occurred to you that there are thirteen million square miles of surface on little Io? And that for all he knows, you might have crashed on any square mile of it? When you're flying from north pole to south pole, there *isn't* any shortest route. You can cross any point on the planet."

Her gray eyes started wide. "But I—"

"Furthermore," said Grant, "this is probably the *last* place a searching party would look. They wouldn't think any one but a loony would try to hurdle Idiots' Hills, in which thesis I quite agree. So it looks very much, Lee Neilan, as if you're marooned here until my supply plane gets here next month!"

"But father will be crazy! He'll think I'm dead!"

"He thinks that now, no doubt."

"But we can't—" She broke off, staring around the tiny shack's single room. After a moment she sighed resignedly, smiled, and said softly, "Well, it might have been worse, Grant. I'll try to earn my keep."

"Good. How do you feel, Lee?"

"Quite normal. I'll start right to work." She flung off the tattered blanket, sat up, and dropped her feet to the floor. "I'll fix dinn— Good night! My dress!" She snatched the blanket about her again.

He grinned. "We had a little run-in with the slinkers after you had passed out. They did for my spare wardrobe too."

"It's ruined!" she wailed.

"Would needle and thread help? They left that, at least, because it was in the table drawer."

"Why, I couldn't make a good swimming suit out of this!" she retorted. "Let me try one of yours."

By dint of cutting, patching, and mending, she at last managed to piece one of Grant's suits to respectable proportions. She looked very lovely in shirt and trousers, but he was troubled to note that a sudden pallor had overtaken her.

It was the *riblancha,* the second spell of fever that usually followed a severe or prolonged attack. His face was serious as he cupped two of his last four ferverin tablets in his hand.

"Take these," he ordered. "And we've got to get some ferva leaves somewhere. The plane took my supply away last week, and I've had bad luck with my loonies ever since. They haven't brought me anything but weeds and rubbish."

Lee puckered her lips at the bitterness of the drug, then closed her eyes against its momentary dizziness and nausea. "Where can you find ferva?" she asked.

He shook his head perplexedly, glancing out at the setting mass of Jupiter, with its bands glowing creamy and brown, and the Red Spot boiling near the western edge. Close above it was the brilliant little disk of Europa. He frowned suddenly, glanced at his watch and then at the almanac on the inside of the cabinet door.

"It'll be Europa light in fifteen minutes," he muttered,

"and true night in twenty-five—the first true night in half a month. I wonder—"

He gazed thoughtfully at Lee's face. He knew where ferva grew. One dared not penetrate the jungle itself, where stinging palms and arrow vines and the deadly worms called toothers made such a venture sheer suicide for any creatures but loonies and slinkers. But he knew where ferva grew—

In Io's rare true night even the clearing might be dangerous. Not merely from slinkers, either; he knew well enough that in the darkness creatures crept out of the jungle who otherwise remained in the eternal shadows of its depths—toothers, bullet-head frogs, and doubtless many unknown slimy, venomous, mysterious beings never seen by man. One heard stories in Herapolis and—

But he had to get ferva, and he knew where it grew. Not even a loony would try to gather it there, but in the little gardens or farms around the tiny slinker towns, there was ferva growing.

He switched on a light in the gathering dusk. "I'm going outside a moment," he told Lee Neilan. "If the *blancha* starts coming back, take the other two tablets. Wouldn't hurt you to take 'em anyway. The slinkers got away with my thermometer, but if you get dizzy again, you take 'em."

"Grant! Where—"

"I'll be back," he called, closing the door behind him.

A loony, purple in the bluish Europa light, bobbed up with a long giggle. He waved the creature aside and set off on a cautious approach to the neighborhood of the slinker village—the old one, for the other could hardly have had time to cultivate its surrounding ground. He crept warily through the bleeding-grass, but he knew his stealth was pure optimism. He was in exactly the position of a hundred-foot giant trying to approach a human city in secrecy—a difficult matter even in the utter darkness of night.

He reached the edge of the slinker clearing. Behind him, Europa, moving as fast as the second hand on his watch, plummeted toward the horizon. He paused in momentary surprise at the sight of the exquisite little town, a hundred feet away across the tiny square fields, with lights flickering in its hand-wide windows. He had not known that slinker culture included the use of lights, but there they were, tiny candles or perhaps diminutive oil lamps.

He blinked in the darkness. The second of the ten-foot fields looked like—it was—ferva. He stooped low, crept out, and reached his hand for the fleshy, white leaves. And at that moment came a shrill giggle and the crackle of grass behind him. The loony! The idiotic purple loony!

Squeaking shrieks sounded. He snatched a double handful of ferva, rose, and dashed toward the lighted window of his shack. He had no wish to face poisoned barbs or disease-bearing teeth, and the slinkers were certainly aroused. Their gibbering sounded in chorus; the ground looked black with them.

He reached the shack, burst in, slammed and latched the door. "Got it!" He grinned. "Let 'em rave outside now."

They were raving. Their gibberish sounded like the creaking of worn machinery. Even Oliver opened his drowsy eyes to listen. "It must be the fever," observed the parcat placidly.

Lee was certainly no paler; the *riblancha* was passing safely. "Ugh!" she said, listening to the tumult without. "I've always hated rats, but slinkers are worse. All the shrewdness and viciousness of rats plus the intelligence of devils."

"Well," said Grant thoughtfully, "I don't see what they can do. They've had it in for me anyway."

"It sounds as if they're going off," said the girl, listening. "The noise is fading."

Grant peered out of the window. "They're still around. They've just passed from swearing to planning, and I wish I knew what. Some day, if this crazy little planet ever becomes worth human occupation, there's going to be a show-down between humans and slinkers."

"Well? They're not civilized enough to be really a serious obstacle, and they're so small, besides."

"But they learn," he said. "They learn so quickly, and they breed like flies. Suppose they pick up the use of gas, or suppose they develop little rifles for their poisonous darts. That's possible, because they work in metals right now, and they know fire. That would put them practically on a par with man as far as offense goes, for what good are our giant cannons and rocket planes against six-inch slinkers? And to be just on even terms would be fatal; one slinker for one man would be a hell of a trade."

Lee yawned. "Well, it's not our problem. I'm hungry, Grant."

"Good. That's a sign the *blancha's* through with you. We'll eat and then sleep a while, for there's five hours of darkness."

"But the slinkers?"

"I don't see what they can do. They couldn't cut through stone-bark walls in five hours, and anyway, Oliver would warn us if one managed to slip in somewhere."

V

It was light when Grant awoke, and he stretched his cramped limps painfully across his two chairs. Something had wakened him, but he didn't know just what.

Oliver was pacing nervously beside him, and now looked anxiously up at him.

"I've had bad luck with my loonies," announced the parcat plaintively. "You're a nice kitty."

"So are you," said Grant. Something had wakened him, but what?

Then he knew, for it came again—the merest trembling of the stone-bark floor. He frowned in puzzlement. Earthquakes? Not on Io, for the tiny sphere had lost its internal heat untold ages ago. Then what?

Comprehension dawned suddenly. He sprang to his feet with so wild a yell that Oliver scrambled sideways with an infernal babble. The startled parcat leaped to the stove and vanished up the flue. His squall drifted faintly back, "It must be the fever!"

Lee had started to a sitting position on the bunk, her gray eyes blinking sleepily.

"Outside!" he roared, pulling her to her feet. "Get out! Quickly!"

"Wh-what—why—"

"Get out!" He thrust her through the door, then spun to seize his belt and weapons, the bag of ferva leaves, a package of chocolate. The floor trembled again, and he burst out of the door with a frantic leap to the side of the dazed girl.

"They've undermined it!" he choked. "The devils undermined the—"

He had no time to say more. A corner of the shack suddenly subsided; the stone-bark logs grated, and the whole structure collapsed like a child's house of blocks. The crash died into silence, and there was no motion save a lazy wisp of vapor, a few black, ratlike forms scurrying toward the grass, and a purple loony bobbing beyond the ruins.

"The dirty devils!" he swore bitterly. "The damn little black rats! The—"

A dart whistled so close that it grazed his ear and then twitched a lock of Lee's tousled brown hair. A chorus of squeaking sounded in the bleeding-grass.

"Come on!" he cried. "They're out to exterminate us this time. No—this way. Toward the hills. There's less jungle this way."

They could outrun the tiny slinkers easily enough. In a few moments they had lost the sound of squeaking voices, and they stopped to gaze ruefully back on the fallen dwelling.

"Now," he said miserably, "we're both where you were to start with."

"Oh, no." Lee looked up at him. "We're together now, Grant. I'm not afraid."

"We'll manage," he said with a show of assurance. "We'll put up a temporary shack somehow. We'll—"

A dart struck his boot with a sharp *blup*. The slinkers had caught up to them.

Again they ran toward Idiots' Hills. When at last they stopped, they could look down a long slope and far over the Ionian jungles. There was the ruined shack, and there, neatly checkered, the fields and towers of the nearer slinker town. But they had scarcely caught their breath when gibbering and squeaking came out of the brush.

They were being driven into Idiots' Hills, a region as unknown to man as the icy wastes of Pluto. It was as if the tiny fiends behind them had determined that this time their enemy, the giant trampler and despoiler of their fields, should be pursued to extinction.

Weapons were useless. Grant could not even glimpse their pursuers, slipping like hooded rats through the vegetation. A bullet, even if chance sped it through a slinker's body, was futile, and his flame pistol, though its lightning stroke should incinerate tons of brush and bleeding-grass, could no more than cut a narrow path through their horde of tormentors. The only weapons that might have availed, the gas bulbs, were lost in the ruins of the shack.

Grant and Lee were forced upward. They had risen a thousand feet above the plain, and the air was thinning. There was no jungle here, but only great stretches of bleeding-grass, across which a few loonies were visible, bobbing their heads on their long necks.

"Toward—the peaks!" gasped Grant, now painfully short of breath. "Perhaps we can stand rarer air than they."

Lee was beyond answer. She panted doggedly along beside him as they plodded now over patches of bare rock. Before them were two low peaks, like the pillars of a gate. Glancing back, Grant caught a glimpse of tiny black forms on a clear area, and in sheer anger he fired a shot. A single slinker leaped convulsively, its cape flapping, but the rest flowed on. There must have been thousands of them.

The peaks were closer, no more than a few hundred yards away. They were sheer, smooth, unscalable.

"Between them," muttered Grant.

The passage that separated them was bare and narrow. The twin peaks had been one in ages past; some forgotten volcanic convulsion had split them, leaving this slender canyon between.

He slipped an arm about Lee, whose breath, from effort and altitude, was a series of rasping gasps. A bright dart tinkled on the rocks as they reached the opening, but looking back, Grant could see only a purple loony plodding upward, and a few more to his right. They raced down a straight fifty-foot passage that debouched suddenly into a sizable valley—and there, thunderstruck for a moment, they paused.

A city lay there. For a brief instant Grant thought

they had burst upon a vast slinker metropolis, but the merest glance showed otherwise. This was no city of medieval blocks, but a poem in marble, classical in beauty, and of human or near-human proportions. White columns, glorious arches, pure curving domes, an architectural loveliness that might have been born on the Acropolis. It took a second look to discern that the city was dead, deserted, in ruins.

Even in her exhaustion, Lee felt its beauty. "How— how exquisite!" she panted. "One could almost forgive them—for being—slinkers!"

"They won't forgive us for being human," he muttered. "We'll have to make a stand somewhere. We'd better pick a building."

But before they could move more than a few feet from the canyon mouth, a wild disturbance halted them. Grant whirled, and for a moment found himself actually paralyzed by amazement. The narrow canyon was filled with a gibbering horde of slinkers, like a nauseous, heaving black carpet. But they came no further than the valley end, for grinning, giggling, and bobbing, blocking the opening with tramping three-toed feet, were our loonies!

It was a battle. The slinkers were biting and stabbing at the miserable defenders, whose shrill keenings of pain were less giggles than shrieks. But with a determination and purpose utterly foreign to loonies, their clawed feet tramped methodically up and down, up and down.

Grant exploded, "I'll be damned!" Then an idea struck him. "Lee! They're packed in the canyon, the whole devil's brood of 'em!"

He rushed toward the opening. He thrust his flame pistol between the skinny legs of a loony, aimed it straight along the canyon, and fired.

VI

Inferno burst. The tiny diamond, giving up all its energy in one terrific blast, shot a jagged stream of fire that filled the canyon from wall to wall and vomited out beyond to cut a fan of fire through the bleeding-grass of the slope.

Idiots' Hills reverberated to the roar, and when the rain of débris settled, there was nothing in the canyon save a few bits of flesh and the head of an unfortunate loony, still bouncing and rolling.

Three of the loonies survived. A purple-faced one was pulling his arm, grinning and giggling in imbecile glee. He waved the thing aside and returned to the girl.

"Thank goodness!" he said. "We're out of that, anyway."

"I wasn't afraid, Grant. Not with you."

He smiled. "Perhaps we can find a place here," he suggested. "The fever ought to be less troublesome at this altitude. But—say, this must have been the capital city of the whole slinker race in ancient times. I can scarcely imagine those fiends creating an architecture as beautiful as this—or as large. Why, these buildings are as colossal in proportion to slinker size as the sky-scrapers of New York to us!"

"But so beautiful," said Lee softly, sweeping her eyes over the glory of the ruins. "One might almost forgive—Grant! Look at those!"

He followed the gesture. On the inner side of the canyon's portals were gigantic carvings. But the thing that set him staring in amazement was the subject of the portrayal. There, towering far up the cliff sides, were the figures, not of slinkers, but of—loonies! Exquisitely carved, smiling rather than grinning, and smiling somehow sadly, regretfully, pityingly—yet beyond doubt loonies!

"Good night!" he whispered. "Do you see, Lee? This

must once have been a loony city. The steps, the doors, the buildings, all are on their scale of size. Somehow, some time, they must have achieved civilization, and the loonies we know are the degenerate residue of a great race."

"And," put in Lee, "the reason those four blocked the way when the slinkers tried to come through is that they still remember. Or probably they don't actually remember, but they have a tradition of past glories, or more likely still, just a superstitious feeling that this place is in some way sacred. They let us pass because, after all, we look more like loonies than like slinkers. But the amazing thing is that they still possess even that dim memory, because this city must have been in ruins for centuries. Or perhaps even for thousands of years."

"But to think that loonies could ever have had the intelligence to create a culture of their own," said Grant, waving away the purple one bobbing and giggling at his side. Suddenly he paused, turning a gaze of new respect on the creature. "This one's been following me for days. All right, old chap, what is it?"

The purple one extended a sorely bedraggled bundle of bleeding-grass and twigs, giggling idiotically. His ridiculous mouth twisted; his eyes popped in an agony of effort at mental concentration.

"Canny!" he giggled triumphantly.

"The imbecile!" flared Grant. "Nitwit! Idiot!" He broke off, then laughed. "Never mind. I guess you deserve it." He tossed his package of chocolate to the three delighted loonies. "Here's your candy."

A scream from Lee startled him. She was waving her arms wildly, and over the crest of Idiots' Hills a rocket plane roared, circled, and nosed its way into the valley.

The door opened. Oliver stalked gravely out, remarking casually, "I'm real and you're real." A man followed the parcat—two men.

"Father!" screamed Lee.

It was some time later that Gustavus Neilan turned to Grant. "I can't thank you," he said. "If there's ever any way I can show my appreciation for—"

"There is. You can cancel my contract."

"Oh, you work for me?"

"I'm Grant Calthorpe, one of your traders, and I'm about sick of this crazy planet."

"Of course, if you wish," said Neilan. "If it's a question of pay—"

"You can pay me for the six months I've worked."

"If you'd care to stay," said the older man, "there won't be trading much longer. We've been able to grow ferva near the polar cities, and I prefer plantations to the uncertainties of relying on loonies. If you'd work out your year, we might be able to put you in charge of a plantation by the end of that time."

Grant met Lee Neilan's gray eyes, and hesitated. "Thanks," he said slowly, "but I'm sick of it." He smiled at the girl, then turned back to her father. "Would you mind telling me how you happened to find us? This is the most unlikely place on the planet."

"That's just the reason," said Neilan. "When Lee didn't get back, I thought things over pretty carefully. At last I decided, knowing her as I did, to search the least likely places first. We tried the shores of the Fever Sea, and then the White Desert, and finally Idiots' Hills. We spotted the ruins of a shack, and on the debris was this chap"—he indicated Oliver—"remarking that 'Ten loonies make one half-wit.' Well, the half-wit part sounded very much like a reference to my daughter, and we cruised about until the roar of your flame pistol attracted our attention."

Lee pouted, then turned her serious gray eyes on Grant. "Do you remember," she said softly, "what I told you there in the jungle?"

"I wouldn't even have mentioned that," he replied. "I knew you were delirious."

"But—perhaps I wasn't. Would companionship make it any easier to work out your year? I mean if—for instance—you were to fly back with us to Junapolis and return with a wife?"

"Lee," he said huskily, "you know what a difference that would make, though I can't understand why you'd ever dream of it."

"It must," suggested Oliver, "be the fever."

1934

HEAVYPLANET
Milton A. Rothman

♃

This is one of the earliest science-fiction stories in this book; when it was written the astronomical notions of the conditions on the surface of Jupiter were rather infirm, and so Milton Rothman hedged his bets a trifle. "Heavyplanet" may be Jupiter, or it may be a similar planet of some other star; he never quite says. But it seemed to us to deserve a place in this collection on its merits . . . and here it is.

Ennis was completing his patrol of Sector EM. Division 426 of the Eastern Ocean. The weather had been unusually fine, the liquid-thick air roaring along in a continuous blast that propelled his craft with a rush as if it were flying, and lifting short, choppy waves that rose and fell with a startling suddenness. A short savage squall whirled about, pounding down on the ocean like a million hammers, flinging the little boat ahead madly.

Ennis tore at the controls, granite-hard muscles standing out in bas-relief over his short, immensely thick body, skin gleaming scalelike in the slashing spray. The heat from the sun that hung like a huge red lantern on the horizon was a tangible intensity, making an inferno of the gale.

The little craft, that Ennis maneuvered by sheer brawn, took a leap into the air and seemed to float for many seconds before burying its keel again in the sea. It often floated for long distances, the air was so dense.

The boundary between air and water was sometimes scarcely defined at all—one merged into the other imperceptibly. The pressure did strange things.

Like a dust mote sparkling in a beam, a tiny speck of light above caught Ennis' eye. A glider, he thought, but he was puzzled. Why so far out here on the ocean? They were nasty things to handle in the violent wind.

The dust mote caught the light again. It was lower, tumbling down with a precipitancy that meant trouble. An upward blast caught it, checked its fall. Then it floated down gently for a space until struck by another howling wind that seemed to distort its very outlines.

Ennis turned the prow of his boat to meet the path of the falling vessel. Curious, he thought; where were its wings? Were they retracted, or broken off? It ballooned closer, and it wasn't a glider. Far larger than any glider ever made, it was of a ridiculous shape that would not stand up for an instant. And with the sharp splash the body made as it struck the water—a splash that fell in almost the same instant it rose—a thought seemed to leap up in his mind. A thought that was more important than anything else on that planet; or was to him, at least. For if it was what he thought it was—and it had to be that—it was what Shadden had been desperately seeking for many years. What a stroke of inconceivable luck, falling from the sky before his very eyes.

The silvery shape rode the ragged waters lightly. Ennis' craft came up with a rush; he skillfully checked its speed and the two came together with a slight jar. The metal of the strange vessel dented as if it were made of rubber. Ennis stared. He put out an arm and felt the curved surface of the strange ship. His finger prodded right through the metal. What manner of people were they who made vessels of such weak materials?

He moored his little boat to the side of the larger one and climbed to an opening. The wall sagged under him.

He knew he must be careful; it was frightfully weak.
It would not hold together very long; he must work fast
if it were to be saved. The atmospheric pressure would
have flattened it out long ago, had it not been for the
jagged rent above which had allowed the pressure to be
equalized.

He reached the opening and lowered himself carefully
into the interior of the vessel. The rent was too small;
he enlarged it by taking the two edges in his hands and
pulling them apart. As he went down he looked askance
at the insignificant plates and beams that were like
tissue paper on his world. Inside was wreckage. Nothing was left in its original shape. Crushed, mutilated
machinery, shattered vacuum tubes, sagging members,
all ruined by the gravity and the pressure.

There was a pulpy mess on the floor that he did not
examine closely. It was like red jelly, thin and stalky,
pulped under a gravity a hundred times stronger and
an atmosphere ten thousand times heavier than that it
had been made for.

He was in a room with many knobs and dials on the
walls, apparently a control room. A table in the center
with a chart on it, the chart of a solar system. It had
nine planets; his had but five.

Then he knew he was right. If they came from another system, what he wanted must be there. It could be
nothing else.

He found a staircase, descended. Large machinery
bulked there. There was no light, but he did not notice
that. He could see well enough by infrared, and the
amount of energy necessary to sustain his compact
gianthood kept him constantly radiating.

Then he went through a door that was of a comfortable massiveness, even for his planet—and there it
was. He recognized it at once. It was big, squat, strong.
The metal was soft, but it was thick enough to stand
solidly under the enormous pull of this world. He had

never seen anything quite like it. It was full of coils, magnets, and devices of shapes unknown to him. But Shadden would know. Shadden, and who-knows-how-many other scientists before him, had tried to make something which would do what this could do, but they had all failed. And without the things this machine could perform, the race of men on Heavyplanet was doomed to stay down on the surface of the planet, chained there immovably by the crushing gravity.

It was atomic energy. That he had known as soon as he knew that the body was not a glider. For nothing else but atomic energy and the fierce winds was capable of lifting a body from the surface of Heavyplanet. Chemicals were impotent. There is no such thing as an explosion where the atmosphere pressed inward with more force than an explosion could press outward. Only atomic, of all the theoretically possible sources of energy, could supply the work necessary to lift a vessel away from the planet. Every other source of energy was simply too weak.

Yes, Shadden—all the scientists—must see this. And quickly, because the forces of sea and storm would quickly tear the ship to shreds, and, even more vital, because the scientists of Bantin and Marak might obtain the secret if there was delay. And that would mean ruin —the loss of its age-old supremacy—for his nation. Bantin and Marak were war nations; if they obtained the secret, they would use it against all the other worlds that abounded in the Universe.

The Universe was big. That was why Ennis was so sure there was atomic energy on this ship. For, even though it might have originated on a planet that was so tiny that *chemical energy*—although that was hard to visualize—would be sufficient to lift it out of the path of gravity, to travel the distance that stretched between the stars only one thing would suffice.

He went back through the ship, trying to see what had happened.

There were pulps lying behind long tubes that pointed out through clever ports in the outer wall. He recognized them as weapons, worth looking into.

There must have been a battle. He visualized the scene. The forces that came from atomic energy must have warped even space in the vicinity. The ship pierced, the occupants killed, the controls wrecked, the vessel darting off at titanic speed, blindly into nothing. Finally it had come near enough to Heavyplanet to be enmeshed in its huge web of gravity.

Weeaao-oow! It was the wailing roar of his alarm siren, which brought him spinning around and dashing for his boat. Beyond, among the waves that leaped and fell so suddenly, he saw a long, low craft making way toward the derelict spaceship. He glimpsed a flash of color on the rounded, gray superstructure, and knew it for a battleship of Marak. Luck was going strong both ways; first good, now bad. He could easily have eluded the battleship in his own small craft, but he couldn't leave the derelict. Once lost to the enemy he could never regain it, and it was too valuable to lose.

The wind howled and buffeted about his head, and he strained his muscles to keep from being blasted away as he crouched there, half on his own boat and half on the derelict. The sun had set and the evening winds were beginning to blow. The bulk scudded before them, its prow denting from the resistence of the water it pushed aside.

He thought furiously fast. With a quick motion he flipped the switch of the radiophone and called Shadden. He waited with fierce impatience until the voice of Shadden was in his ear. At last he heard it, then: "Shadden! This is Ennis. Get your glider, Shadden, fly to a45j on my route! Quickly! It's come, Shadden! But I have no time. Come!"

He flipped the switch off and pounded the valve out of the bottom of his craft, clutching at the side of the derelict. With a rush the ocean came up and flooded his little boat and in an instant it was gone, on its way down to the bottom. That would save him from being detected for a short time.

Back into the darkness of the spaceship. He didn't think he had been noticed climbing through the opening. Where could he hide? Should he hide? He couldn't defeat the entire battleship singlehanded, without weapons. There were no weapons that could be carried anyway. A beam of concentrated actinic light that ate away the eyes and the nervous system had to be powered by the entire output of a battleship's generators. Weapons for striking and cutting had never been developed on a world where flesh was tougher than metal. Ennis was skilled in personal combat, but how could he overcome all that would enter the derelict?

Down again, into the dark chamber where the huge atomic generator towered over his head. This time he looked for something he had missed before. He crawled around it, peering into its recesses. And then, some feet above, he saw the opening, and pulled himself up to it, carefully, not to destroy the precious thing with his own mass. The opening was shielded with a heavy, darkly transparent substance through which seeped a dim glow from within. He was satisfied then. Somehow, matter was still being disintegrated in there, and energy could be drawn off if he knew how.

There were leads—wires of all sizes, and busbars, and thick, heavy tubes that bent under their own weight. Some must lead in and some must lead out; it was not good to tamper with them. He chose another track. Upstairs again, and to the places where he had seen the weapons.

They were all mounted on heavy, rigid swivels. He carefully detached the tubes from the bases. The first time he tried it he was not quite careful enough, and part of the projector itself was ripped away, but next time he knew what he was doing and it came away nicely. It was a large thing, nearly as thick as his arm and twice as long. Heavy leads trailed from its lower end, and a lever projected from behind. He hoped it was in working condition. He dared not try it; all he could do was to trace the leads back and make sure they were intact.

He ran out of time. There came a thud from the side, and then smaller thuds, as the boarding party incautiously leaped over. Once there was a heavy sound, as someone went all the way through the side of the ship.

"Idiots!" Ennis muttered, and moved forward with his weapon toward the stairway. Noises came from overhead, and then a loud crash buckled the plates of the ceiling. Ennis leaped out of the way, but the entire section came down, with two men on it. The floor sagged, but held for the moment. Ennis, caught beneath the downcoming mass, beat his way free. He came up with a girder in his hand, which he bent over the head of one of the Maraks. The man shook himself and struck out for Ennis, who took the blow rolling and countered with a buffet that left a black splotch on a skin that was like armor plate and sent the man through the opposite wall. The other was upon Ennis, who whirled with the quickness of one who maneuvers habitually under a pressure of ten thousand atmospheres, and shook the Marak from him, leaving him unconscious with a twist in a sensitive spot.

The first opponent returned, and the two grappled,

searching for nerve centers to beat upon. Ennis twisted
frantically, conscious of the real danger that the frail
vessel might break to pieces beneath his feet. The
railing of a staircase gave behind the two, and they
hurtled down it, crashing through the steps to the floor
below. Their weight and momentum carried them
through. Ennis released his grip on the Marak, stopped
his fall by grasping one of the girders that was part of
the ship's framework. The other continued his devastat-
ing way down, demolishing the inner shell, and then
the outer shell gave way with a grinding crash that
ominously became a burbling rush of liquid.

Ennis looked down into the space where the Marak
had fallen, hissed with a sudden intake of breath, then
dove down himself. He met rising water, gushing in
through a rent in the keel. He braced himself against a
girder which sagged under his hand and moved onward
against the rushing water. It geysered through the hole
in a heavy stream that pushed him back and started to
fill the bottom level of the ship. Against that terrific
pressure he strained forward slowly, beating against the
resisting waves, and then, with a mighty flounder, was
at the opening. Its edges had been folded back upon
themselves by the inrushing water, and they gaped inward like a jagged maw. He grasped them in a huge
hand and exerted force. They strained for a moment
and began to straighten. Irresistibly he pushed and
stretched them into their former position, and then took
the broken ends in his hands and *squeezed*. The metal
grew soft under his grip and began to flow. The edges
of the plate welded under that mighty pressure. He
moved down the crack and soon it was watertight. He
flexed his hands as he rose. They ached; even his
strength was beginning to be taxed.
      Noises from above; pounding feet. Men were coming

down to investigate the commotion. He stood for a moment in thought, then turned to a blank wall, battered his way through it, and shoved the plates and girders back into position. Down to the other end of the craft, and up a staircase there. The corridor above was deserted, and he stole along it, hunting for the place he had left the weapon he had prepared. There was a commotion ahead as the Maraks found the unconscious man.

Two men came pounding up the passageway, giving him barely enough time to slip into a doorway to the side. The room he found himself in was a sleeping chamber. There were two red pulps there, and nothing that could help him, so he stayed in there only long enough to make sure that he would not be seen emerging into the hall. He crept down it again, with as little noise as possible. The racket ahead helped him: it sounded as though they were tearing the ship apart. Again he cursed their idiocy. Couldn't they see how valuable this was?

They were in the control room, ripping apart the machinery with the curiosity of children, wondering at the strange weakness of the paperlike metal, not realizing that, on the world where it was fabricated, it was sufficiently strong for any strain the builders could put upon it.

The strange weapon Ennis had prepared was on the floor of the passage, and just outside the control room. He looked anxiously at the trailing cables. Had they been stepped on and broken? Was the instrument in working condition? He had to get it and be away; no time to experiment to see if it would work.

A noise from behind, and Ennis again slunk into a doorway as a large Marak with a colored belt around his waist strode jarringly through the corridor into the control room. Sharp orders were barked, and the men ceased their havoc with the machinery of the room. All

but a few left and scattered through the ship. Ennis'
face twisted into a scowl. This made things more difficult. He couldn't overcome them all singlehanded, and
he couldn't use the weapon inside the ship if it was
what he thought it was from the size of the cables.

A Marak was standing immediately outside the
room in which Ennis lurked. No exit that way. He
looked around the room; there were no other doors.
A porthole in the outer wall was a tiny disk of trans-
parency. He looked at it, felt it with his hands, and
suddenly pushed his hands right through it. As quietly
as he could, he worked at the edges of the circle until
the hole was large enough for him to squeeze through.
The jagged edges did not bother him. They felt soft,
like a ragged pat of butter.

The Marak vessel was moored to the other side of
the spaceship. On this side the wind howled blankly,
and the sawtooth waves stretched on and on to a
horizon that was many miles distant. He cautiously
made his way around the glistening rotundity of the
derelict, past the prow, straining silently against the
vicious backward sweep of the water that tore at every
inch of his body. The darker hump of the battleship
loomed up as he rounded the curve, and he swam across
the tiny space to grasp a row of projections that curved
up over the surface of the craft. He climbed up them,
muscles that were hard as carborundum straining to
hold against all the forces of gravity and wind that
fought him down. Near the top of the curve was a
rounded, streamlined projection. He felt around its
base and found a lever there, which he moved. The metal
hump slid back, revealing a rugged swivel mounting
with a stubby cylindrical projector atop it.

He swung the mounting around and let loose a short,
sudden blast of white fire along the naked deck of the

battleship. Deep voices yelled within and men sprang out, to fall back with abrupt screams clogged in their throats as Ennis caught them in the intolerable blast from the projector. Men, shielded from actinic light, used to receiving only red and infrared, were painfully vulnerable to this frightful concentration of ultraviolet.

Noise and shouts burst from the derelict spaceship alongside, sweeping away eerily in the thundering wind that seemed to pound down upon them with new vigor in that moment. Heads appeared from the openings in the craft.

Ennis suddenly stood up to his full height, bracing himself against the wind, so dense it made him buoyant. With a deep bellow he bridged the space to the derelict. Then, as a squad of Maraks made their difficult, slippery way across the flank of the battleship toward him, and as the band that had boarded the spaceship crowded out on its battered deck to see what the noise was about, he dropped down into a crouch behind his ultraviolet projector, and whirled it around, pulling the firing lever.

That was what he wanted. Make a lot of noise and disturbance, get them all on deck, and then blow them to pieces. The ravening blast spat from the nozzle of the weapon, and the men on the battleship dropped flat on the deck. He found he could not depress the projector enough to reach them. He spun it to point at the spaceship. The incandescence reached out, and then seemed to waver and die. The current was shut off at the switchboard.

Ennis rose from behind the projector, and then hurtled from the flank of the battleship as he was struck by two Maraks leaping on him from behind the hump of the vessel. The three struck the water and sank, Ennis struggling violently. He was on the last lap, and he gave all his strength to the spurt. The water swirled around them in little choppy waves that fell more quickly than the eye could follow. Heavier blows than those from an Earthly trip hammer were scoring Ennis' face and head. He was in a bad position to strike back, and suddenly he became limp and sank below the surface. The pressure of the water around him was enormous, and it increased very rapidly as he went lower and lower. He saw the shadowy bulk of the spaceship above him. His lungs were fighting for air, but he shook off his pretended stupor and swam doggedly through the water beneath the derelict. He went on and on. It seemed as though the distance were endless, following the metal curve. It was so big from beneath, and trying to swim the width without air made it bigger.

Clear, finally, his lungs drew in the saving breaths. No time to rest, though. He must make use of his advantage while it was his; it wouldn't last long. He swam along the side of the ship looking for an opening. There was none within reach from the water, so he made one, digging his stubby fingers into the metal, climbing up until it was safe to tear a rent in the thick outer and inner walls of the ship.

He found himself in one of the machine rooms of the second level. He went out into the corridor and up the stairway which was half-wrecked, and found himself in the main passage near the control room. He darted down it, into the room. There was nobody there, although the noises from above indicated that the Maraks were again descending. There was his weapon on the floor, where he had left it. He was glad that they had not gotten around to pulling that instrument apart. There would be one thing saved for intelligent examination.

The clatter from the descending crowd turned into a clamor of anger as they discovered him in the passageway. They stopped there for a moment, puzzled. He had been in the ocean, and had somehow magically reappeared within the derelict. It gave him time to pick up the weapon.

Ennis debated rapidly and decided to risk the unknown. How powerful the weapon was he did not know,
but with atomic energy it would be powerful. He dis-
liked using it inside the spaceship; he wanted to have
enough left to float on the water until Shadden arrived;
but they were beginning to advance on him, and he had
to start something.

He pulled a lever. The cylinder in his arms jerked
back with great force; a bolt of fierce, blinding energy
tore out of it and passed with the quickness of light
down the length of the corridor.

When he could see again there was no corridor.
Everything that had been in the way of the projector
was gone, simply disappeared.

Unmindful of the heat from the object in his hands,
he turned and directed it at the battleship that was
plainly outlined through the space that had been once
the walls of the derelict. Before the men on the deck
could move, he pulled the lever again.

And the winds were silent for a moment. The natural
elements were still in fear at the incredible forces that
came from the destruction of atoms. Then with an
agonized scream the hurricane struck again, tore through
the spot where there had been a battleship.

Far off in the sky Ennis detected motion. It was
Shadden, speeding in a glider.

Now would come the work that was important. Shadden would take the big machine apart and see how it
ran. That was what history would remember.

1939

THE LOTUS-ENGINE
Raymond Z. Gallun

21

Ray Gallun has written science fiction over a period of many years, but it has always been a very part-time affair for him. Gallun is a rover, and his stories are always written in bits and pieces in Paris, aboard ship, in some small town in the United States, somewhere in the Pacific—wherever he happens to be when the mood strikes him. For that reason most of them are short—the peripatetic author has trouble keeping manuscripts together—but memorable.

"We've got it started, Milt! The sun-engine's running, after a billion years! Look! Darn it, look, Milt! . . ."

My pal, old Russ Abfall, was dancing up and down there, in that dusty valley on the surface of Io, first large moon of the planet Jupiter. I could hear his high, cracked voice through the helmet radiophones of my space suit. His normally small eyes seemed very big, through the window of his own headgear, as he looked back at me along the cold, arid trail.

And his thin face was red with excitement, and maybe a touch of scare, too. Russ is past sixty. He's been a hopeful space rover for better than forty years. But now he was acting as tickled as a kid.

I didn't blame him, though I'm more phlegmatic than he is, and bigger—and red-headed and less than half his age. He used to say sometimes, that I—Milt Claire's my name, by the way—missed a lot of the pleasures of life by not letting my feelings go, enough.

But I was plenty thrilled just then, too—and a bit uneasy and tense. I realized that we were confronted by a mystery that might easily prove dangerous.

A big, ugly-looking machine was working once more there in that valley, after its creators, the humans of Io—large-chested, furry, and goblin-like—had been extinct for an inconceivable time—the victims of a water famine on their dying world.

The thousands of reflecting mirrors of that solar motor, mounted on their slanted, circular frame, were collecting the feeble rays of the tiny, far-distant sun, and concentrating them on the blackened boiler at the center of the frame. The boiler was made like a squatting image of one of those last natives. It had a great beard carved out of iron, ruby eyes, long goblin nose and ears, and a strange, mocking, secret grin on its lips —a grin that was sinister in itself.

Steam, generated by focused solar heat, was turning a turbine, flywheel, and dynamo, the last shaped like a gigantic pocket-watch. Condenser coils were cooling the spent steam, and returning the water efficiently to the boiler.

It was all a most interesting spectacle—interesting, with a secretive threat in it somewhere . . .

Russ Abfall and I had gone out there to Io in a rickety space ship, *Sun Spot,* three months back. Our hope had been to explore that almost untouched Jovian satellite, and maybe find a deposit of some rich metal. Free-lance space wanderers generally don't brave the rigors of near-dead worlds, except for the very human reason of making money. That was our idea, backed up by certain life-long dreams.

Our luck had exceeded our wildest optimisms. No, we

hadn't discovered a mine. Instead, we'd located a deserted, underground city. Its galleries and chambers had been dug out of the sullen, almost airless hills, by those final Ionians. In it was a treasure-trove of small, easily transportable relics. Bowls, beautiful vases, queer clocks. Odd, ornate lamps that didn't give light any more, because the radium salts in them had worn out with age. There was a fortune in the stuff, selling to museums on Earth, and to wealthy individuals making collections.

But we had stopped our feverish crating of ordinary antiques when Russ had found that solar engine, all but buried by an ancient rockslide from the desolate mountains. On two Ionian days—forty-two hours long, they are—we put in protracted work-shifts, digging the thing out of the rubble that had preserved it.

It must have weighed a hundred tons, even in that weak gravity. We could never get it carted back to Earth. It didn't look like a good financial prospect. But lots of times enigmas are more fascinating than filthy lucre.

"We'll never have any peace until we see whether the engine'll run, Milt," old Russ had told me. And I knew he was right. Though later I was aware we should have left well-enough alone.

So we'd polished the reflecting mirrors of the sun-plant. We'd patched and repaired the leaks and dents in the boiler, turbine, and other parts. We'd filled the dried-out boiler from our ship's precious supply of water. We'd applied oil liberally, where necessary. Just at evening we'd got that huge, tip-tilted reflector frame turned around on its pivot, so it would face the sun at dawn.

And now, coming back from our ship in the early afternoon, we were flabbergasted to see that world-old engine already in operation, its throttle evidently opened by an automatic device!

Russ Abfall scrambled around to the dynamo.

"Is it really delivering juice, Russ?" I demanded, running after him.

"Yeah! Plenty!" he responded after a moment, pointing through a glass-covered peephole in its side. Peering there, I saw fat blue sparks of electricity playing steadily about some peculiarly-formed metal brushes.

"But where is all that juice going?" I asked. "The Ionians didn't use electricity much. They had those radioactive lamps to light up their digs, for instance."

Russ shrugged and pointed to the enamel-insulated wires leading out of the generator, and into a heavy iron pipe that went right down into the rocky ground, to some hidden destination. Tracing it to its end would be difficult, if we wanted to avoid the possibility of breaking an important part of the whole mechanism.

"We'll find out one way or another what's happening to the current," Russ reassured me. "Right now let's watch—here. There's enough to see."

He spoke briskly, but I could tell he was getting worried. As for myself, I felt an unpleasant tautening of the hide along my back, and the nape of my neck. It was like a premonition of disaster.

There really was plenty to see, just watching the sun-engine itself. As the hours went by, a gear-system became active, turning and tilting the reflector frame on its pivot and gimbals, keeping the great iron ring and its mirrors faced toward the sun, so as to collect all the heat possible for the boiler.

After a while I went to a grotto nearby—part of that last Ionian city—while Russ, who is a much better mechanic and scientist than I am, stayed behind to keep an eye on the solar engine. For hours and hours I walked down bas-relief-flanked passages, and through gloomy halls, searching for some sign of where that electric current was disappearing to; but long search by the light of my ato-flash revealed no trace of an answer.

It was there, in that dust and silence, and wreckage of quaint household fittings, that a definite wave of intense mental discomfort came over me. It was as sudden as a hammer-blow. I hurried back to the surface, a vague suspicion in me becoming half conviction. It was already late afternoon.

Russ was walking around and around the sun-plant, his nerves and mind evidently responding to the same weird influence as were mine.

He had one arm drawn out of the sleeve of his space suit. His hand, thus freed, was thrust up under the collar of his oxygen helmet, and this way he was smoking a cigarette.

"Something's happened, Russ," I grated. "But what?"

"I know it!" he returned, swinging around to face me. "I feel queer as the deuce, Milt! I'm all tense and tight inside; I want to do something, though just what it is I can't say. I've got to get these arms and legs of mine busy. I can't relax at all. It's like I was about ready to explode!".

The sun plant. We both stared at it, accusation in our hearts. Russ was fingering the pistol at his belt, as though he wanted to fire a dynamium capsule at that ancient mechanism, and blow it to smithereens.

"Maybe," he said slowly, his voice shriller, even, than usual. "—maybe we ought to anyway shut this damned thing off. That electricity the dynamo is delivering—It's going down there under ground. It's energizing something. It's making us feel the way we do . . ."

"I suppose we should trace that pipe—that carries those wires—right away, Russ," I added. "We'll have to, eventually, I suppose, to see what kind of a funny apparatus they're hooked to."

Rocking on his metal-shod heels, Russ seemed to consider; but he vetoed what I had suggested, at last, just as we'd both vetoed it before.

"No, not yet, Milt," he said, barely audible, as though his heavy breathing made it hard for him to speak. "Some circumstance might turn up by itself, to explain everything to us. Meanwhile we can't take the chance of wrecking any important works. If we did, we might never learn the—truth. This seems to be big stuff, Milt."

That ugly, bearded image, which was the boiler of the solar engine, grinned its secret grin. The sun was dropping lower and lower in the dark firmament. It was already very close to the sullen hills. Soon, frigid darkness would come. Jupiter, as always, hung with just about one fourth of its great grey-and-red streaked disc above the horizon.

"It'll be sundown soon, Russ," I said, trying to reassure not only him, but myself as well—trying to ignore that increasing and nameless tension within me. "Then, deprived of energy to keep up steam, the engine'll have to stop."

I was right, of course. True to my predictions, the turbine and generator ceased turning at sunset. But the sinister spell that had come over Russ and me didn't quit! Somewhere, energy from the power-plant must have been stored up, to operate whatever apparatus and force it was, that was acting on our nervous systems.

"I guess it's about time to do something about—all this!" Russ grumbled, his voice wavering.

"Yeah!" I seconded.

I was thinking, somehow, of all the skeletons I'd seen on Io—and mummies, too. White-furred bodies, dehydrated and preserved by the dryness. Everywhere those old Ionians had died at their tasks. Digging canals and reservoirs to collect and hoard the precious water of the rare snows. The conditions under which they had lived, in those final days, must have been terrible. Yet many of the mummies still wore eternal and mysteriously happy smiles on their withered faces. The Ionians seemed to have perished in joy. But why? How? In that question there was a blood-chilling enigma.

Well, we started back for our ship, to get our blast-excavators. We were going to dig down and see just what was hidden under the solar engine. But as we hurried through the swift-gathering night, I heard a dim rattle behind me, transmitted by the tenuous atmosphere.

Startled, we looked back at the machine—the sun-plant—which was now a hundred yards away. The whole frame of it was turning around slowly, majestically, a black, bizarre silhouette against the still-lighted west. It was turning to face the east—to wait for the dawn. Gears were moving it. As to where the power came from—well, I could guess on that point. An electric generator is built just about like a motor, and can serve as one, if electricity is fed back to it. So I figured juice was coming up along those wires that led into the ground—enough stored juice to revolve the dynamo and work the gears, turning the ring, and the reflector of the power plant east.

At sight of that eerie, automatic motion, Russ gave an inarticulate gurgle. We both knew then, that with its efficient steam condensers keeping the boiler always full, the engine could run every day, indefinitely, till it wore out. But we didn't get a chance to discuss the situation, or to act. Strange events happened too suddenly, bewildering us.

I can't say just what it was that reminded me, not of those final Ionians, but of their still more ancient ancestors, who had lived in the warm age of Io's youth.

Maybe it was my increasing hatred of the starkness of my surroundings, and of the greater and greater menace in them.

I glanced along the mountain gorge, toward the small desert plain beyond, where those last cultivated fields of Io had been. I expected to see, in the harsh, bluish twilight, only those dry irrigation trenches, and the twisted iron pillars that had supported the glass roofs of those hothouse fields, smashed long ago by infrequent meteor showers. Beyond that mass of rock there, the cigar-shape of the *Sun Spot* should be resting, still hidden from view.

But—there was something else—collecting and forming against the picture of that dreary scene. Call it a kind of mirage—something that resembled a photograph superimposed upon another photograph by double-exposure. And the second of the two was becoming more solid, more real, every moment.

There was a lake there, on that dry plain—or there seemed to be. It was a beautiful lake ruffled by little moving wavelets. Along its shores were odd trees. Beyond them loomed a city wall, covered with vines. And rearing up over the rampart were high buildings topped by carved pavilion-like structures, ornate as Burmese pagodas. Over it all was a sky, soft and blue as if it belonged to a summer evening on Earth—except for the many moons that hung in it, not almost-airless moons like those of the present, for each was clad in the cloudy veil of an atmosphere.

And there was Jupiter, still three-quarters hidden below the horizon, but not streaked and cold anymore. It glowed with a dusky, luminous redness, and it seemed that I could feel its warmth.

I knew then, at least, what the mirage, or whatever you care to call it, represented. Primitive Io, long before the last days—when the whole Jovian system was new. I had thought of those times, and here, somehow, it was crystallizing before me. Real.

"Russ," I gasped. "Russ—I see a city—like the ruins of the most ancient cities here on Io. The ones whose foundations you can hardly trace! Down there on the plain at the end of the gorge!"

I pointed with an extended arm, while I babbled on, describing what I seemed to see. I was too bewildered to think of danger.

Russ, beside me, gave a nervous grunt. Then he stammered: "No, I can't make out—anything—Milt. But I feel damned—funny! . . ."

He paused there, as if startled. Pretty soon he gasped in sheer surprise. "You're right, Milt!" he grated. "I see it now—the city—the details filling themselves in, each one as you describe it. The lake, the wall, the vines! It's what you'd imagine one of those oldest cities to be— from the ruins . . . And I see a city gate. People are coming out of it—goblin people, very slender and pallid, and without the great lungs and chests of their descendants. They're like those original folk must have been! Except for their natural fur, white, and much less heavy than that of the last men, they wear no clothing—only metal ornaments. And I hear strange music . . ."

Russ and I stood there, staring, at the mouth of the gorge. And—it was funny! I hadn't seen that gate my pal spoke of, before! But I did now! I hadn't seen the people either, or heard the music. But these parts of the vision were all there, now, clear and vivid! It was as though everything was imaginary, somehow, though it all seemed so real, and that Russ' descriptive words were helping my imagination to fill in the details. From what Russ had just said, it had been the same with him. He hadn't seen the ancient city at all, until I had described it to him. Apparently, then, I had reached the nameless stage of being able to observe the impossible, a moment or so ahead of Russ.

I was in a kind of drunken fuddle. The lake there, fascinated me. I saw goblin-folk wading into it, the cool water splashing around their thin knees . . . Suddenly I was aware of a tremendous yearning, stronger than any perhaps more logical fear.

"Russ," I mumbled. "The lake . . . Let's go swimming. It's been so damned long. Out here on Io we never could—before. Dust, and skeletons, and cold stars. That's all we've been living with—for a month . . ."

Well, right then Russ Abfall began to swear at me. "You loony nut!" he shrilled at last in his cracked voice. "Don't you realize this is all a fake—a mental phantasmagoria of some kind? It's one of the enigmas of a dying race—something they must have employed in desperation! You don't want to get mixed up any more than you are with something like that, do you? . . . That damned sun-plant—and what ever its underground-wires are attached to! Visions! Hallucinations! Somehow that hidden apparatus causes them! And we can't even guess what kind of a hellish end this thing we've tangled with, can have! It must be like a drug— opium or hashish! It can't work like them of course— but—"

He stopped and stared at me. His tone was changed utterly, when he spoke again. "Milt," he said in wondering simplicity. "You've got a swim-suit on."

I examined myself quickly. Yep, it was true! My heavy space armor had apparently vanished. And I was clad in a one-piece outfit of blue cellutex fabric, common on Earthly beaches. Looking at Russ, through that antique dusk and its weird illumination, I saw that he was rigged out just as I was! We were two contemporary Earthmen on primal Io!

"You're ready for the water too, I see, Russ," I told him.

His confusion was almost humorous when he looked down at himself. He swore rather weakly. Then he wheeled about, as if to search for the sun engine with his eyes. I looked too, but what I saw was—not a desolate expanse at the foot of the northern cliffs, but a dense forest. A soft mild wind blew against my body. And the stars overhead were pale . . . The mirage or hallucination had closed in on me almost completely.

Russ' voice was a bit odd, and far away, when he spoke; but I was sure that it, at least, was still real. Sure because of the worry in it, and the momentary groping for fact.

"It isn't there, Milt!" he was stammering. "The sun-plant, I mean . . . At least I can't see it. Can you?"

"No!" I shouted, straining, so that I would be sure to reach him. "I see just trees . . ."

"So do I, Milt," he returned. "It's natural we'd imagine the same thing, there. Old Io. We both know the archeology, Milt. How things were . . ." And then Russ sighed in capitulation. "I wonder if it matters—really," he continued. "Maybe you were right, Milt—about a swim. I've been a space-man off and on for forty-one years. You get sick of things out here on these damned silent worlds sometimes—damned sick . . ." His voice seemed to trail away.

But I knew from my own experience just what was back of what he had said. Space. That awful nostalgia that grows on you. It was largely the humanness in old Russ, and the intriguing pull of the visions that had surrounded us, that had made him give up. And it was the same with me. We both knew that we were toying with something that justly should have made our flesh crawl; but we didn't care. I wasn't worried a bit. And

I had the oddest idea that anything I wanted would happen.

Russ and I walked down to the lake together. Or anyway seemed to. Perhaps we were already going our separate ways, along separate dream-channels, as our individual fancies dictated. We waded out into the water, mingling with those ancient Ionians. Their voices echoed around me, speaking a beautiful, liquid language. Or was it a language at all? Probably it was just a lot of pleasing sounds which my mind created for itself. But those ancients paid no attention to me, however— most likely because I wanted to think, alone—then. I swam far out from the shore, feeling the heady glory of that tropic night . . .

Yes, I knew it was just a dream. But what did that matter? Pretty soon I began to wish that I wasn't on Io—that I was back on Earth instead. Almost at once, then, the scene around me, vanished. I was riding a San Francisco belt-walk—one I knew well. Ahead of me, in the morning sunshine, was the new Farwell building, finished in 2314. Chet Robbins, an old friend of mine, was with me. He works for the Wenz Rocket Motor Company, and he likes magic.

"Got a new card trick to spring on the gang tonight, Milt," he was saying, his broad face all pleased good-nature. "It's a real honey! Boy, it'll make your eyes pop!"

I'd never been able to catch on to those clever stunts of Chet's, and sometimes this had made me kind of mad. But now, in this dream, I was sure I had him. All I had to do was imagine—for instance—the Farwell building floating up into the sky . . .

I saw that two thousand foot spire doing just that. I heard a rending of metal, as the aerial street-spans connecting it with other buildings, parted. I heard people scream distantly. And I could see Chet's face turn suddenly pale and foolish. He gasped, speechless.

"Never mind, Chet," I said, laughing. "I'll bring it down again. And I did. A moment later the Farwell building was back in place on the ground once more, and the street-spans were intact. Chet was looking at me utterly flabbergasted.

It made me feel a little silly. This wasn't the real Chet Robbins at all. Petty revenge was out of place. So I shifted the scene again—I don't remember to what.

But it's easy to see what I'd started for myself. Anything was possible in my imaginary environment. I could imagine myself Caesar or Alexander the Great, if I wanted to, and my fancies would seem perfectly real around me. Historical accuracy would depend on my limited knowledge in each case, if history happened to be involved. For instance, I don't know much about how Caesar's Roman legions were organized, and their equipment is hazy to me—but still I could construct for myself a vivid living picture.

I didn't ever try Roman times more than briefly, but I tried countless other things. Pulled by a strong nostalgia, I relived fragments of my own life. I'd played football for California Tech, and I did so again, now. Saturday afternoons. Yelling crowds. Coach McKay giving us his hardboiled lectures. Fun and fight all over again. And then the training school at Vananis, Mars, where I'd learned to fly rockets. We'd had some nice blowouts—our class—in that quaint old city, which twenty-five thousand Earth people had colonized, replacing the Martian race, dead in some ancient plague. Dances. Parties. The faces of friends.

Maybe it was all sort of silly. But it was relief from that lonely stay on Io, where not a real thing grew any more, except some rock lichens. And I could enjoy luxuries I'd never had before.

Sometimes I remembered—danger. But not till I was aware of the passage of time, as dream succeeded dream, literally in thousands. Weeks, maybe months, must have already been used up by now. And I'd never emerged from that curtain of rosy visions, which I realized was the result of a science of the mind developed by the last men of Io, for a purpose of their own.

And I wondered: "Where am I really? Where is my actual body? How is it feeding itself? What is it doing? There are air-purifiers in its space suit, of course; but there are so many other things to consider!"

I didn't know how to answer these questions. So, in moments of panic, I tried to break the spell of dreams, and fight my way back to the truth. It was then that I discovered that I was in a trap. I couldn't get rid of those visions—or if it was possible to do so, it would require a tremendous effort. And I didn't seem equal to that, now. Still, it didn't seem to trouble me much. "What of it?" I kept telling myself. "What of it?" So my visionary magic carpet continued to function.

But I wondered about old Russ Abfall. How was he faring? Doubtless his situation was the same as mine. Doubtless he was lost in a web of dreams, too. What were they like? I was pretty sure I could guess. Old Russ, weary of the life of a space man, wanted to retire. He wanted to build himself a laboratory on Earth, and spend the rest of his days in research for the improvement of space craft. It had been a dream of his since he was a kid. He'd hoped to win enough money from his various ventures in out-of-the-way corners of the solar system, to finance his costly experiments. So doubtless, now, he was getting a kind of vivid if unsubstantial fulfillment to his ambitions, just as I was frequently imagining the success of that interplanetary

tourist line I wanted to start, if I ever had the means.
There'd be contacts, people, movement and color. I'd
own ships. I wouldn't be just a space bum any more.

Another thing about Russ. He'd had a wife once,
when he was young. But she'd been killed, when they
were married a year. Killed in the smash of a rocket
plane racer she was piloting. Rhoda, her name had
been. Once in a great while, Russ used to rave about
her. He'd show me her picture then. She'd been dark
and snappy, and pretty. Perhaps Russ was imagining
himself with her now, young again . . .

I was on the bridge of a big Earth–Mars Liner,
giving orders as its captain, when, finally, the break
in the dream-curtain came. From out of nowhere, I
knew that a hand was on my shoulder, shaking it with
insistent violence.

"Hey, Milt!" someone was calling, in tones as faint
as if they originated a thousand miles away. "Good
night! We've got to snap out of this! If we don't, it's
our finish, sure!"

It was Russ, of course. I knew that voice was truly
his, and not another phantom. I couldn't see him, but
I could tell how hoarse he was. When he stopped
speaking, he began to cough. It was a hollow, horrible
sort of cough, that made my blood run cold for a
second. But terror starting up in me, caused me to
make a mighty effort to win my way back to solid
reality, and find out just what sort of a predicament we
were in. I struggled furiously, using all the will I could
muster. And the dream fought back.

But at last those instruments on the control panels
of my make-believe space liner began to grow faint and
transparent. So did the comfortable fitting of the bridge.
Sleek chromium fittings, and soft dark rugs and chairs,

turned to ghosts, hovering at the vanishing-point. And around me, maintained only by force of will, was grim fact!

I was in a deep, vertical shaft—a sort of well. Jagged walls of stone were around me, towering up toward a circle of daylight, far aloft. I was clad in space armor again. Russ Abfall was there beside me, leaning weakly against the wall of the pit. Io, it was, the real Io, though I'd never seen this excavation before.

Instead of feeling languid and comfortable, though in tip-top shape, as I had a moment ago, I felt rotten! I was sick, and worn out with work and half starvation. My hands and arms—my whole body, in fact—were so emaciated they fairly rattled inside my space armor. Still I didn't get the significance of all this—quite. Though I was pretty certain that, weak as I was, I could never climb out of this pit. I'd starve here—die of thirst.

Naturally I looked to Russ for explanations—because he's smart, figuring things out. "What's it—all about, Russ?" I grumbled thickly, still battling to keep those comfortable visions out of my tired brain—visions I yearned for now in this hell-hole, as I had never yearned for anything before.

Russ Abfall, probably because of his age, was in even worse shape than I was. His face, in his oxygen helmet, looked like the face of a corpse in a coffin. But he came through with the answers. He was too tired to be excited any more. But he spoke, swiftly, tensely, in his cracked and now hoarse voice, aware that we couldn't hold onto real things for long.

"You know what reverie, or daydreaming is, Milt?" he asked. "Naturally you do, but let me give my own definition: It's a mental mechanism which enables one to escape from something unpleasant. If you've a routine kind of job that you don't like, you generally do it while thinking about something nice.

"The phenomenon that has tricked us is just a kind of reverie, enormously improved by artificial means. To understand its purpose here, you've got to understand the position of those last Ionians. The climate was bitterly cold. They had little food or water. The future prospect was hopeless. But still they wanted to keep going as long as they could—getting as much out of life as they could.

"Some genius of a scientist found them the means. But in some respects, it's an old trick to us on Earth. In a crude way, drugs like opium and hashish accomplish the same thing—produce dreams of strange beauty and vividness.

"But agents other than drugs might do this far more perfectly, without, in themselves, putting one's body out of kilter. We're both sick, but from different causes.

"The brain responds to quite a number of stimuli. When one has a fever—when one's brain is being thrown off balance by heat—there's a tendency toward the hallucinations of delirium. Sun spot radiations have long been believed to cause mental and emotional excitement, producing wars and other forms of mass and individual violence. Music—sound waves, enriched by tone and mathematical rhythm—soothe the mind and emotions, generally.

"We must be dealing with a form of radiation here, Milt. Something that beats on the nerve and brain cells. The sun-plant, you know, and that concealed apparatus its electricity is fed into. It detaches the visionary part of our minds from fact, and allows our imaginations to roam, free, while the mechanical portions of our brain, and our bodies, can go on with unpleasant tasks.

"That's the way I've doped it out, Milt. It's beautiful and insidious. But of course the mess we're in isn't the fault of the old Ionians—or their intention. We just got tangled with the Lethean influence they used on themselves, probably at the very last. We monkeyed with their sun-plant—and so, liberated again what might be called the drug of a hopelessly doomed and dying race."

Russ Abfall stopped speaking. He was panting heavily. My will tensed against the blur of visions trying to envelope me once more. I was looking around. Some of Russ' explanation, I had worked out myself, when I had pondered in that dream region.

I saw the walls of that deep well around me, grey and stark. Tools—blast excavators, which we had brought from our ship—were lying in the thick dust. We'd been digging here, perhaps for months. In the wall of the pit, chinks were cut, one above the other—a kind of ladder, going up and up. We'd been out of the pit often, going back to the ship for supplies, driven by some perhaps subconscious urge like sleep-walkers. We'd been working here, using up our strength until we were no longer able to climb out of that deep hole which we'd been digging deeper from some ancient Ionian beginning. We'd even rigged up a system of buckets and cables to remove the dust our blast-excavators knocked loose from the rock.

"Digging down for water," I grumbled. "Subterranean water which can't be there any more. The Ionians wanted water The urge to get it was stamped in the radiations of their reverie machine and—we got a dose of it too . . ."

"I think so" Russ commented.

"But" I asked "what was it that snapped you out of the dream-world in the first place? Did you just realize and fight your way out or—?"

Russ raised his right arm. I could see, even with the space suit sleeve around it, that it was badly swelled. "A falling rock dropped on my wrist," he told me. "And the pain was strong enough to get through to me.

It almost woke me up, so to speak—showed me how things were. And I was scared enough to use every bit of will I had, to go the rest of the way . . ."

Well, what were we to do now? Starvation and death in that pit was staring us in the face, if we couldn't climb out of that hole. We tried doing just this, using that crude ladder of chinks. But we could do only a few steps before dizziness and the weakness in our muscles overcame us, and we had to drop back. Then, impelled by a forlorn idea, we staggered around, half-awake, searching for some sign of that Ionian reverie machine. We blasted into the walls with our excavators, but we found nothing tangible to smash—to fight. But in the dust under our booted feet, we stumbled on more mummified Ionian corpses, each elfin face smiling a happy smile which we understood now. Maybe we'd be like that soon—mummies. The tools of those Ionians were beside them—complicated, sharp-ended rods, which may have employed some powerful principle. But they were useless now.

And as we plied the disintegrating flame of our excavators, our wills grew tired.

The strain of hanging on to cold, uninviting facts was too strong.

"T'hell with it!" Russ croaked at last. And then he muttered a name—"Rhoda." His young wife, of long ago.

"No, Russ!" I grated. "Don't slip! Try not to—think —"

But my voice trailed off—and I was somewhere else—reminiscing. I was a kid again, reading a book. There was sunshine on the piano keys in the living room.

And my brain was saying: "What's the difference? The Ionian scientist who made the dreams possible, was a great guy. His invention can give a beautiful, quiet death. Better than feeling starvation creeping on you, anyway. Better than seeing this hole, and that circle of stars, way up there . . ."

Like that. I guess anyone can understand how it was with Russ and me, all right. We were exhausted physically from the strain of constant work. And Russ had been chasing an ambition in the void for more than forty years, seeking the funds to set up that lab he wanted. No one could criticize that tough old bird for lack of nerve because he had crumpled. The trail had been too long and too hard. Besides, there was Rhoda, whom he could reach only in fancy.

But suddenly I wanted things real, myself. The real Earth, and not these empty phantoms. I wanted the real people I had known. It would be the same with Russ, if he had the chance. And he was my pal.

So, after a little while I gained some strength back. I didn't know whether it would accomplish any good, but I brought my will into play again, for all I was worth. The well materialized around me, with its grey, volcanic stone. I felt as ill as before. And I thought desperately: "What'll I do? What'll I do?"

There was adrenalin in the emergency pack of my space suit. I'd of course remembered all the time that it was there, but I hadn't thought that injecting some of this powerful gland extract into my blood would do much good. Nor did I think so now. I just hoped.

Everything was swaying and blurred around me. But I got out the emergency pack. Filling a hypodermic syringe with that powerful, treacherous fluid, was no snap, since my fingers were trembling like castanets. And always I had to keep those visions out of my eyes, and those softening dream-sounds of music and wind and water, out of my ears. It was like balancing on a tightrope, when you're a novice.

Grimly I unfastened the wrist-band of my space suit

sleeve, exposing part of my arm to the cold half-vacuum. Quivering, I jabbed the needle home, and pressed the plunger. Then I fumbled to refasten the wrist-band.

Russ was lying there, half imbedded in the dust, like a drunken sot. I kicked him in the ribs to try to bring him around, but it was no good. So I had to doctor him without his assistance. Never before had I had to fight so hard to concentrate on a purpose. But after some minutes I got an adrenalin shot into him too.

By the time I was finished with him, the gland extract was beginning to take effect on me. My heart was pounding until I thought it would burst itself wide open. But otherwise I felt a little more competent. Maybe that was an illusion produced by the adrenalin. My arms waved crazily, as if to push back, by physical action, the mental phantasms of Ionian mind magic, still hammering in my imagination. They seemed to cling around me like smoke, trying to develop solidity again.

Suddenly, though, I was more sure than ever that all my efforts were going to fail. I was certain that the adrenalin wouldn't do any good—that I couldn't have taken enough to have the needed effect of combating the weakness in my body, and that, still, I had injected too much into my veins—enough to kill me.

Then I heard Russ in my helmet phones. I looked around. He had staggered to his feet, braced to that extent by the adrenalin.

"What—?" he stammered thickly.

"I gave you a shot in the arm," I told him. "Now come on—quick! Let's try again to climb out of this hole!"

"How?" he questioned. "Don't be dumb, Milt! Don't be crazy!"

But he came forward anyway. I put his foot in the first step of the chink-ladder, and boosted him—one step up. Oh, it looked like a futile business, all right! He slipped on that first chink, and whacked his shin. He cursed with the pain of the jolt. I was nearly thrown off my feet, as his body came down upon me.

Then, however, all at once, his face took on a furious, mad brightness. "That's it, Milt!" he growled weakly, coughing a little. "That's our one chance! Get angry—think of things to make us angry. Concentrate on hating! It's wonderful what emotions like that can do to strengthen an enfeebled carcass! Come on, boy! Hate! Hate Io! Hate the cold of it, and the loneliness! Hate the circumstances that are killing us! Hate those damned dreams! Hate the sun-plant, working up there! We've got to smash it! Let your blood boil with just that one idea! Don't think about life or death. Think of the fun we're going to have, blasting that ugly contraption to bits! Come on Milt! If it's the last thing we do . . ."

Like half-starved cats we clawed our way over the lip of the well. Madness was in us, filming dreams tried to enfold us again. We were exhausted there on the cold plain among the hills. But our job wasn't finished yet. We couldn't delay, because if we did we'd slip back into the clutch of that Ionian mind magic that had enslaved us, making us work beyond our limits. And if we did slip, there never would be another chance. We had to hang on—somehow.

We hardly knew where we were. We didn't remember being in this spot before. Getting oriented properly took more time, there in the confusing labyrinth of passes between the hills and mountains. But our tracks in the dust, made when we were like sleep-walking robots, finally offered a solution. Following them, we found our way to the sun machine, a quarter-mile distant.

The thing's flywheel still spun steadily. Peering at it with blurred, wobbly vision, I saw the secret grin on the face of the boiler image. Then Russ and I raised our pistols. As twin dynamium capsules struck the machine, there was a thin, distant-sounding, though mighty, explosion. Iron, reflector fragments, and bits of the generator, boiler, steam condenser and turbine flew in every direction. And there was a white puff of steam that expanded quickly into rainbow frost crystals there in the weak sunshine.

It wasn't quite over even yet—for there was that unknown thing underground, and still active, for it stored electricity. Without speaking, we fired more dynamium capsules, until we had a hole fifty feet deep blasted in the crust of Io. In it there were just a few pieces of metal and other materials that could tell little about the miracle that had been concealed there, throwing off strange radiations. Bits of wire, there were. Some pitchy, insulating substance, and glass. The latter may have been part of a storage battery.

Russ gave one look down into the hole. Then he sagged to his knees and rolled over on the rocky ground. When I tried to rouse him, he grumbled sleepily: "All over, Milt. Beat it. Nuts!" In the next instant the plucky old devil was snoring, and I had to drag him back to the ship as best I could. I was sleepy as hell. Maybe we'd slept on our feet before, but it couldn't have been quite natural sleep.

I guess that's about all. Our trade in Ionian relics was a financial success. We're back on Earth. Russ has the lab he wanted all these years—testing new space craft principles. And I'm negotiating to buy some ships for my interplanetary tourist line . . .

1940

CALL ME JOE
Poul Anderson

21

Poul Anderson, with his writer wife Karen, is the heart
and soul of the West Coast division of the Society for
Creative Anachronism. Their greatest joy is organizing
medieval fetes and tourneys, where the men flail away at
each other with (wooden) broadswords and (foam plastic)
morningstars, while the women languorously recreate the
court of Eleanor of Aquitaine. But if Poul Anderson's
heart is in the past, his head is in the future. There are
few like him in matching the hardware of science and the
implications of theory to the color and excitement of interplanetary adventure.

The wind came whooping out of eastern darkness,
driving a lash of ammonia dust before it. In minutes,
Edward Anglesey was blinded.

He clawed all four feet into the broken shards which
were soil, hunched down and groped for his little
smelter. The wind was an idiot bassoon in his skull.
Something whipped across his back, drawing blood, a
tree yanked up by the roots and spat a hundred miles.
Lightning cracked, immensely far overhead where
clouds boiled with night.

As if to reply, thunder toned in the ice mountains and
a red gout of flame jumped and a hillside came booming down, spilling itself across the valley. The earth
shivered.

Sodium explosion, thought Anglesey in the drumbeat noise. The fire and the lightning gave him enough illumination to find his apparatus. He picked up tools in muscular hands, his tail gripped the trough, and he battered his way to the tunnel and thus to his dugout.

It had walls and roof of water, frozen by sun-remoteness and compressed by tons of atmosphere jammed on to every square inch. Ventilated by a tiny smokehole, a lamp of tree oil burning in hydrogen made a dull light for the single room.

Anglesey sprawled his slate-blue form on the floor, panting. It was no use to swear at the storm. These ammonia gales often came at sunset, and there was nothing to do but wait them out. He was tired anyway.

It would be morning in five hours or so. He had hoped to cast an axehead, his first, this evening, but maybe it was better to do the job by daylight.

He pulled a dekapod body off a shelf and ate the meat raw, pausing for long gulps of liquid methane from a jug. Things would improve once he had proper tools; so far, everything had been painfully grubbed and hacked to shape with teeth, claws, chance icicles, and what detestably weak and crumbling fragments remained of the spaceship. Give him a few years and he'd be living as a man should.

He sighed, stretched, and lay down to sleep.

Somewhat more than one hundred and twelve thousand miles away, Edward Anglesey took off his helmet.

He looked around, blinking. After the Jovian surface, it was always a little unreal to find himself here again, in the clean quiet orderliness of the control room.

His muscles ached. They shouldn't. He had not really been fighting a gale of several hundred miles an hour, under three gravities and a temperature of 140 Absolute. He had been here, in the almost non-existent pull of Jupiter V, breathing oxynitrogen. It was Joe who lived down there and filled his lungs with hydrogen and helium at a pressure which could still only be estimated because it broke aneroids and deranged piezoelectrics.

Nevertheless, his body felt worn and beaten. Tension, no doubt—psychosomatics; after all, for a good many hours now he had, in a sense, been Joe, and Joe had been working hard.

With the helmet off, Anglesey held only a thread of identification. The esprojector was still tuned to Joe's brain but no longer focused on his own. Somewhere in the back of his mind, he knew an indescribable feeling of sleep. Now and then, vague forms or colors drifted in the soft black—dreams? Not impossible, that Joe's brain should dream a little when Anglesey's mind wasn't using it.

A light flickered red on the esprojector panel, and a bell whined electronic fear. Anglesey cursed. Thin fingers danced over the controls of his chair, he slewed around and shot across to the bank of dials. Yes— there—K-tube oscillating again! The circuit blew out. He wrenched the faceplate off with one hand and fumbled in a drawer with the other.

Inside his mind he could feel the contact with Joe fading. If he once lost it entirely, he wasn't sure he could regain it. And Joe was an investment of several million dollars and quite a few highly skilled man-years.

Anglesey pulled the offending K-tube from its socket and threw it on the floor. Glass exploded. It eased his temper a bit, just enough so he could find a replacement, plug it in, switch on the current again—as the machine warmed up, once again amplifying, the Joeness in the back alleys of his brain strengthened.

Slowly, then, the man in the electric wheel chair rolled out of the room, into the hall. Let somebody else sweep up the broken tube. To hell with it. To hell with everybody.

Jan Cornelius had never been farther from Earth than some comfortable Lunar resort. He felt much put upon that the Psionics Corporation should tap him for a thirteen-months exile. The fact that he knew as much about esprojectors and their cranky innards as any other man alive, was no excuse. Why send anyone at all? Who cared?

Obviously the Federation Science Authority did. It had seemingly given those bearded hermits a blank check on the taxpayer's account.

Thus did Cornelius grumble to himself, all the long hyperbolic path to Jupiter. Then the shifting accelerations of approach to its tiny inner satellite left him too wretched for further complaint.

And when he finally, just prior to disembarkation, went up to the greenhouse for a look at Jupiter, he said not a word. Nobody does, the first time.

Arne Viken waited patiently while Cornelius stared. *It still gets me, too,* he remembered. *By the throat. Sometimes I'm afraid to look.*

At length Cornelius turned around. He had a faintly Jovian appearance himself, being a large man with an imposing girth. "I had no idea," he whispered. "I never thought . . . I had seen pictures, but—"

Viken nodded. "Sure, Dr. Cornelius. Pictures don't convey it."

Where they stood, they could see the dark broken rock of the satellite, jumbled for a short way beyond the landing slip and then chopped off sheer. This moon was scarcely even a platform, it seemed, and cold constellations went streaming past it, around it. Jupiter lay across a fifth of that sky, softly ambrous, banded with colors, spotted with the shadows of planet-sized moons and with whirlwinds as broad as Earth. If there had been any gravity to speak of, Cornelius would have thought, instinctively, that the great planet was falling on him. As it was, he felt as if sucked upward, his hands were still sore where he had grabbed a rail to hold on.

"You live here ... all alone ... with this?" He spoke feebly.

"Oh, well, there are some fifty of us all told, pretty congenial," said Viken. "It's not so bad. You sign up for four-cycle hitches—four ship arrivals—and believe it or not, Dr. Cornelius, this is my third enlistment."

The newcomer forbore to inquire more deeply. There was something not quite understandable about the men on Jupiter V. They were mostly bearded, though otherwise careful to remain neat; their low-gravity movements were somehow dreamlike to watch; they hoarded their conversation, as if to stretch it through the year and month between ships. Their monkish existence had changed them—or did they take what amounted to vows of poverty, chastity, and obedience, because they had never felt quite at home on green Earth?

Thirteen months! Cornelius shuddered. It was going to be a long cold wait, and the pay and bonuses accumulating for him were scant comfort now, four hundred and eighty million miles from the sun.

"Wonderful place to do research," continued Viken. "All the facilities, hand-picked colleagues, no distractions ... and of course—" He jerked his thumb at the planet and turned to leave.

Cornelius followed, wallowing awkwardly. "It is very interesting, no doubt," he puffed. "Fascinating. But really, Dr. Viken, to drag me way out here and make me spend a year-plus waiting for the next ship ... to do a job which may take me a few weeks—"

"Are you sure it's that simple?" asked Viken gently. His face swivelled around, and there was something in his eyes that silenced Cornelius. "After all my time here, I've yet to see any problem, however complicated, which when you looked at it the right way didn't become still more complicated."

They went through the ship's air lock and the tube joining it to the station entrance. Nearly everything was underground. Rooms, laboratories, even halls had a degree of luxuriousness—why, there was a fireplace with a real fire in the common room! God alone knew what *that* cost!

Thinking of the huge chill emptiness where the king planet laired, and of his own year's sentence, Cornelius decided that such luxuries were, in truth, biological necessities.

Viken showed him to a pleasantly furnished chamber which would be his own. "We'll fetch your luggage soon, and unload your psionic stuff. Right now, everybody's either talking to the ship's crew or reading his mail."

Cornelius nodded absently and sat down. The chair, like all low-gee furniture, was a mere spidery skeleton, but it held his bulk comfortably enough. He felt in his tunic hoping to bribe the other man into keeping him company for a while. "Cigar? I brought some from Amsterdam."

"Thanks." Viken accepted with disappointing casualness, crossed long thin legs and blew greyish clouds.

"Ah . . . are you in charge here?"

"Not exactly. No one is. We do have one administrator, the cook, to handle what little work of that type may come up. Don't forget, this is a research station, first, last, and always."

"What is your field, then?"

Viken frowned. "Don't question anyone else so bluntly, Dr. Cornelius," he warned. "They'd rather spin the gossip out as long as possible with each newcomer. It's a rare treat to have someone whose every last conceivable reaction hasn't been— No, no apologies to me. 'S all right. I'm a physicist, specializing in the solid state at ultra-high pressures." He nodded at the wall. "Plenty of it to be observed—there!"

"I see." Cornelius smoked quietly for a while. Then: "I'm supposed to be the psionics expert, but frankly, at present, I've no idea why your machine should misbehave as reported."

"You mean those, uh, K-tubes have a stable output on Earth?"

"And on Luna, Mars, Venus . . . everywhere, apparently, but here." Cornelius shrugged. "Of course, psibeams are always pernickety, and sometimes you get an unwanted feedback when— No. I'll get the facts before I theorize. Who are your psimen?"

"Just Anglesey, who's not a formally trained esman at all. But he took it up after he was crippled, and showed such a natural aptitude that he was shipped out here when he volunteered. It's so hard to get anyone for Jupiter V that we aren't fussy about degrees. At that, Ed seems to be operating Joe as well as a Ps.D. could."

"Ah, yes. Your pseudojovian. I'll have to examine that angle pretty carefully too," said Cornelius. In spite of himself, he was getting interested. "Maybe the trouble comes from something in Joe's biochemistry. Who knows? I'll let you into a carefully guarded little secret, Dr. Viken: psionics is not an exact science."

"Neither is physics," grinned the other man. After a moment, he added more soberly: "Not my brand of physics, anyway. I hope to make it exact. That's why I'm here, you know. It's the reason we're all here."

Edward Anglesey was a bit of a shock, the first time. He was a head, a pair of arms, and a disconcertingly intense blue stare. The rest of him was mere detail, enclosed in a wheeled machine.

"Biophysicist originally," Viken had told Cornelius. "Studying atmospheric spores at Earth Station when he was still a young man—accident crushed him up, nothing below his chest will ever work again. Snappish type, you have to go slow with him."

Seated on a wisp of stool in the esprojector control room, Cornelius realized that Viken had been soft-pedaling the truth.

Anglesey ate as he talked, gracelessly, letting the chair's tentacles wipe up after him. "Got to," he explained. "This stupid place is officially on Earth time, GMT. Jupiter isn't. I've got to be here whenever Joe wakes, ready to take him over."

"Couldn't you have someone spell you?" asked Cornelius.

"Bah!" Anglesey stabbed a piece of prot and waggled it at the other man. Since it was native to him, he could spit out English, the common language of the station, with unmeasured ferocity. "Look here. You ever done therapeutic esping? Not just listening in, or even communication, but actual pedagogic control?"

"No, not I. It requires a certain natural talent, like yours." Cornelius smiled. His ingratiating little phrase was swallowed without being noticed by the scored face opposite him. "I take it you mean cases like, oh, re-educating the nervous system of a palsied child?"

"Yes, yes. Good enough example. Has anyone ever tried to suppress the child's personality, take him over in the most literal sense?"

"Good God, no!"

"Even as a scientific experiment?" Anglesey grinned. "Has any esprojector operative ever poured on the juice and swamped the child's brain with his own thoughts? Come on, Cornelius, I won't snitch on you."

"Well . . . it's out of my line, you understand." The psionicist looked carefully away, found a bland meter face and screwed his eyes to that. "I have, uh, heard something about . . . well, yes, there were attempts made in some pathological cases to, uh, bull through . . . break down the patient's delusions by sheer force—"

"And it didn't work," said Anglesey. He laughed. "It *can't* work, not even on a child, let alone an adult with a fully developed personality. Why, it took a decade of refinement, didn't it, before the machine was debugged to the point where a psychiatrist could even 'listen in' without the normal variation between his pattern of thought and the patient's . . . without that variation setting up an interference scrambling the very thing he wanted to study. The machine has to make automatic compensations for the differences between individuals. We still can't bridge the differences between species.

"If someone else is willing to co-operate, you can very gently guide his thinking. And that's all. If you try to seize control of another brain, a brain with its own background of experience, its own ego—you risk your very sanity. The other brain will fight back, instinctively. A fully developed, matured, hardening human personality is just too complex for outside control. It has too many resources, too much hell the subconscious can call to its defense if its integrity is threatened. Blazes, man, we can't even master our own minds, let alone anyone else's!"

Anglesey's cracked-voice tirade broke off. He sat brooding at the instrument panel, tapping the console of his mechanical mother.

"Well?" said Cornelius after a while.

He should not, perhaps, have spoken. But he found it hard to remain mute. There was too much silence—half a billion miles of it, from here to the sun. If you kept your mouth closed five minutes at a time, the silence began creeping in like a fog.

"Well," gibed Anglesey. "So our pseudojovian, Joe, has a physically adult brain. The only reason I can control him is that his brain has never been given a chance to develop its own ego. I *am* Joe. From the moment he was 'born' into consciousness, I have been there. The psibeam sends me all his sense data and sends him back my motor-nerve impulses. But nevertheless, he has that excellent brain, and its cells are recording every trace of experience, even as yours and mine; his synapses have assumed the topography which is my 'personality pattern.'

"Anyone else, taking him over from me, would find it was like an attempt to oust me myself from my own brain. It couldn't be done. To be sure, he doubtless has only a rudimentary set of Anglesey-memories—I do not, for instance, repeat trigonometric theorems while controlling him—but he has enough to be, potentially, a distinct personality.

"As a matter of fact, whenever he wakes up from sleep—there's usually a lag of a few minutes, while I sense the change through my normal psi faculties and get the amplifying helmet adjusted—I have a bit of a struggle. I feel almost a . . . a resistance . . . until I've brought his mental currents completely into phase with mine. Merely dreaming has been enough of a different experience to—"

Anglesey didn't bother to finish the sentence.

"I see," murmured Cornelius. "Yes, it's clear enough. In fact, it's astonishing that you can have such total contact with a being of such alien metabolism."

"I won't for much longer," said the esman sarcastically, "unless you can correct whatever is burning out those K-tubes. I don't have an unlimited supply of spares."

"I have some working hypotheses," said Cornelius, "but there's so little known about psibeam transmission —is the velocity infinite or merely very great, is the beam strength actually independent of distance? How about the possible effects of transmission . . . oh, through the degenerate matter in the Jovian core? Good

Lord, a planet where water is a heavy mineral and hydrogen is a metal? What do we know?"

"We're supposed to find out," snapped Anglesey. "That's what this whole project is for. Knowledge. Bull!" Almost, he spat on the floor. "Apparently what little we have learned doesn't even get through to people. Hydrogen is still a gas where Joe lives. He'd have to dig down a few miles to reach the solid phase. And I'm expected to make a scientic analysis of Jovian conditions!"

Cornelius waited it out, letting Anglesey storm on while he himself turned over the problem of K-tube oscillation:

"They don't understand back on Earth. Even here they don't. Sometimes I think they refuse to understand. Joe's down there without much more than his bare hands. He, I, we started with no more knowledge than that he could probably eat the local life. He has to spend nearly all his time hunting for food. It's a miracle he's come as far as he has in these few weeks— made a shelter, grown familiar with the immediate region, begun on metallurgy, hydrurgy, whatever you want to call it. What more do they want me to do, for crying in the beer?"

"Yes, yes—" mumbled Cornelius. "Yes, I—"

Anglesey raised his white bony face. Something filmed over in his eyes.

"What—?" began Cornelius.

"Shut up!" Anglesey whipped the chair around, groped for the helmet, slapped it down over his skull. "Joe's waking. Get out of here."

"But if you'll only let me work while he sleeps, how can I—"

Anglesey snarled and threw a wrench at him. It was a feeble toss, even in low-gee. Cornelius backed towards the door. Anglesey was tuning in the esprojector. Suddenly he jerked.

"Cornelius!"

"Whatisit?" The psionicist tried to run back, overdid it, and skidded in a heap to end up against the panel.

"K-tube again." Anglesey yanked off the helmet. It must have hurt like blazes, having a mental squeal build up uncontrolled and amplified in your own brain, but he said merely: "Change it for me. Fast. And then get out and leave me alone. Joe didn't wake up of himself. Something crawled into the dugout with me—I'm in trouble down there!"

It had been a hard day's work, and Joe slept heavily. He did not wake until the hands closed on his throat.

For a moment, then, he knew only a crazy smothering wave of panic. He thought he was back on Earth Station, floating in null-gee at the end of a cable while a thousand frosty stars haloed the planet before him. He thought the great I-beam had broken from its moorings and started towards him, slowly, but with all the inertia of its cold tons, spinning and shimmering in the Earth-light, and the only sound himself screaming and screaming in his helmet trying to break from the cable the beam nudged him ever so gently but it kept on moving he moved with it he was crushed against the station wall nuzzled into it his mangled suit frothed as it tried to seal its wounded self there was blood mingled with the foam his blood *Joe roared*.

His convulsive reaction tore the hands off his neck and sent a black shape spinning across the dugout. It struck the wall, thunderously, and the lamp fell to the floor and went out.

Joe stood in darkness, breathing hard, aware in a vague fashion that the wind had died from a shriek to a low snarling while he slept.

The thing he had tossed away mumbled in pain and

crawled along the wall. Joe felt through lightlessness after his club.

Something else scrabbled. The tunnel! They were coming through the tunnel! Joe groped blindly to meet them. His heart drummed thickly and his nose drank an alien stench.

The thing that emerged, as Joe's hands closed on it, was only about half his size, but it had six monstrously taloned feet and a pair of three-fingered hands that reached after his eyes. Joe cursed, lifted it while it writhed, and dashed it to the floor. It screamed, and he heard bones splinter.

"Come on, then!" Joe arched his back and spat at them, like a tiger menaced by giant caterpillars.

They flowed through his tunnel and into the room, a dozen of them entered while he wrestled one that had curled around his shoulders and anchored its sinuous body with claws. They pulled at his legs, trying to crawl up on his back. He struck out with claws of his own, with his tail, rolled over and went down beneath a heap of them and stood up with the heap still clinging to him.

They swayed in darkness. The legged seething of them struck the dugout wall. It shivered, a rafter cracked, the roof came down. Anglesey stood in a pit, among broken ice plates, under the wan light of a sinking Ganymede.

He could see, now, that the monsters were black in color and that they had heads big enough to accommodate some brains, less than human but probably more than apes. There were a score of them or so, they struggled from beneath the wreckage and flowed at him with the same shrieking malice.

Why?

Baboon reaction, thought Anglesey somewhere in the back of himself. See the stranger, fear the stranger, hate the stranger, kill the stranger. His chest heaved, pumping air through a raw throat. He yanked a whole rafter to him, snapped it in half, and twirled the iron-hard wood.

The nearest creature got its head bashed in. The next had its back broken. The third was hurled with shattered ribs into a fourth, they went down together. Joe began to laugh. It was getting to be fun.

"Yeee-ow! Ti-i-i-iger!" He ran across the icy ground, towards the pack. They scattered, howling. He hunted them until the last one had vanished into the forest.

Panting, Joe looked at the dead. He himself was bleeding, he ached, he was cold and hungry and his shelter had been wrecked . . . but, he'd whipped them! He had a sudden impulse to beat his chest and howl. For a moment, he hesitated—why not? Anglesey threw back his head and bayed victory at the dim shield of Ganymede.

Thereafter he went to work. First build a fire, in the lee of the spaceship—which was little more by now than a hill of corrosion. The monster pack cried in darkness; they had not given up on him, they would return.

He tore a haunch off one of the slain and took a bite. Pretty good. Better yet if properly cooked. Heh! They'd made a big mistake in calling his attention to their existence! He finished breakfast while Ganymede slipped under the western ice mountains. It would be morning soon. The air was almost still, and a flock of pancake-shaped skyskimmers, as Anglesey called them, went overhead, burnished copper color in the first pale dawn streaks.

Joe rummaged in the ruins of his hut until he had recovered the water-smelting equipment. It wasn't harmed. That was the first order of business, melt some ice and cast it in the moulds of axe, knife, saw, hammer he had painfully prepared. Under Jovian conditions, methane was a liquid that you drank and water was a

dense hard mineral. It would make good tools. Later on
he would try alloying it with other materials.

Next—yes. To hell with the dugout, he could sleep
in the open again for a while. Make a bow, set traps, be
ready to massacre the black caterpillars when they
attacked him again. There was a chasm not far from
here, going down a long way towards the bitter cold of
the metallic-hydrogen strata: a natural icebox, a place
to store the several weeks' worth of meat his enemies
would supply. This would give him leisure to— Oh,
a hell of a lot!

Joe laughed, exultantly, and lay down to watch the
sunrise.

It struck him afresh how lovely a place this was.
See how the small brilliant spark of the sun swam up
out of eastern fogbanks colored dusky purple and veined
with rose and gold; see how the light strengthened until
the great hollow arch of the sky became one shout of
radiance; see how the light spilled warm and living over
a broad fair land, the million square miles of rustling
low forests and wave-blinking lakes and feather-plumed
hydrogen geysers; and see, see, see how the ice mountains of the west flashed like blued steel!

Anglesey drew the wild morning wind deep into his
lungs and shouted with a boy's joy.

"I'm not a biologist myself," said Viken carefully.
"But maybe for that reason I can better give you the
general picture. Then Lopez or Matsumoto can answer
any questions of detail."

"Excellent," nodded Cornelius. "Why don't you assume I am totally ignorant of this project? I very nearly
am, you know."

"If you wish," laughed Viken.

They stood in an outer office of the xenobiology section. No one else was around, for the station's clocks

said 1730 GMT and there was only one shift. No point in having more, until Anglesey's half of the enterprise had actually begun gathering quantitative data.

The physicist bent over and took a paperweight off a desk. "One of the boys made this for fun," he said, "but it's a pretty good model of Joe. He stands about five feet tall at the head."

Cornelius turned the plastic image over in his hands. If you could imagine such a thing as a feline centaur with a thick prehensile tail— The torso was squat, long-armed, immensely muscular; the hairless head was round, wide-nosed, with big deep-set eyes and heavy jaws, but it was really quite a human face. The overall color was bluish grey.

"Male, I see," he remarked.

"Of course. Perhaps you don't understand. Joe is the complete pseudojovian: as far as we can tell, the final model, with all the bugs worked out. He's the answer to a research question that took fifty years to ask." Viken looked sideways at Cornelius. "So you realize the importance of your job, don't you?"

"I'll do my best," said the psionicist. "But if . . . well, let's say that tube failure or something causes you to lose Joe before I've solved the oscillation problem. You do have other pseudos in reserve, don't you?"

"Oh, yes," said Viken moodily. "But the cost— We're not on an unlimited budget. We do go through a lot of money, because it's expensive to stand up and sneeze this far from Earth. But for that same reason our margin is slim."

He jammed hands in pockets and slouched towards the inner door, the laboratories, head down and talking in a low, hurried voice:

"Perhaps you don't realize what a nightmare planet Jupiter is. Not just the surface gravity—a shade under three gees, what's that? But the gravitational potential, ten times Earth's. The temperature. The pressure . . .

above all, the atmosphere, and the storms, and the darkness!

"When a spaceship goes down to the Jovian surface, it's a radio-controlled job; it leaks like a sieve, to equalize pressure, but otherwise it's the sturdiest, most utterly powerful model ever designed; it's loaded with every instrument, every servo-mechanism, every safety device the human mind has yet thought up to protect a million-dollar hunk of precision equipment.

"And what happens? Half the ships never reach the surface at all. A storm snatches them and throws them away, or they collide with a floating chunk of Ice VII— small version of the Red Spot—or, so help me, what passes for a flock of *birds* rams one and stoves it in!

"As for the fifty per cent which does land, it's a one-way trip. We don't even try to bring them back. If the stresses coming down haven't sprung something, the corrosion has doomed them anyway. Hydrogen at Jovian pressure does funny things to metals.

"It cost a total of—about five million dollars—to set Joe, one pseudo, down there. Each pseudo to follow will cost, if we're lucky, a couple of million more."

Viken kicked open the door and led the way through. Beyond was a big room, low-ceilinged, coldly lit and murmurous with ventilators. It reminded Cornelius of a nucleonics lab; for a moment he wasn't sure why, then recognized the intricacies of remote control, remote observation, walls enclosing forces which could destroy the entire moon.

"These are required by the pressure, of course," said Viken, pointing to a row of shields. "And the cold. And the hydrogen itself, as a minor hazard. We have units here duplicating conditions in the Jovian, uh, stratosphere. This is where the whole project really began."

"I've heard something about that," nodded Cornelius. "Didn't you scoop up airborne spores?"

"Not I." Viken chuckled. "Totti's crew did, about

fifty years ago. Proved there was life on Jupiter. A life using liquid methane as its basic solvent, solid ammonia as a starting point for nitrate synthesis—the plants use solar energy to build unsaturated carbon compounds, releasing hydrogen; the animals eat the plants and reduce those compounds again to the saturated form. There is even an equivalent of combustion. The reactions involve complex enzymes and . . . well, it's out of my line."

"Jovian biochemistry is pretty well understood, then."

"Oh, yes. Even in Totti's day, they had a highly developed biotic technology: Earth bacteria had already been synthesized, and most gene structures pretty well mapped. The only reason it took so long to diagram Jovian life processes was the technical difficulty, high pressure and so on."

"When did you actually get a look at Jupiter's surface?"

"Gray managed that, about thirty years ago. Set a televisor ship down, a ship that lasted long enough to flash him quite a series of pictures. Since then, the technique has improved. We know that Jupiter is crawling with its own weird kind of life, probably more fertile than Earth. Extrapolating from the airborne microorganisms, our team made trial syntheses of metazoans and—"

Viken sighed. "Damn it, if only there were intelligent native life! Think what they could tell us, Cornelius, the data, the— Just think back how far we've gone since Lavoisier, with the low-pressure chemistry of Earth. Here's a chance to learn a high-pressure chemistry and physics at least as rich with possibilities!"

After a moment, Cornelius murmured slyly: "Are you certain there *aren't* any Jovians?"

"Oh, sure, there could be several billion of them," shrugged Viken. "Cities, empires, anything you like. Jupiter has the surface area of a hundred Earths, and we've only seen maybe a dozen small regions. But we do know there aren't any Jovians using radio. Considering their atmosphere, it's unlikely they ever would invent it for themselves—imagine how thick a vacuum tube has to be, how strong a pump you need! So it was finally decided we'd better make our own Jovians."

Cornelius followed him through the lab, into another room. This was less cluttered, it had a more finished appearance: the experimenter's haywire rig had yielded to the assured precision of an engineer.

Viken went over to one of the panels which lined the walls and looked at its gauges. "Beyond this lies another pseudo," he said. "Female, in this instance. She's at a pressure of two hundred atmospheres and a temperature of 194 Absolute. There's a . . . an umbilical arrangement, I guess you'd call it, to keep her alive. She was grown to adulthood in this, uh, fetal stage—we patterned our Jovians after the terrestrial mammal. She's never been conscious, she won't ever be till she's 'born.' We have a total of twenty males and sixty females waiting here. We can count on about half reaching the surface. More can be created as required.

"It isn't the pseudos that are so expensive, it's their transportation. So Joe is down there alone till we're sure that his kind *can* survive."

"I take it you experimented with lower forms first," said Cornelius.

"Of course. It took twenty years, even with forced-catalysis techniques, to work from an artificial air-borne spore to Joe. We've used the psibeam to control everything from pseudoinsects on up. Interspecies control is possible, you know, if your puppet's nervous system is deliberately designed for it, and isn't given a chance to grow into a pattern different from the esman's."

"And Joe is the first specimen who's given trouble?"

"Yes."

"Scratch one hypothesis." Cornelius sat down on a

workbench, dangling thick legs and running a hand through thin sandy hair. "I thought maybe some physical effect of Jupiter was responsible. Now it looks as if the difficulty is with Joe himself."

"We've all suspected that much," said Viken. He struck a cigarette and sucked in his cheeks around the smoke. His eyes were gloomy. "Hard to see how. The biotics engineers tell me *Pseudocentaurus Sapiens* has been more carefully designed than any product of natural evolution."

"Even the brain?"

"Yes. It's patterned directly on the human, to make psibeam control possible, but there are improvements— greater stability."

"There are still the psychological aspects, though," said Cornelius. "In spite of all our amplifiers and other fancy gadgets, psi is essentially a branch of psychology, even today . . . or maybe it's the other way around. Let's consider traumatic experiences. I take it the . . . the adult Jovian's fetus has a rough trip going down?"

"The ship does," said Viken. "Not the pseudo itself, which is wrapped up in fluid just like you were before birth."

"Nevertheless," said Cornelius, "the two hundred atmospheres pressure here is not the same as whatever unthinkable pressure exists down on Jupiter. Could the change be injurious?"

Viken gave him a look of respect. "Not likely," he answered. "I told you the J-ships are designed leaky. External pressure is transmitted to the, uh, uterine mechanism through a series of diaphragms, in a gradual fashion. It takes hours to make the descent, you realize."

"Well, what happens next?" went on Cornelius. "The ship lands, the uterine mechanism opens, the umbilical connection disengages, and Joe is, shall we say, born. But he has an adult brain. He is not protected by the only half-developed infant brain from the shock of sudden awareness."

"We thought of that," said Viken. "Anglesey was on the psibeam, in phase with Joe, when the ship left this moon. So it wasn't really Joe who emerged, who perceived. Joe has never been much more than a biological waldo. He can only suffer mental shock to the extent that Ed does, because it *is* Ed down there!"

"As you will," said Cornelius. "Still, you didn't plan for a race of puppets, did you?"

"Oh, heavens, no," said Viken. "Out of the question. Once we know Joe is well established, we'll import a few more esmen and get him some assistance in the form of other pseudos. Eventually females will be sent down, and uncontrolled males, to be educated by the puppets. A new generation will be born normally— Well, anyhow, the ultimate aim is a small civilization of Jovians. There will be hunters, miners, artisans, farmers, housewives, the works. They will support a few key members, a kind of priesthood. And that priesthood will be esp-controlled, as Joe is. It will exist solely to make instruments, take readings, perform experiments, and tell us what we want to know!"

Cornelius nodded. In a general way, this was the Jovian project as he had understood it. He could appreciate the importance of his own assignment.

Only, he still had no clue to the cause of that positive feedback in the K-tubes.

And what could he do about it?

His hands were still bruised. *Oh, God,* he thought with a groan, for the hundredth time, *does it affect me that much? While Joe was fighting down there, did I really hammer my fists on metal up here?*

His eyes smouldered across the room, to the bench

where Cornelius worked. He didn't like Cornelius, fat cigar-sucking slob, interminably talking and talking. He had about given up trying to be civil to the Earthworm.

The psionicist laid down a screwdriver and flexed cramped fingers. *"Whuff!"* he smiled. "I'm going to take a break."

The half-assembled esprojector made a gaunt backdrop for his wide soft body, where it squatted toadfashion on the bench. Anglesey detested the whole idea of anyone sharing this room, even for a few hours a day. Of late he had been demanding his meals brought here, left outside the door of his adjoining bedroom-bath. He had not gone beyond for quite some time now.

And why should I?

"Couldn't you hurry it up a little?" snapped Anglesey.

Cornelius flushed. "If you'd had an assembled spare machine, instead of loose parts—" he began. Shrugging, he took out a cigar stub and relit it carefully; his supply had to last a long time. Anglesey wondered if those stinking clouds were blown from his mouth on malicious purpose. *I don't like you, Mr. Earthman Cornelius, and it is doubtless quite mutual.*

"There was no obvious need for one, until the other esmen arrive," said Anglesey in a sullen voice. "And the testing instruments report this one in perfectly good order."

"Nevertheless," said Cornelius, "at irregular intervals it goes into wild oscillations which burn out the K-tube. The problem is why. I'll have you try out this new machine as soon as it is ready, but frankly, I don't believe the trouble lies in electronic failure at all—or even in unsuspected physical effects."

"Where, then?" Anglesey felt more at ease as the discussion grew purely technical.

"Well, look. What exactly is the K-tube? It's the heart of the esprojector. It amplifies your natural psionic pulses, uses them to modulate the carrier wave, and shoots the whole beam down at Joe. It also picks up Joe's resonating impulses and amplifies them for your benefit. Everything else is auxiliary to the K-tube."

"Spare me the lecture," snarled Anglesey.

"I was only rehearsing the obvious," said Cornelius, "because every now and then it is the obvious answer which is hardest to see. Maybe it isn't the K-tube which is misbehaving. Maybe it is you."

"What?" The white face gaped at him. A dawning rage crept red across its thin bones.

"Nothing personal intended," said Cornelius hastily. "But you know what a tricky beast the subconscious is. Suppose, just as a working hypothesis, that way down underneath, you don't *want* to be on Jupiter. I imagine it is a rather terrifying environment. Or there may be some obscure Freudian element involved. Or, quite simply and naturally, your subconscious may fail to understand that Joe's death does not entail your own."

"Um-m-m—" *Mirabile dictu,* Anglesey remained calm. He rubbed his chin with one skeletal hand. "Can you be more explicit?"

"Only in a rough way," replied Cornelius. "Your conscious mind sends a motor impulse along the psi-beam to Joe. Simultaneously, your subconscious mind, being scared of the whole business, emits the glandular-vascular-cardiac-visceral impulses associated with fear. These react on Joe, whose tension is transmitted back along the beam. Feeling Joe's somatic fear-symptoms, your subconscious gets still more worried, thereby increasing the symptoms— Get it? It's exactly similar to ordinary neurasthenia, with this exception: that since there is a powerful amplifier, the K-tube, involved, the oscillations can build up uncontrollably within a second or two. You should be thankful the tube does burn out—otherwise your brain might do so!"

For a moment Anglesey was quiet. Then he laughed.

It was a hard, barbaric laughter. Cornelius started as it struck his eardrums.

"Nice idea," said the esman. "But I'm afraid it won't fit all the data. You see, I like it down there. I like being Joe."

He paused for a while, then continued in a dry impersonal tone: "Don't judge the environment from my notes. They're just idiotic things like estimates of wind velocity, temperature variations, mineral properties —insignificant. What I can't put in is how Jupiter looks through a Jovian's infrared-seeing eyes."

"Different, I should think," ventured Cornelius after a minute's clumsy silence.

"Yes and no. It's hard to put into language. Some of it I can't because man hasn't got the concepts. But . . . oh, I can't describe it. Shakespeare himself couldn't. Just remember that everything about Jupiter which is cold and poisonous and gloomy to us is *right* for Joe."

Anglesey's tone grew remote, as if he spoke to himself:

"Imagine walking under a glowing violet sky, where great flashing clouds sweep the earth with shadow and rain strides beneath them. Imagine walking on the slopes of a mountain like polished metal, with a clean red flame exploding above you and thunder laughing in the ground. Imagine a cool wild stream, and low trees with dark coppery flowers, and a waterful, methane-fall . . . whatever you like . . . leaping off a cliff, and the strong live wind shakes its mane full of rainbows! Imagine a whole forest, dark and breathing, and here and there you glimpse a pale-red wavering will-o'-the-wisp, which is the life radiation of some fleet shy animal, and . . . and—"

Anglesey croaked into silence. He stared down at his clenched fists, then he closed his eyes tight and tears ran out between the lids.

"Imagine being *strong!*"

Suddenly he snatched up the helmet, crammed it on his head and twirled the control knobs. Joe had been sleeping, down in the night, but Joe was about to wake up and—roar under the four great moons till all the forest feared him?

Cornelius slipped quietly out of the room.

In the long brazen sunset light, beneath dusky cloud banks brooding storm, he strode up the hillslope wi h a sense of day's work done. Across his back, two woven baskets balanced each other, one laden with the pungent black fruit of the thorntree and one with cable-thick creepers to be used as rope. The axe on his shoulder caught the waning sunlight and tossed it blindingly back.

It had not been hard labor, but weariness dragged at his mind and he did not relish the household chores yet to be performed, cooking and cleaning and all the rest. Why couldn't they hurry up and get him some helpers?

His eyes sought the sky, resentfully. The moon Five was hidden—down here, at the bottom of the air ocean, you saw nothing but the sun and the four Galilean satellites. He wasn't even sure where Five was just now, in relation to himself . . . *wait a minute, it's sunset here, but if I went out to the viewdome I'd see Jupiter in the last quarter, or would I, oh, hell, it only takes us half an Earth-day to swing around the planet anyhow*—

Joe shook his head. After all this time, it was still damnably hard, now and then, to keep his thoughts straight. *I, the essential I, am up in heaven, riding Jupiter V between coldstars. Remember that. Open your eyes, if you will, and see the dead control room superimposed on a living hillside.*

He didn't, though. Instead, he regarded the boulders strewn wind-blasted grey over the tough mossy vegetation of the slope. They were not much like Earth rocks, nor was the soil beneath his feet like terrestrial humus.

For a moment Anglesey speculated on the origin of the silicates, aluminates, and other stony compounds. Theoretically, all such materials should be inaccessibly locked in the Jovian core, down where the pressure got vast enough for atoms to buckle and collapse. Above the core should lie thousands of miles of allotropic ice, and then the metallic hydrogen layer. There should not be complex minerals this far up, but there were.

Well, possibly Jupiter had formed according to theory, but had thereafter sucked enough cosmic dust, meteors, gases and vapours, down its great throat of gravitation, to form a crust several miles thick. Or more likely the theory was altogether wrong. What did they know, what *would* they know, the soft pale worms of Earth?

Anglesey stuck his—Joe's—fingers in his mouth and whistled. A baying sounded in the brush, and two midnight forms leaped towards him. He grinned and stroked their heads; training was progressing faster than he'd hoped, with these pups of the black caterpillar beasts he had taken. They would make guardians for him, herders, servants.

On the crest of the hill, Joe was building himself a home. He had logged off an acre of ground and erected a stockade. Within the grounds there now stood a lean-to for himself and his stores, a methane well, and the beginnings of a large comfortable cabin.

But there was too much work for one being. Even with the half-intelligent caterpillars to help, and with cold storage for meat, most of his time would still go to hunting. The game wouldn't last forever, either; he had to start agriculture within the next year or so—Jupiter year, twelve Earth years, thought Anglesey. There was the cabin to finish and furnish; he wanted to put a waterwheel, no, methane wheel in the river to turn any of a dozen machines he had in mind, he wanted to experiment with alloyed ice and—

And, quite apart from his need of help, why should he remain alone, the single thinking creature on an entire planet? He was a male in this body, with male instincts—in the long run, his health was bound to suffer if he remained a hermit, and right now the whole project depended on Joe's health.

It wasn't right!

But I am not alone. There are fifty men on the satellite with me. I can talk to any of them, any time I wish. It's only that I seldom wish it, these days. I would rather be Joe.

Nevertheless . . . I, cripple, feel all the tiredness, anger, hurt, frustration, of that wonderful biological machine called Joe. The others don't understand. When the ammonia gale flays open his skin, it is I who bleed.

Joe lay down on the ground, sighing. Fangs flashed in the mouth of the black beast which humped over to lick his face. His belly growled with hunger, but he was too tired to fix a meal. Once he had the dogs trained—

Another pseudo would be so much more rewarding to educate.

He could almost see it, in the weary darkening of his brain. Down there, in the valley below the hill, fire and thunder as the ship came to rest. And the steel egg would crack open, the steel arms—already crumbling, puny work of worms!—lift out the shape within and lay it on the earth.

She would stir, shrieking in her first lungful of air, looking about with blank mindless eyes. And Joe would come carry her home. And he would feed her, care for her, show her how to walk—it wouldn't take long, an adult body would learn those things very fast. In a few weeks she would even be talking, be an individual, a soul.

Did you ever think, Edward Anglesey, in the days

when you also walked, that your wife would be a grey, four-legged monster?

Never mind that. The important thing was to get others of his kind down here, female *and* male. The station's niggling little plan would have him wait two more Earth-years, and then send him only another dummy like himself, a contemptible human mind looking through eyes which belonged rightfully to a Jovian. It was not to be tolerated!

If he weren't so tired—

Joe sat up. Sleep drained from him as the realization entered. *He* wasn't tired, not to speak of. Anglesey was. Anglesey, the human side of him, who for months had only slept in catnaps, whose rest had lately been interrupted by Cornelius—it was the human body which drooped, gave up, and sent wave after soft wave of sleep down the psibeam to Joe.

Somatic tension travelled skyward; Anglesey jerked awake.

He swore. As he sat there beneath the helmet, the vividness of Jupiter faded with his scattering concentration, as if it grew transparent; the steel prison which was his laboratory strengthened behind it. He was losing contact— Rapidly, with the skill of experience, he brought himself back into phase with the neutral currents of the other brain. He willed sleepiness on Joe, exactly as a man wills it on himself.

And, like any other insomniac, he failed. The Joe-body was too hungry. It got up and walked across the compound towards its shack.

The K-tube went wild and blew itself out.

The night before the ships left, Viken and Cornelius sat up late.

It was not truly a night, of course. In twelve hours the tiny moon was hurled clear around Jupiter, from darkness back to darkness, and there might well be a pallid little sun over its crags when the clocks said witches were abroad in Greenwich. But most of the personnel were asleep at this hour.

Viken scowled. "I don't like it," he said. "Too sudden a change of plans. Too big a gamble."

"You are only risking—how many?—three male and a dozen female pseudos," Cornelius replied.

"And fifteen J-ships. All we have. If Anglesey's notion doesn't work, it will be months, a year or more, till we can have others built and resume aerial survey."

"But if it does work," said Cornelius, "you won't need any J-ships, except to carry down more pseudos. You will be too busy evaluating data from the surface to piddle around in the upper atmosphere."

"Of course. But we never expected it so soon. We were going to bring more esmen out here, to operate some more pseudos—"

"But they aren't *needed*," said Cornelius. He struck a cigar to life and took a long pull on it, while his mind sought carefully for words. "Not for a while, anyhow. Joe has reached a point where, given help, he can leap several thousand years of history—he may even have a radio of sorts operating in the fairly near future, which would eliminate the necessity of much of your esping. But without help, he'll just have to mark time. And it's stupid to make a highly trained human esman perform manual labor, which is all that the other pseudos are needed for at this moment. Once the Jovian settlement is well established, certainly, then you can send down more puppets."

"The question is, though," persisted Viken, "can Anglesey himself educate all those pseudos at once? They'll be helpless as infants for days. It will be weeks before they really start thinking and acting for themselves. Can Joe take care of them meanwhile?"

"He has food and fuel stored for months ahead,"

said Cornelius. "As for what Joe's capabilities are, well, hm-m-m . . . we just have to take Anglesey's judgment. He has the only inside information."

"And once those Jovians do become personalities," worried Viken, "are they necessarily going to string along with Joe? Don't forget, the pseudos are not carbon copies of each other. The uncertainty principle assures each one a unique set of genes. If there is only one human mind on Jupiter, among all those aliens—"

"One *human* mind?" It was barely audible. Viken opened his mouth inquiringly. The other man hurried on.

"Oh, I'm sure Anglesey can continue to dominate them," said Cornelius. "His own personality is rather—tremendous."

Viken looked startled. "You really think so?"

The psionicist nodded. "Yes. I've seen more of him in the past weeks than anyone else. And my profession naturally orients me more towards a man's psychology than his body or his habits. You see a waspish cripple. I see a mind which has reacted to its physical handicaps by developing such a hellish energy, such an inhuman power of concentration, that it almost frightens me. Give that mind a sound body for its use and nothing is impossible to it."

"You may be right, at that," murmured Viken after a pause. "Not that it matters. The decision is taken, the rockets go down tomorrow. I hope it all works out."

He waited for another while. The whirring of ventilators in his little room seemed unnaturally loud, the colors of a girlie picture on the wall shockingly garish. Then he said, slowly:

"You've been rather close-mouthed yourself, Jan. When do you expect to finish your own esprojector and start making the tests?"

Cornelius looked around. The door stood open to an empty hallway, but he reached out and closed it before he answered with a slight grin: "It's been ready for the past few days. But don't tell anyone."

"How's that?" Viken started. The movement, in low-gee, took him out of his chair and halfway across the table between the men. He shoved himself back and waited.

"I have been making meaningless tinkering motions," said Cornelius, "but what I waited for was a highly emotional moment, a time when I can be sure Anglesey's entire attention will be focused on Joe. This business tomorrow is exactly what I need."

"Why?"

"You see, I have pretty well convinced myself that the trouble in the machine is psychological, not physical. I think that for some reason, buried in his subconscious, Anglesey doesn't want to experience Jupiter. A conflict of that type might well set a psionic amplifier circuit oscillating."

"Hm-m-m." Viken rubbed his chin. "Could be. Lately Ed has been changing more and more. When he first came here, he was peppery enough, and he would at least play an occasional game of poker. Now he's pulled so far into his shell you can't even see him. I never thought of it before, but . . . yes, by God, Jupiter must be having some effect on him."

"Hm-m-m," nodded Cornelius. He did not elaborate: did not, for instance, mention that one altogether uncharacteristic episode when Anglesey had tried to describe what it was like to be a Jovian.

"Of course," said Viken thoughtfully, "the previous men were not affected especially. Nor was Ed at first, while he was still controlling lower-type pseudos. It's only since Joe went down to the surface that he's become so different."

"Yes, yes," said Cornelius hastily. "I've learned that much. But enough shop talk—"

"No. Wait a minute." Viken spoke in a low, hurried

tone, looking past him. "For the first time, I'm starting to think clearly about this . . . never really stopped to analyse it before, just accepted a bad situation. There *is* something peculiar about Joe. It can't very well involve his physical structure, or the environment, because lower forms didn't give this trouble. Could it be the fact that—Joe is the first puppet in all history with a potentially human intelligence?"

"We speculate in a vacuum," said Cornelius. "Tomorrow, maybe, I can tell you. Now I know nothing."

Viken sat up straight. His pale eyes focused on the other man and stayed there, unblinking. "One minute," he said.

"Yes?" Cornelius shifted, half rising. "Quickly, please. It is past my bedtime."

"You know a good deal more than you've admitted," said Viken. "Don't you?"

"What makes you think that?"

"You aren't the most gifted liar in the universe. And then—you argued very strongly for Anglesey's scheme, this sending down the other pseudos. More strongly than a newcomer should."

"I told you, I want his attention focused elsewhere when—"

"Do you want it that badly?" snapped Viken.

Cornelius was still for a minute. Then he sighed and leaned back.

"All right," he said. "I shall have to trust your discretion. I wasn't sure, you see, how any of you old-time station personnel would react. So I didn't want to blabber out my speculations, which may be wrong. The confirmed facts, yes, I will tell them; but I don't wish to attack a man's religion with a mere theory."

Viken scowled. "What the devil do you mean?"

Cornelius puffed hard on his cigar, its tip waxed and waned like a miniature red demon star. "This Jupiter V is more than a research station," he said gently. "It is a way of life, is it not? No one would come here for even one hitch unless the work was important to him. Those who re-enlist, they must find something in the work, something which Earth with all her riches cannot offer them. No?"

"Yes," answered Viken. It was almost a whisper. "I didn't think you would understand so well. But what of it?"

"Well, I don't want to tell you, unless I can prove it, that maybe this has all gone for nothing. Maybe you have wasted your lives and a lot of money and will have to pack up and go home."

Viken's long face did not flicker a muscle. It seemed to have congealed. But he said calmly enough: "Why?"

"Consider Joe," said Cornelius. "His brain has as much capactiy as any adult human's. It has been recording every sense datum that came to it, from the moment of 'birth'—making a record in itself, in its own cells, not merely in Anglesey's physical memory bank up here. Also, you know, a thought is a sense datum too. And thoughts are not separated into neat little railway tracks; they form a continuous field. Every time Anglesey is in rapport with Joe, and thinks, the thought goes through Joe's synapses as well as his own—and every thought carries its own associations, and every associated memory is recorded. Like if Joe is building a hut, the shape of the logs might remind Anglesey of some geometric figure, which in turn would remind him of the Pythagorean theorem—"

"I get the idea," said Viken in a cautious way. "Given time, Joe's brain will have stored everything that ever was in Ed's."

"Correct. Now a functioning nervous system with an engrammatic pattern of experience—in this case, a *non-*

human nervous system—isn't that a pretty good definition of a personality?"

"I suppose so—Good Lord!" Viken jumped. "You mean Joe is—taking over?"

"In a way. A subtle, automatic, unconscious way." Cornelius drew a deep breath and plunged into it. "The pseudojovian is so nearly perfect a life form: your biologists engineered into it all the experiences gained from nature's mistakes in designing *us*. At first, Joe was only a remote-controlled biological machine. Then Anglesey and Joe became two facets of a single personality. Then, oh, very slowly, the stronger, healthier body . . . more amplitude to its thoughts . . . do you see? Joe is becoming the dominant side. Like this business of sending down the other pseudos—Anglesey only thinks he has logical reasons for wanting it done. Actually, his 'reasons' are mere rationlizations for the instinctive desires of the Joe-facet.

"Anglesey's subconscious must comprehend the situation, in a dim reactive way; it must feel his human ego gradually being submerged by the steamroller force of *Joe's* instincts and *Joe's* wishes. It tries to defend its own identity, and is swatted down by the superior force of Joe's own nascent subconscious.

"I put it crudely," he finished in an apologetic tone, "but it will account for that oscillation in the K-tubes."

Viken nodded slowly, like an old man. "Yes, I see it," he answered. "The alien environment down there . . . the different brain structure . . . good God! Ed's being swallowed up in Joe! The puppet master is becoming the puppet!" He looked ill.

"Only speculation on my part," said Cornelius. All at once, he felt very tired. It was not pleasant to do this to Viken, whom he liked. "But you see the dilemma, no? If I am right, then any esman will gradually become a Jovian—a monster with two bodies, of which the human body is the unimportant auxiliary one. This means no esman will ever agree to control a pseudo— therefore the end of your project."

He stood up. "I'm sorry, Arne. You made me tell you what I think, and now you will lie awake worrying, and I am maybe quite wrong and you worry for nothing."

"It's all right," mumbled Viken. "Maybe you're not wrong."

"I don't know." Cornelius drifted towards the door. "I am going to try to find some answers tomorrow. Good night."

The moon-shaking thunder of the rockets, crash, crash, crash, leaping from their cradles, was long past. Now the fleet glided on metal wings, with straining secondary ramjets, through the rage of the Jovian sky.

As Cornelius opened the control-room door, he looked at his telltale board. Elsewhere a voice tolled the word to all the stations, *one ship wrecked, two ships wrecked,* but Anglesey would let no sound enter his presence when he wore the helmet. An obliging technician had haywired a panel of fifteen red and fifteen blue lights above Cornelius' esprojector, to keep him informed, too. Ostensibly, of course, they were only there for Anglesey's benefit, though the esman had insisted he wouldn't be looking at them.

Four of the red bulbs were dark and thus four blue ones would not shine for a safe landing. A whirlwind, a thunderbolt, a floating ice meteor, a flock of mantalike birds with flesh as dense and hard as iron—there could be a hundred things which had crumpled four ships and tossed them tattered across the poison forests.

Four ships, hell! Think of four living creatures, with an excellence of brain to rival your own, damned first to years in unconscious night and then, never awakening save for one uncomprehending instant, dashed in bloody splinters against an ice mountain. The wasteful callousness of it was a cold knot in Cornelius' belly. It had to be done, no doubt, if there was to be any thinking life on Jupiter at all; but then let it be done quickly and minimally, he thought, so the next generation could be begotten by love and not by machines!

He closed the door behind him and waited for a breathless moment. Anglesey was a wheelchair and a coppery curve of helmet, facing the opposite wall. No movement, no awareness whatsoever. Good!

It would be awkward, perhaps ruinous, if Anglesey learned of this most intimate peering. But he needn't, ever. He was blindfolded and ear-plugged by his own concentration.

Nevertheless, the psionicist moved his bulky form with care, across the room to the new esprojector. He did not much like his snooper's role, he would not have assumed it at all if he had seen any other hope. But neither did it make him feel especially guilty. If what he suspected was true, then Anglesey was all unawares being twisted into something not human; to spy on him might be to save him.

Gently, Cornelius activated the meters and started his tubes warming up. The oscilloscope built into Anglesey's machine gave him the other man's exact alpha rhythm, his basic biological clock. First you adjusted to that, then you discovered the subtler elements by feel, and when your set was fully in phase you could probe undetected and—

Find out what was wrong. Read Anglesey's tortured subconscious and see what there was on Jupiter that both drew and terrified him.

Five ships wrecked.

But it must be very nearly time for them to land.

Maybe only five would be lost in all. Maybe ten would get through. Ten comrades for—Joe?

Cornelius sighed. He looked at the cripple, seated blind and deaf to the human world which had crippled him, and felt a pity and an anger. It wasn't fair, none of it was.

Not even to Joe. Joe wasn't any kind of soul-eating devil. He did not even realise, as yet, that he *was* Joe, that Anglesey was becoming a mere appendage. He hadn't asked to be created, and to withdraw his human counterpart from him would be very likely to destroy him.

Somehow, there were always penalties for everybody, when men exceeded the decent limits.

Cornelius swore at himself, voicelessly. Work to do. He sat down and fitted the helmet on his own head. The carrier wave made a faint pulse, inaudible, the trembling of neurones low in his awareness. You couldn't describe it.

Reaching up, he turned to Anglesey's alpha. His own had a somewhat lower frequency. It was necessary to carry the signals through a heterodyning process. Still no reception . . . well, of course, he had to find the exact wave form, timbre was as basic to thought as to music. He adjusted the dials, slowly, with enormous care.

Something flashed through his consciousness, a vision of clouds rolled in a violet-red sky, a wind that galloped across horizonless immensity—he lost it. His fingers shook as he turned back.

The psibeam between Joe and Anglesey broadened. It took Cornelius into the circuit. He looked through Joe's eyes, he stood on a hill and stared into the sky above the ice mountains, straining for a sign of the first rocket; and simultaneously, he was still Jan Cornelius, blurrily seeing the meters, probing about for emotions,

symbols, any key to the locked terror in Anglesey's soul.
The terror rose up and struck him in the face.

Psionic detection is not a matter of passive listening
in. Much as a radio receiver is necessarily also a weak
transmitter, the nervous system in resonance with a
source of psionic-spectrum energy is itself emitting.
Normally, of course, this effect is unimportant; but
when you pass the impulses, either way, through a set
of heterodyning and amplifying units, with a high
negative feedback—

In the early day, psionic psychotherapy vitiated itself
because the amplified thoughts of one man, entering
the brain of another, would combine with the latter's
own neural cycles according to the ordinary vector
laws. The result was that both men felt the new beat
frequencies as a nightmarish fluttering of their very
thoughts. An analyst, trained into self-control, could
ignore it; his patient could not, and reacted violently.

But eventually the basic human wave-timbres were
measured, and psionic therapy resumed. The modern
esprojector analysed an incoming signal and shifted its
characteristics over to the "listener's" pattern. The
really different pulses of the transmitting brain, those
which could not possibly be mapped on to the pattern of the receiving neurones—as an exponential
signal cannot very practicably be mapped on to a
sinusoid—those were filtered out.

Thus compensated, the other thought could be appre-
hended as comfortably as one's own. If the patient were
on a psibeam circuit, a skilled operator could tune in
without the patient being necessarily aware of it. The
operator could either probe the other man's thoughts
or implant thoughts of his own.

Cornelius' plan, an obvious one to any psionicist,
had depended on this. He would receive from an un-

witting Anglesey-Joe. If his theory were right, and the esman's personality was being distorted into that of a monster—his thinking would be too alien to come through the filters. Cornelius would receive spottily or not at all. If his theory was wrong, and Anglesey was still Anglesey, he would receive only a normal human stream-of-consciousness, and could probe for other trouble-making factors.

His brain roared!

What's happening to me?

For a moment, the interference which turned his thoughts to saw-toothed gibberish struck him down with panic. He gulped for breath, there in the Jovian wind, and his dreadful dogs sensed the alienness in him and whined.

Then, recognition, remembrance, and a blaze of anger so great that it left no room for fear. Joe filled his lungs and shouted it aloud, the hillside boomed with echoes:

"Get out of my mind!"

He felt Cornelius spiral down towards unconsciousness. The overwhelming force of his own mental blow had been too much. He laughed, it was more like a snarl, and eased the pressure.

Above him, between thunderous clouds, winked the first thin descending rocket flare.

Cornelius' mind groped back towards the light. It broke a watery surface, the man's mouth snapped after air and his hands reached for the dials, to turn his machine off and escape.

"Not so fast, you." Grimly, Joe drove home a command that locked Cornelius' muscles rigid. "I want to know the meaning of this. Hold still and let me look!" He smashed home an impulse which could be rendered, perhaps, as an incandescent question mark. Remembrance exploded in shards through the psionicist's forebrain.

"So. That's all there is? You thought I was afraid to come down here and be Joe, and wanted to know why? But I *told* you I wasn't!"

I should have believed—whispered Cornelius.

"Well, get out of the circuit, then." Joe continued growling it vocally. "And don't ever come back in the control-room, understand? K-tubes or no, I don't want to see you again. And I may be a cripple, but I can still take you apart cell by cell. Now—sign off—leave me alone. The first ship will be landing in minutes."

You a cripple . . . you, Joe Anglesey?

"What?" The great grey being on the hill lifted his barbaric head as if to sudden trumpets. "What do you mean?"

Don't you understand? said the weak, dragging thought. *You know how the esprojector works. You know I could have probed Anglesey's mind in Anglesey's brain without making enough interference to be noticed. And I could not have probed a wholly nonhuman mind at all, nor could it have been aware of me. The filters would not have passed such a signal. Yet you felt me in the first fractional second. It can only mean a human mind in a nonhuman brain.*

You are not the half-corpse on Jupiter V any longer. You're Joe—Joe Anglesey.

"Well, I'll be damned," said Joe. "You're right."

He turned Anglesey off, kicked Cornelius out of his mind with a single brutal impulse, and ran down the hill to meet the space ship.

Cornelius woke up minutes afterwards. His skull felt ready to split apart. He groped for the main switch before him, clashed it down, ripped the helmet off his head and threw it clanging on the floor. But it took a little while to gather the strength to do the same for Anglesey. The other man was unable to do anything for himself.

They sat outside sickbay and waited. It was a harshly lit barrenness of metal and plastic, smelling of antiseptics: down near the heart of the satellite, with miles of rock to hide the terrible face of Jupiter.

Only Viken and Cornelius were in that cramped little room. The rest of the station went about its business mechanically, filling in the time till it could learn what had happened. Beyond the door, three bio-technicians, who were also the station's medical staff, fought with death's angel for the thing which had been Edward Anglesey.

"Nine ships got down," said Viken dully. "Two males, seven females. It's enough to start a colony."

"It would be genetically desirable to have more," pointed out Cornelius. He kept his own voice low, in spite of its underlying cheerfulness. There was a certain awesome quality to all this.

"I still don't understand," said Viken.

"Oh, it's clear enough—now. I should have guessed it before, maybe. We had all the facts, it was only that we couldn't make the simple, obvious interpretation of them. No, we had to conjure up Frankenstein's monster."

"Well," Viken's words grated, "we have played Frankenstein, haven't we? Ed is dying in there."

"It depends on how you define death." Cornelius drew hard on his cigar, needing anything that might steady him. His tone grew purposely dry of emotion:

"Look here. Consider the data. Joe, now: a creature with a brain of human capacity, but without a mind—a perfect Lockean *tabula rasa,* for Anglesey's psibeam to write on. We deduced, correctly enough—if very belatedly—that when enough had been written, there would be a personality. But the question was: whose? Because, I suppose, of normal human fear of the unknown, we assumed that any personality in so alien a body had to be monstrous. Therefore it must be hostile to Anglesey, must be swamping him—"

The door opened. Both men jerked to their feet.

The chief surgeon shook his head. "No use. Typical deep-shock traumata, close to terminus now. If we had better facilities, maybe—"

"No," said Cornelius. "You cannot save a man who has decided not to live any more."

"I know." The doctor removed his mask. "I need a cigarette. Who's got one?" His hands shook a little as he accepted it from Viken.

"But how could he—decide—anything?" choked the physicist. "He's been unconscious ever since Jan pulled him away from that . . . that thing."

"It was decided before then," said Cornelius. "As a matter of fact, that hulk in there on the operating table no longer has a mind. I know. I was there." He shuddered a little. A stiff shot of tranquilizer was all that held nightmare away from him. Later he would have to have that memory exorcised.

The doctor took a long drag of smoke, held it in his lungs a moment, and exhaled gustily. "I guess this winds up the project," he said. "We'll never get another esman."

"I'll say we won't." Viken's tone sounded rusty. "I'm going to smash that devil's engine myself."

"Hold on a minute," exclaimed Cornelius. "Don't you understand? This isn't the end. It's the beginning!"

"I'd better get back," said the doctor. He stubbed out his cigarette and went through the door. It closed behind him with a deathlike quietness.

"What do you mean?" Viken said it as if erecting a barrier.

"Won't you understand?" roared Cornelius. "Joe has all Anglesey's habits, thoughts, memories, prejudices, interests . . . oh, yes, the different body and the different environment, they do cause some changes—but no

more than any man might undergo on Earth. If you were suddenly cured of a wasting disease, wou'dn't you maybe get a little boisterous and rough? There is nothing abnormal in it. Nor is it abnormal to want to stay healthy—no? Do you see?"

Viken sat down. He spent a while without speaking.

Then, enormously slow and careful: "Do you mean Joe is Ed?"

"Or Ed is Joe. Whatever you like. He calls himself Joe now, I think—as a symbol of freedom—but he is still himself. What *is* the ego but continuity of existence?"

"He himself did not fully understand this. He only knew—he told me, and I should have believed him— that on Jupiter he was strong and happy. Why did the K-tube oscillate? A hysterical symptom! Anglesey's subconscious was not afraid to stay on Jupiter—it was afraid to come back!

"And then, today, I listened in. By now, his whole self was focused on Joe. That is, the primary source of libido was Joe's virile body, not Angelesy's sick one. This meant a different pattern of impulses—not too alien to pass the filters, but alien enough to set up interference. So he felt my presence. And he saw the truth, just as I did—

"Do you know the last emotion I felt, as Joe threw me out of his mind? Not anger any more. He plays rough, him, but all he had room to feel was joy.

"I *knew* how strong a personality Anglesey has! Whatever made me think an overgrown child-brain like Joe's could override it? In there, the doctors—bah! They're trying to salvage a hulk which has been shed because it is useless!"

Cornelius stopped. His throat was quite raw from talking. He paced the floor, rolled cigar smoke around his mouth but did not draw it any farther in.

When a few minutes had passed, Viken said cautiously: "All right. You should know—as you said, you were there. But what do we do now? How do we get in touch with Ed? Will he even be interested in contacting us?"

"Oh, yes, of course," said Cornelius. "He is still himself, remember. Now that he has none of the cripple's frustrations, he should be more amiable. When the novelty of his new friends wears off, he will want someone who can talk to him as an equal."

"And precisely who will operate another pseudo?" asked Viken sarcastically. "I'm quite happy with this skinny frame of mine, thank you!"

"Was Anglesey the only hopeless cripple on Earth?" asked Cornelius quietly.

Viken gaped at him.

"And there are aging men, too," went on the psionicist, half to himself. "Someday, my friend, when you and I feel the years close in, and so much we would like to learn—maybe we, too, would enjoy an extra lifetime in a Jovian body." He nodded at his cigar. "A hard, lusty, stormy kind of life, granted—dangerous, brawling, violent—but life as no human, perhaps, has lived it since the days of Elizabeth the First. Oh, yes, there will be small trouble finding Jovians."

He turned his head as the surgeon came out again.

"Well?" croaked Viken.

The doctor sat down. "It's finished," he said.

They waited for a moment, awkwardly.

"Odd," said the doctor. He groped after a cigarette he didn't have. Silently, Viken offered him one. "Odd. I've seen these cases before. People who simply resign from life. This is the first one I ever saw that went out smiling—smiling all the time."

1957

HABIT
Lester del Rey

♃

Science-fiction writers are a durable lot (a quick calculation shows that the nine writers represented in this book have amassed a grand total among them of some two and a half centuries of writing time!), and so the fact that Lester del Rey is busily writing as hard as ever some thirty-five years after his first story was published is not particularly surprising. It is not even surprising that his newest work is as exciting and innovative as his first—his most recent novel, **Pstalemate,** is one of his best. "Habit" does not actually take place **on** Jupiter, or even on one of its moons; but it does suggest some of the complicated navigation problems in the complex Jovian system—problems that Pioneer 10 is facing right now!

Habit is a wonderful thing. Back in the days of ape-like men, one of them invented a piece of flint that made life a little easier; then another found something else. Labor-saving ideas were nice, and it got to be a habit, figuring them out, until the result was what we call civilization, as exemplified by rocket racing.

Only, sometimes, habits backfire in the darnedest way. Look at what happened to the eight-day rocket race out of Kor on Mars.

I was down there, entered in the open-class main

event, with a little five-ton soup can of rare vintage, equipped with quartz tube linings and an inch of rust all over. How I'd ever sneaked it past the examiners was a miracle in four dimensions, to begin with.

Anyway, I was down in the engine well, welding a new brace between the rocket stanchion and the main thrust girder when I heard steps on the tilly ladder outside. I tumbled out of the dog port to find a little shriveled fellow with streaked hair and sharp gray eyes giving the *Umatila* the once-over.

"Hi, Len," he said casually, around his cigarette. "Been making repairs, eh? Well, not meaning any offense, son, she looks to me like she needs it. Darned if I'd risk my neck in her, not in the opens. Kind of a habit with me, being fond of my neck."

I mopped the sweat and grease off the available parts of my anatomy. "Would if you had to. Since you seem to know me, how about furnishing your handle?"

"Sure. Name's Jimmy Shark—used to be thick as thieves with your father, Brad Masters. I saw by the bulletin you'd sneaked in just before they closed the entries, so I came down to look you over."

Dad had told me plenty about Jimmy Shark. As a matter of fact, my father had been staked to the *Umatila* by this man, when racing was still new. "Glad to meet you." I stuck out my hand and dug up my best grin.

"Call me Jimmy when you get around to it—it's a habit." His smile was as easy and casual as an old acquaintance. "I'd 'a' known you anywhere; look just like your father. Never thought I'd see you in this game, though. Brad told me he was fixing you up in style."

"He was, only—" I shrugged. "Well, he figured one more race would sweeten the pot, so he blew the bank roll on himself in the *Runabout*. You heard what happened."

"Um-hm-m-m. Blew up rounding Ceres. I was sorry

to hear it. Didn't leave you anything but the old *Umatila,* eh?"

"Engineering ticket that won't draw a job, and some debts. Since I couldn't get scrap-iron prices for the old soup can, I made a dicker for the soup on credit. Back at the beginning, starting all over—and going to win this race."

Jimmy nodded. "Um-hm-m-m. Racing kind of gets to be a habit. Still quartz tubes on her, eh? Well, they're faster, when they hold up. Since you aren't using duratherm, I suppose your soup is straight Dynatomic IV?"

I had to admit he knew his tubes and fuels. They haven't used quartz tube linings for ten years, so only a few people know that Dynatomic can be used in them straight to give a forty-percent-efficient drive, if the refractory holds up. In the new models, duratherm lining is used, and the danger of blowing a tube is nil. But the metal in duratherm acts as an anticatalyst on the soup, and cuts the power way down. To get around that, they add a little powdered platinum and acid, which brings the efficiency up to about thirty-five per cent, but still isn't the perfect fuel it should be.

Jimmy ran his hand up a tube, tapped it and listened to the coyote howl it gave off. "A nice job, son. You put that lining in yourself, I take it. Well, Brad won a lot of races in the old shell using home-lined quartz tubes. Must have learned the technique from him."

"I did," I agreed, "with a couple of little tricks of my own thrown in for good measure."

"How about looking at the cockpit, Len?"

I hoisted him up and helped him through the port. There wasn't room for two in there, so I stood on the tilly ladder while he looked her over.

"Um-hm-m-m. Nice and cozy, some ways. Still using Brad's old baby autopilot, I see, and the old calculator.

Only that brace there—it's too low. The springs of your shock hammock might give enough to throw you against it when you reverse, and you'd be minus backbone. By the way, you can't win races by sleeping in your shock mattress—you ought to know that." He held up my duffel and a half can of beans. "And that isn't grub for a meteor dodger, either."

"Heck, Jimmy, I'm tough." I knew he was right, of course, but I also knew how far a ten-spot went on Mars.

"Um-hm-m-m. Be like old times with a Masters in the running. Got to be a habit, seeing that name on the list." He crawled out of the port and succeeded in lighting a cigarette that stung acridly in the dry air. "You know, Len, I just happened to think; I was supposed to have a partner this trip, but he backed down. There's room and board paid for two over at Mom Doughan's place, and only me to use it. We'd better go over there before her other boarders clean the table and leave us without supper. Eating's sort of a habit with me."

He had me by the arm and was dragging me across the rocket pit before I could open my mouth. "Now, Jimmy, I'm used—"

"Shut up. You're used to decent living, same as anyone else, so you might as well take it and like it. I told you I'd paid for them already, didn't I? All right. Anyhow, I'm not used to staying alone; sort of a habit, having somebody to talk to."

I was beginning to gather that he had a few habits scattered around at odd places.

Jimmy was right; shock cushions and beans don't make winners. With a decent meal inside me, and an air-conditioned room around me, my chances looked a lot rosier. Some of the old cocksureness came back.

"Jimmy," I said, lying back and letting the bed ease

my back lazily, "I'm going to win that race. That hundred-thousand first looks mighty good."

"Um-hm-m-m." Jimmy was opening a can of cigarettes, and he finished before answering. "Better stick to the second, kid. This race is fixed."

"I'll change that, then. Who told you it was fixed?"

He grinned sourly. "Nobody. I fixed it myself." He watched my mouth run around and end up in an open circle. "Maybe Brad forgot to tell you, and it's not common news, but I'm a professional bettor."

It was news to me. "But I thought dad— Did he know?"

"Sure, he knew. Oh, he wasn't connected with it, if that's what you're wondering. When he switched from jockeying to dodging, I left the ponies to handicap the soup cans. Learned the gambling end from my father, the best handicapper in the business. It's a habit in the family."

There was pride in his voice. Maybe I was screwy; after all, some people have a pretty low opinion of rocket dodgers. I decided to let Jimmy spill his side without foolish questions.

"Um-hm-m-m. Natural-born handicapper, I am. I won twice every time I lost. Never cheated a man, welshed on a bet, or bribed a dodger to throw a race. Anything wrong with that?"

I had to admit there wasn't. After all, dad used to do some betting himself, as I should know. "How about the race being crooked?"

Jimmy snorted. "Not crooked—fixed. Don't go twisting my words, Len." He stretched out on the bed and took the cigarette out of his mouth. "Always wanted to be famous, son. You know, big philanthropist, endow libraries and schools. Got to be a habit, planning on that; and you can't make that kind of money just handicapping. Your dad ever tell you about that fuel he was working on?"

I began to see light. "We knew he'd been doing something of that sort, though the formula couldn't be found. Matter of fact, he was using it in the *Runabout* when it went out."

"That's it." Jimmy nodded. "A little bit of the compound in the fuel boosts the speed way up. There were a couple of kinks in the original formula, but I got them straightened out. I picked the winner—the fellow who needs to win most, if that's any comfort to you—and sell him on the new fuel. Only the thing won't work in quartz tubes—burns 'em out."

"I won't need it. I'll win this race fair and square." All the same, that did mess things up: I knew dad had thought a lot of that fuel.

"No rules against better fuels. A man can pick the fuel he wants, the same as he can travel any course he wants to, no matter how long, if he goes past the markers." He grunted. "Brad didn't want you racing, so he sent me the formula. Had a hunch about going out, I guess; dodgers get a habit of hunches."

"And we Masters have a habit of winning. Better change your bets, Jimmy."

"It's all fixed, too late to change, and the odds are big. After this race, I'm going back and get the habit of being a big philanthropist. Look, kid, you're not sore about my using Brad's formula?"

"If he gave it to you, that was his business." I pulled the sheet up and reached for the light switch. "Only don't blame me when you lose your bet."

But the morning of the start, I had to confess I wasn't feeling so cocky, in spite of living high on Jimmy for a week. I'd seen the favorite—*Bouncing Betty*—and Jimmy's fix, the *Tar Baby,* and the both looked mighty good to me.

"What's the *Tar Baby* pulling?" I asked Jimmy. Or do you know?"

"Olsen says he's driving her at better than two G's all the way. The *Bouncing Betty*'s pulling straight two which is tough enough, but Olsen thinks he can stand the strain at two and a quarter."

I looked them over again. An extra quarter gravity of acceleration, even if it is only an extra four feet per second per second, uses a lot of additional fuel, even for a sixteen-ton soup can. "How about that mixture, Jimmy? Does it pep up the efficiency, or just the speed —combustion rate and exhaust velocity?"

"She'll throw out a fifty-percent mixture I gave Olsen; optimum is good for eighty." Something began to click in my head then, but his next words sidetracked it. "You'd better draw out, kid. An eight-day race is bad, even if you can hold two G's. How's your supplies?"

I was worried a little myself, but I wouldn't admit it. "They'll last. I've stocked enough soup to carry me to Jupiter and back at two G's, if I had to, and the marker station is forty million miles this side of the big fellow, on a direct line from here. I've got plenty of oxygen, water, and concentrates."

They'd given out the course that morning. We were to head out from Kor, point straight at Jupiter with a climb out of the plane of the ecliptic, dive down and hit a beacon rocket they were holding on a direct line with the big planet, forty million miles this side of him; that made about an even three-hundred-trillion-mile course from Mars, out and back, figured for eight days at a constant acceleration and deceleration of two gravities. It had been advertised as the longest and toughest race in rocket history, and they were certainly living up to the publicity.

"That's a tough haul on a youngster, Len," Jimmy grumbled. "And with quartz lining, it's worse."

"I've had plenty of practice at high acceleration, and the tubes are practically safe for six days' firing. I think they'll last the other two."

"Then you're matching the *Bouncing Betty's* speed?"

I nodded glumly. "I'll have to. The *Tar Baby*'ll probably run into trouble at the speed she's meaning to make, but the *Betty*'s built to stand two."

The starter was singing out his orders, and the field was being cleared. Jimmy grabbed my hand. "Good luck, Len. Don't ride her harder'n she'll carry. You Masters make too much of a habit of being crazy."

Then they forced him off the field, and I was climbing into the cockpit, tightening the anchor straps of the shock hammock about the straightjacket I wore.

And I expected to need them. Two gravities mean double weight, during eight days, fighting your lungs and heart. If you take it lengthwise, it can't be done, but by lying stretched out on the hammock at right angles to the flight line, it's just possible.

The *Betty* roared up first, foaming out without a falter. Olsen took the *Tar Baby* up a little uncertainly, but straightened sharply and headed up. Finally, I got the signal and gave her the gun, leaving Mars dangling in space while I tried to keep my stomach off my backbone. The first ten minutes are always the toughest.

When that passed, I began feeding the tape into the baby autopilot that would take over when I had to sleep, which was about three quarters of the time, under the gravity drag. There wasn't anything exciting to the takeoff, and I was out in space before I knew it, with the automatic guiding her. I might have to make a correction or two, but she'd hold at the two-G mark on course for days at a stretch.

I'd been fool enough to dream about excitement, but I knew already I wasn't going to get it. By the time I was half an hour out, I was bored stiff, or felt that way. The automat ran the ship, space looked all alike, and the only sensation was weight pressing against me. I looked around for the *Betty*, and spotted her blast some fifty miles away, holding evenly abreast of me. The others were strung out behind in a little cluster, except for Olsen. His blast was way up ahead, forging along at a good quarter gravity more than I could use. At the end of an hour, he was a full ten thousand miles away from me; there was no mistaking the harsh white glare of his jets. Olsen had decided to duck over the ecliptic, as I was doing, but the *Bouncing Betty* had headed below it, so it was drawing out of sight. That left me out of touch with what I hoped was my leading competitor.

Of course, the radio signals came through on the ultra-wave every so often, but the pep-talk description of the thrilling contest for endurance racing didn't mean much when I put it up against the facts. A racing ship in space on a long haul is the loneliest, most God-forsaken spot under the stars. For excitement, I'll take marbles.

Having nothing better to do, I turned over and went to sleep on my stomach. You can kill a lot of time sleeping, and I meant to do it.

The howler was banging in my ear when I woke up. I reached over and cut on, noting that the chronometer said sixteen hours out of Kor.

"Special bulletin to all pilots," said the ultra-wave set. "The *Bouncing Betty*, piloted by James MacIntyre, is now out of the race. MacIntyre reports that, in cutting too close to the ecliptic, he was struck by a small meteor, and has suffered the loss of three main tubes. While out of the running, he feels confident of reaching Kor safely on his own power.

"This leaves Olsen of the *Tar Baby* and Masters of the *Umatila* in the lead by a long margin. Come in, Olsen."

Olsen's voice held a note of unholy glee that the obvious fatigue he was feeling couldn't hide. "Still holding two and a quarter, heart good, breathing only slightly labored; no head pains. Position at approximately twenty-two and a half million miles from Kor; speed, two million eight hundred thousand per hour. Confident of winning."

"Report acknowledged, Olsen. Come in, Masters."

I tried to sound careless, but I guess I failed. "Acceleration at two, holding course beautifully on autopilot, rising over ecliptic. Body and ship standing up O.K. Pyrometer indications of tube lining very satisfactory. Position, twenty million miles out; speed, two and a half million. No signs of meteors up here. Can you give next highest acceleration below me?"

Already it took time for the messages to reach Kor and return, and I tried to locate Olsen with his two-and-a-half-million-mile lead. Even if he cut down to two now, the race seemed a certainty for him—unless something happened. Finally the report came back.

"Burkes, on the *Salvador,* reports one and three quarters, refuses to try higher. No others above that except yourself and Olsen. Are you going to match the *Tar Baby*?"

Match the *Tar Baby,* indeed, and run short of fuel or blow-up! "No chance. Still expect to win, though."

Well, at least it would sound nice back home, and it might worry Olsen a little. He was too conceited about his speed. But I couldn't see myself making good. Even if I cut closer to the ecliptic, it wouldn't save enough time to count, and the risk wasn't worth while. I dug into my store of concentrates and satisfied a raving hunger—double weight takes double energy, just as it does sleep. The only thing I could think of was to wish I could maintain acceleration all the way, instead of just half.

That's the trouble with racing. You accelerate with

all you've got half the way, then turn around and decelerate just as hard until you reach your goal; then you repeat the whole thing in getting back. The result is that as soon as you reach top speed, you have to check it, and you average only a part of what you can do. If there were just something a man could get a grip on in space to slew around, instead of stopping dead, every record made would go to pieces the next day.

I checked over the automat, found it ticking cheerfully, and fiddled around with the calculator. But the results were the same as they'd been back in Kor. It still said I'd have to decelerate after about forty-four hours. Then I messed around with imaginary courses to kill time, listened to the thrilling reports of the race—it must have been nice to listen to—and gave up. Setting the alarm, I went back to sleep, with the announcer's voice concluding some laudatory remark about the "fearless young man out there giving his ship everything he's got in a frantic effort to win."

But I was awake when the next bulletin came in from Kor at the end of the forty-hour mark. "Special bulletin! We've just received word from Dynatomic Fuels that there's a prize of fifty thousand additional to any and every man who makes the course in less than eight full days! Olsen and Masters are now way ahead in the field, and about to do their reversing. Come on, Masters, we're pulling for you; make it a close race! All right, Olsen, come in."

"Tell Dynatomic the prize is due me already, and give 'em my thanks. Holding up fine here, fuel running better than I expected. Hundred and forty million out; speed, seven million. Reversing in two hours."

"O. K., Olsen. Come in. Masters—and don't forget that special; you're still in line for it."

By a tight margin, I might make it, since it applied to as many as came in within the time period. "I'll be in the special field, Kor. Everything like clockwork here, standing it fine. Pyrometer still says tubes O. K. Position, one twenty-five millions; speed, six and a quarter. Reversing in four hours."

"O. K., Masters; hope you make it. Watch out for Jupiter, both of you; even at forty million miles, he'll play tricks with your steering when you hit the beacon. Signing off at Kor."

Jupiter! Right then a thought I'd been trying to nurse into consciousness came up and knocked on my dome. I dug my fingers into the calculator; the more the tape said, the better things looked.

Finally I hit the halfway. Olsen had reversed a couple of hours before with no bad effects from the change. But I was busy dialing Mars. They came in, after a good long wait. "Acknowledging Masters. Trouble?"

"Clear sailing, here and ahead, Kor." It's nice to feel confident after staring second prize in the face all the trip. "Is there any rule about the course, provided a man passes the beacon inside of a hundred thousand miles? Otherwise, do I have free course?"

"Absolutely free course, Masters. Anything you do after the beacon is O. K., if you get back. Advise you don't cut into asteroids, however."

"No danger of that. Thanks, Kor."

I'd already passed the reversing point, but that wasn't worrying me. I snapped off the power, leaving only the automat cut into the steering tubes, and gazed straight ahead. Sure enough, there was Jupiter, with his markings and all; the fellow that was going to let me maintain full speed over halfway, and make the long course the faster one. I was remembering Jimmy's remark that put the idea into my head: "A man can pick the fuel he wants, the same as he can travel any course he wants, no matter how long."

With power cut off, I was still ticking off about seven million miles an hour, but I couldn't feel it. Instead, I felt plenty sick, without any feeling of weight at all. But I couldn't bother about that. Kor was calling again, but I shut them up with a few words. If I was crazy, that was my business, and the ship was doing O. K.

I set the buzzer to wake me when I figured I'd be near Olsen. Looking out, when the thing went off, I could see his jets shooting out away off side, and a little ahead. But he was cutting his speed sharply, while I was riding free, and I began sliding past him.

I was all set to gloat when his voice barked in over the ultra-set: "Masters! Calling Masters!"

"O. K., Olsen."

"Man, decelerate! You'll crack up on Jupiter at that rate. If something's wrong, say so. We're way out ahead, and there's plenty of time. Give me the word and I'll try to cut in on you. The *Tar Baby*'s strong enough to hold back your soup can. How about it, Masters?"

That was the guy I'd been hating for a glory hound, figuring him as out for himself only. "No need, Olsen, but a load of thanks. I'm trying out a hunch to steal first place away from you."

The relief in his voice was as unquestionable as his bewilderment. "It's O. K. if you can do it, mister. I'll still make the special. Why not let me in on the hunch? I won't crib your idea."

"O. K., but I don't know how it'll work, for sure. I'm going around Jupiter at full speed instead of cutting to the beacon."

"You're crazy, Masters." The idea didn't appeal to him at all. "Hope your tubes hold up under the extra eighty million miles. So long!"

Sixty-seven hours out of Kor I passed the beacon at the required hundred thousand miles—which isn't as wide a margin at full speed as it sounds—and headed out. Olsen must have called ahead to tell them what I was doing, because they acknowledged my call, verified my distance, and signed off without questions.

I caught an hour's sleep again, and then Jupiter was growing uncomfortably close. I'd already been over my calculations twenty times, but so darned much depended on them that I wasn't taking chances. I ran them through again. The big fellow was coming up alongside like a mountain rolling toward an ant, and I was already closer than anyone I'd ever heard of.

But it worked out all right, at first. I gazed around the side, was caught in his gravity, and began to swing in an orbit. That's what I'd been looking for, something to catch hold of out in space to swing me around without loss of momentum, and that's what I'd found; Jupiter's gravity pulled me around like a lead weight on a swung rope.

Which was fine—if I had enough speed to make him let go again, as close as I was to his surface. Fortunately, he hasn't any atmosphere to speak of in proportion to his diameter, or I'd have been warmed up entirely too much for pleasant living. In no time I was coming around and facing back in the general direction of Mars; and then two things happened at once.

Jupiter wasn't letting me go on schedule; he seemed to think he needed a little more time for observation of this queer satellite he'd just caught. And Io swung up right where it shouldn't have been. I'd forgotten the moons!

That's when I began counting heartbeats. Either Jupiter pulled me too far, or he threw me square into Io, and I didn't like either prospect. The steering tubes were worthless in the short space I had at that speed. I waited, and Jupiter began to let go—with Io coming up!

Whishh! I could hear the outer edges of the moon's atmosphere whistle briefly past the sides of my soup can, and then silence. When I opened my eyes, Io lay behind, with Jupiter, and I was heading straight for the beacon. Dear old Io! Light as its gravity was, it had still been enough to correct the slight error in my calculations and set me back on my course, even if I did come too close for my peace of mind.

I was asleep when I passed the beacon again, so I don't know what they had to say. It was Olsen's call that woke me up.

"Congratulations, Masters! When you reach Mars, tell them to hold the special and second prizes for me. And I'll remember the trick. Clear dodging!" He was still heading in toward the beacon on deceleration, and less than eighty hours had passed.

Well, there wasn't much more to it, except for the sleeping and the ravings of that fool announcer back on Kor. I reversed without any trouble at about the point where I'd stopped accelerating, and began braking down for Mars. Then the monotony of the trip began again, with the automat doing all the work. The tubes, safe for six days, would be used only about three and a half and I had soup to spare.

Miraculously, they had the landing pit cleared when I settled down over Kor, and the sweetest-looking white ambulance was waiting. I set her down without a jolt, slipped out, and was inside the car before the crowds could get to me. They've finally learned to protect the winning dodger that way.

Jimmy was inside, chewing on an unlit cigarette. "O. K." he told the ambulance driver, "take us to Mom Doughan's. Hi, kid. Made it in a hundred and forty-five hours. That gives you first and special, so you're out of the red. Nice work!"

I couldn't help rubbing it in a little. "Next time, Jimmy, bet on a Masters if you want to go through with those endowments of yours."

Jimmy's face was glum, and the cigarette bobbed up and down in his mouth in a dull rhythm, but his eyes crinkled up and he showed no rancor at the crack. "There won't be any endowments, kid. Should have stuck to the old handicapping, instead of trying to start something new. I'm cleaned, lock, stock, and barrel. Anyway, those endowments dreams were just sort of a habit."

"You've still got your formula."

"Um-hm-m-m. Your fuel formula; I'm sticking to the old habits and letting the newfangled ideas go hang."

I stopped playing with him then. "That's where you're wrong, Jimmy. I did a lot of thinking out there, and I've decided some habits are things to get rid of."

"Maybe." He didn't sound very convinced. "How'd you mean?"

"Well, take the old idea that the shortest time is made on the shortest possible course; that's a habit with pilots, and one I had a hard time breaking. But look what happened. And dad had one habit, you another, and you'd both have been better off without those fixations."

"Um-hm-m-m. Go on."

"Dad thought a fuel was good only in racing, because he was used to thinking in terms of the perambulating soup cans," I explained. I'd done plenty of thinking on the way in, when I was awake, so I knew what I was talking about. "You had a habit of thinking of everything in terms of betting. Take that fuel. You say it gives eighty-percent efficiency. Did you ever stop to think there'd be a fortune in it for sale to the commercials? The less load they carry in fuel, the more pay cargo."

"Well, I'll be——" He mulled it over slowly, letting the

idea seep in. Then he noticed the cigarette dangling in his mouth and started to light it.

I amplified my scheme. "We'll market it fifty-fifty. You put up the fuel and salesmanship; I'll put up the prize money and technical knowledge. And if you're looking for fame, there ought to be some of that mixed in there, too."

"Um-hm-m-m." Jimmy stuck out his hand. "Shake on the partnership, Len. But, if you don't mind, I'll use the money like I said. These endowment ideas sort of get to be a habit with me."

1939

A MEETING WITH MEDUSA
Arthur C. Clarke

21

We have enjoyed the company of Arthur Clarke in all sorts of exotic places—Rio de Janeiro, London, a small hotel on Lake Biwa, Japan, and heaven knows where all. It began to seem to us that Arthur was everywhere, and so when we found ourselves in Moscow and Leningrad a year or two ago, the first person we looked for was Arthur Clarke. "Clarke?" said our hosts. "Oh, no. He isn't here. He has never been in the Soviet Union." But then, just as we began to feel a real triumph, they added, "But he is expected shortly."

(This particular story is one about which I have quite mixed feelings. On the one hand I have to think it is a masterpiece, since it beat out my story, "The Gold at the Starbow's End," for the Nebula award for best of its class. On the other hand, for the same reason I sometimes wish that it had never been written.)

A DAY TO REMEMBER

The Queen Elizabeth was five kilometers above the Grand Canyon, dawdling along at a comfortable 180, when Howard Falcon spotted the camera platform closing in from the right. He had been expecting it—nothing else was cleared to fly at this altitude—but he was not too happy to have company. Although he welcomed any signs of public interest, he also wanted as much empty sky as he could get. After all, he was the first man in history to navigate a ship half a kilometer long.

So far, this first test flight had gone perfectly; ironically enough, the only problem had been the century-old aircraft carrier Chairman Mao, borrowed from the San Diego naval museum for support operations. Only one of Mao's four nuclear reactors was still operating, and the old battlewagon's top speed was barely thirty knots. Luckily, wind speed at sea level had been less than half this, so it had not been too difficult to maintain still air on the flight deck. Though there had been a few anxious moments during gusts, when the mooring lines had been dropped, the great dirigible had risen smoothly, straight up into the sky, as if on an invisible elevator. If all went well, Queen Elizabeth IV would not meet Chairman Mao for another week.

Everything was under control: all test instruments gave normal readings. Commander Falcon decided to go upstairs and watch the rendezvous. He handed over to his second officer and walked out into the transparent tubeway that led through the heart of the ship. There, as always, he was overwhelmed by the spectacle of the largest space ever enclosed by man.

The ten spherical gas cells, each more than 100 meters across, were ranged one behind the other like a line of gigantic soap bubbles. The tough plastic was so clear that he could see through the whole length of the array and make out details of the elevator mechanism almost half a kilometer from his vantage point. All around him, like a three-dimensional maze, was the structural framework of the ship—the great longitudinal girders running from nose to tail, the fifteen hoops that were the ribs of this skyborne colossus, whose varying sizes defined its graceful, streamlined profile.

At this low speed, there was very little sound—merely the soft rush of wind over the envelope and an occasional creak of metal as the pattern of stresses changed. The shadowless light from the rows of lamps far overhead gave the whole scene a curiously submarine quality, and to Falcon this was enhanced by the spectacle of the translucent gasbags. He had once encountered a squadron of large but harmless jellyfish, pulsing their mindless way above a shallow tropical reef, and the plastic bubbles that gave Queen Elizabeth her lift often reminded him of these—especially when changing pressures made them crinkle and scatter new patterns of light.

He walked fifty meters down the axis of the ship, until he came to the forward elevator, between gas cells one and two. Riding up to the observation deck, he noticed that it was uncomfortably hot and dictated a brief memo to himself on his pocket recorder. The Queen obtained almost a quarter of her buoyancy from the unlimited amounts of waste heat produced by her fusion power plant; on this lightly loaded flight, indeed, only six of the ten gas cells contained helium and the remaining four were full of air; yet she still carried 200 tons of water as ballast. However, running the cells at high temperatures did produce problems in refrigerating the accessways; it was obvious that a little more work would have to be done here.

A refreshing blast of cooler air hit him in the face when he stepped out onto the observation deck and into the dazzling sunlight streaming through the Plexiglas roof. Half a dozen workmen, with an equal number of superchimp assistants, were busily laying the partly completed dance floor, while others were installing electric wiring and fixing furniture. It was a scene of controlled chaos and Falcon found it hard to believe that everything would be ready for the maiden voyage, only four weeks ahead. Well, that was not *his* problem, thank goodness. He was merely the captain, not the cruise director.

The human workers waved to him and the simps flashed toothy smiles as he walked through the confusion into the already completed sky lounge. This was his favorite place in the whole ship and he knew that once she was operating, he would never again have it all to himself. He would allow himself just five minutes of private enjoyment.

He called the bridge, checked that everything was still in order and relaxed into one of the comfortable swivel chairs. Below, in a curve that delighted the eye, was the unbroken silver sweep of the ship's envelope. He was perched at the highest point, surveying the whole immensity of the largest vehicle ever built. And when he had tired of *that*—all the way out to the horizon was the fantastic wilderness carved by the Colorado River in half a billion years of time.

Apart from the camera platform (it had now fallen back and was filming from amidships), he had the sky to himself. It was blue and empty, clear down to the horizon. In his grandfather's day, Falcon knew, it would have been streaked with vapor trails and stained with smoke. Both had gone; the aerial garbage had vanished with the primitive technologies that spawned it, and the long-distance transportation of this age arced too far beyond the stratosphere for any sight or sound of it to reach Earth. Once again, the lower atmosphere belonged to the birds and the clouds—and now to Queen Elizabeth IV.

It was true, as the old pioneers had said at the beginning of the twentieth century; this was the only way to travel—in silence and luxury, breathing the air around you and not cut off from it, near enough to the surface to watch the ever-changing beauty of land and sea. The subsonic jets of the 1980s, packed with hundreds of passengers seated ten abreast, could not even begin to match such comfort and spaciousness.

Of course, the Q. E. would never be an economic proposition; and even if her projected sister ships were built, only a few of the world's quarter of a billion inhabitants would ever enjoy this silent gliding through the sky. But a secure and prosperous global society could afford such follies and, indeed, needed them for its novelty and entertainment. There were at least a million men on Earth whose discretionary income exceeded a thousand new dollars a year, so the Queen would not lack for passengers.

Falcon's pocket communicator beeped; the copilot was calling from the bridge.

"OK for rendezvous, Captain? We've got all the data we need from this run and the TV people are getting impatient."

Falcon glanced at the camera platform, now matching his speed a quarter of a kilometer away.

"OK," he replied. "Proceed as arranged. I'll watch from here."

He walked back through the busy chaos of the observation deck, so that he could have a better view amidships. As he did so, he could feel the change of vibration underfoot; by the time he had reached the rear of the lounge, the ship had come to rest. Using his master key, he let himself out onto the small external platform flaring from the end of the deck; half a dozen people could stand there, with only low guardrails separating them from the vast sweep of the envelope—and from the ground, thousands of meters below. It was an exciting place to be and perfectly safe even when the ship was traveling at speed, for it was in the dead air behind the huge dorsal blister of the observation deck. Nevertheless, it was not intended that the passengers would have access to it; the view was a little too vertiginous.

The covers of the forward cargo hatch had already opened like giant trap doors and the camera platform was hovering above them, preparing to descend. Along this route, in the years to come, would travel thousands of passengers and tons of supplies; only on rare occasions would the Queen drop down to sea level and dock with her floating base.

A sudden gust of crosswind slapped Falcon's cheek and he tightened his grip on the guardrail. The Grand Canyon was a bad place for turbulence, though he did not expect much at this altitude. Without any real anxiety, he focused his attention on the descending platform, now about fifty meters above the ship. He knew that the highly skilled operator who was flying the remotely controlled vehicle had performed this very simple maneuver a dozen times already; it was inconceivable that he would have any difficulties.

Yet he seemed to be reacting rather sluggishly; that last gust had drifted the platform almost to the edge of the open hatchway. Surely the pilot could have corrected before this . . . did he have a control problem? It was very unlikely; these remotes had multiple-redundancy, fail-safe take-overs and any number of backup systems. Accidents were almost unheard of.

But there he went again, off to the left. Could the pilot be *drunk?* Improbable though that seemed, Falcon considered it seriously for a moment. Then he reached for his microphone switch.

Once again, without warning, he was slapped violently in the face. He hardly felt it, for he was staring in horror at the camera platform. The distant operator was fighting for control, trying to balance the craft on its jets—but he was only making matters worse. The oscillations increased—twenty degrees, forty, sixty, ninety . . .

"Switch to automatic, you fool!" Falcon shouted uselessly into his microphone. "Your manual control's not working!"

The platform flipped over onto its back; the jets no longer supported it but drove it swiftly downward. They had suddenly become allies of the gravity they had fought until this moment.

Falcon never heard the crash, though he felt it; he

was already inside the observation deck, racing for the elevator that would take him down to the bridge. Workmen shouted at him anxiously, asking what had happened. It would be many months before he knew the answer to that question.

Just as he was stepping into the elevator cage, he changed his mind. What if there were a power failure? Better be on the safe side, even if it took longer and time was of the essence. He began to run down the spiral stairway enclosing the shaft.

Halfway down, he paused for a second to inspect the damage. That damned platform had gone clear through the ship, rupturing two of the gas cells as it did so. They were still collapsing slowly, in great falling veils of plastic. He was not worried about the loss of lift—the ballast could easily take care of that, as long as eight cells remained intact. Far more serious was the possibility of structural damage; already he could hear the great latticework around him groaning and protesting under its abnormal loads. It was not enough to have sufficient lift; unless it was properly distributed, the ship would break her back.

He was just resuming his descent when a superchimp, shrieking with fright, came racing down the elevator shaft, moving with incredible speed hand over hand along the *outside* of the latticework. In its terror, the poor beast had torn off its company uniform, perhaps in an unconscious attempt to regain the freedom of its ancestors.

Falcon, still descending as swiftly as he could, watched its approach with some alarm; a distraught simp was a powerful and potentially dangerous animal, especially if fear overcame its conditioning. As it overtook him, it started to call out a string of words, but they were all jumbled together and the only one he could recognize was a plaintive, frequently repeated "Boss." Even now, Falcon realized, it looked toward humans for guidance; he felt sorry for the creature, involved in a man-made disaster beyond its comprehension and for which it bore no responsibility.

It stopped opposite him, on the other side of the lattice; there was nothing to prevent it from coming through the open framework if it wished. Now its face was only inches from his and he was looking straight into the terrified eyes. Never before had he been so close to a simp and able to study its features in such detail; he felt that strange mingling of kinship and discomfort that all men experience when they gaze thus into the mirror of time.

His presence seemed to have calmed the creature; Falcoln pointed up the shaft, back toward the observation deck, and said very clearly and precisely: "Boss—boss—*go.*" To his relief, the simp understood; it gave him a grimace that might have been a smile and at once started to race back the way it had come. Falcon had given it the best advice he could; if any safety remained aboard the Queen, it was in that direction. But his duty lay in the other.

He had almost completed his descent when, with a sound of rending metal, the vessel pitched nose down and the lights went out. But he could still see quite well, for a shaft of sunlight streamed through the open hatch and the huge tear in the envelope. Many years ago, he had stood in a great cathedral nave, watching the light pouring through the stained-glass windows and forming pools of multicolored radiance on the ancient flagstones. The dazzling shaft of sunlight through the ruined fabric high above reminded him of that moment. He was in a cathedral of metal, falling down the sky.

When he reached the bridge and was able for the first time to look outside, he was horrified to see how close the ship was to the ground. Only a thousand meters below were the beautiful and deadly pinnacles of rock and the red rivers of mud that were still carving their way down into the past. There was no level area anywhere in sight where a ship as large as the Queen could come to rest on an even keel.

A glance at the display board told him that all the ballast had gone. However, rate of descent had been reduced to a few meters a second; they still had a fighting chance.

Without a word, Falcon eased himself into the pilot's seat and took over such control as remained. The instrument board showed him everything he wished to know; speech was superfluous. In the background, he could hear the communications officer giving a running report over the radio. By this time, all the news channels of Earth would have been preempted and he could imagine the utter frustration of the program controllers. One of the most spectacular wrecks in history was occurring —without a single camera to record it. The last moments of the Queen would never fill millions with awe and terror, as had those of the Hindenburg a century and a half before.

Now the ground was only half a kilometer away, still coming up slowly. Though he had full thrust, he had not dared use it, lest the weakened structure collapse; but now he realized that he had no choice. The wind was taking them toward a fork in the canyon, where the river was split by a wedge of rock, like the prow of some gigantic, fossilized ship of stone. If she continued on her present course, the Queen would straddle that triangular plateau and come to rest with at least a third of her length jutting out over nothingness; she would snap like a rotten stick.

From far away, above the sound of straining metal and escaping gas, came the familiar whistle of the jets as Falcon opened up the lateral thrusters. The ship staggered and began to slew to port. The shriek of tearing metal was now almost continuous—and the rate of descent had started to increase ominously. A glance at the damage-control board showed that cell number five had just gone.

The ground was only meters away; even now, he could not tell whether his maneuver would succeed or fail. He switched the thrust vectors over to vertical, giving maximum lift to reduce the force of impact.

The crash seemed to last forever. It was not violent—merely prolonged and irresistible. It seemed that the whole universe was falling about them.

The sound of crunching metal came nearer, as if some great beast were eating its way through the dying ship.

Then floor and ceiling closed upon him like a vise.

"BECAUSE IT'S THERE"

"Why do you want to go to Jupiter?"

"As Springer said when he lifted for Pluto—because it's there."

"Thanks. Now we've got *that* out of the way—the real reason." Howard Falcon smiled, though only those who knew him well could have interpreted the slight, leathery grimace. Webster was one of them; for more than twenty years, they had been involved in each other's projects. They had shared triumphs and disasters—including the greatest disaster of all.

"Well, Springer's cliché is still valid. We've landed on all the terrestrial planets but none of the gas giants. They are the only real challenge left in the Solar System."

"An expensive one. Have you worked out the cost?"

"As well as I can; here are the estimates. But remember—this isn't a one-shot mission but a transportation system. Once it's proved out, it can be used over and over again. And it will open up not merely Jupiter but *all* the giants."

Webster looked at the figures and whistled.

"Why not start with an easier planet—Uranus, for example? Half the gravity and less than half the escape velocity. Quieter weather, too—if that's the right word for it."

Webster had certainly done his homework. But that, of course, was why he was head of Long Range Planning.

"There's very little saving, when you allow for the extra distance and the logistics problems. For Jupiter, we can use the facilities on Ganymede. Beyond Saturn, we'd have to establish a new supply base."

Logical, thought Webster; but he was sure that it was not the important reason. Jupiter was lord of the Solar System; Falcon would be interested in no lesser challenge.

"Besides," Falcon continued, "Jupiter is a major scientific scandal. It's more than a hundred years since its radio storms were discovered, but we still don't know what causes them—and the Great Red Spot is as big a mystery as ever. That's why I can get matching funds from the Bureau of Astronautics. Do you know how many probes they have dropped into that atmosphere?"

"A couple of hundred, I believe."

"*Three* hundred and twenty-six, over the past fifty years—about a quarter of them total failures. Of course, they've learned a hell of a lot, but they've barely scratched the planet. Do you realize how *big* it is?"

"More than ten times the size of Earth."

"Yes, yes—but do you know what that really means?"

Falcon pointed to the large globe in the corner of Webster's office.

"Look at India—how small it seems. Well, if you skinned Earth and spread it out on the surface of Jupiter, it would look about as big as India does here."

There was a long silence while Webster contemplated

the equation: Jupiter is to Earth as Earth is to India. Falcon had—deliberately, of course—chosen the best possible example . . .

Was it already ten years ago? Yes, it must have been. The crash lay seven years in the past (*that* date was engraved on his heart) and those initial tests had taken place three years before the first and last flight of the Queen Elizabeth.

Ten years ago, then, Commander (no, Lieutenant) Falcon had invited him to a preview—a three-day drift across the northern plains of India, within sight of the Himalayas. "Perfectly safe," he had promised. "It will get you away from the office—and will teach you what this whole thing is about."

Webster had not been disappointed. Next to his first journey to the Moon, it had been the most memorable experience of his life. And yet, as Falcon had assured him, it had been perfectly safe and quite uneventful.

They had taken off from Srinagar just before dawn, with the huge silver bubble of the balloon already catching the first light of the Sun. The ascent had been made in total silence; there were none of the roaring propane burners that had lifted the hot-air balloons of an earlier age. All the heat they needed came from the little pulsed-fusion reactor, weighing only a hundred kilograms, hanging in the open mouth of the envelope. While they were climbing, its laser was zapping ten times a second, igniting the merest whiff of deuterium fuel; once they had reached altitude, it would fire only a few times a minute, making up for the heat lost through the great gasbag overhead.

And so, even while they were a kilometer above the ground, they could hear dogs barking, people shouting, bells ringing. Slowly the vast, Sun-smitten landscape expanded around them; two hours later, they had leveled out at five kilometers and were taking frequent draughts of oxygen. They could relax and admire the scenery;

the on-board instrumentation was doing all the work—gathering the information that would be required by the designers of the still-unnamed liner of the skies.

It was a perfect day; the southwest monsoon would not break for another month and there was hardly a cloud in the sky. Time seemed to have come to a stop; they resented the hourly radio reports that interrupted their reverie. And all around, to the horizon and far beyond, was that infinite, ancient landscape drenched with history—a patchwork of villages, fields, temples, lakes, irrigation canals.

With a real effort, Webster broke the hypnotic spell of that ten-year-old memory. It had converted him to lighter-than-air flight—and it had made him realize the enormous size of India, even in a world that could be circled within ninety minutes. And yet, he repeated to himself, Jupiter is to Earth as Earth is to India.

"Granted your argument," he said, "and supposing the funds are available, there's another question you have to answer. Why should you do better than the—what is it—three hundred and twenty-six robot probes that have already made the trip?"

"I am better qualified than they were—as an observer and as a pilot. *Especially* as a pilot; don't forget —I've more experience of lighter-than-air flight than anyone in the world."

"You could still serve as controller and sit safely on Ganymede."

"*But that's just the point!* They've already done that. Don't you remember what killed the Queen?"

Webster knew perfectly well, but he merely answered, "Go on."

"Time lag—*time lag!* That idiot of a platform controller thought he was using a local radio circuit. But he'd been accidentally switched through a satellite—oh, maybe it wasn't his fault, but he should have noticed. That's a half-second time lag for the round trip. Even then it wouldn't have mattered, flying in calm air. It was the turbulence over the Grand Canyon that did it. When the platform tipped and he corrected for that—it had already tipped the other way. Ever tried to drive a car over a bumpy road with a half-second delay in the steering?"

"No, and I don't intend to try. But I can imagine it."

"Well, Ganymede is more than a million kilometers from Jupiter. That means a round-trip delay of six seconds. No, you need a controller on the spot—to handle emergencies in real time. Let me show you something. Mind if I use this?"

"Go ahead."

Falcon picked up a postcard that was lying on Webster's desk; they were almost obsolete on Earth, but this one showed a 3-D view of a Martian landscape and was decorated with exotic and expensive stamps. He held it so that it dangled vertically.

"This is an old trick but helps make my point. Place your thumb and finger on either side, not quite touching. That's right."

Webster put out his hand, almost but not quite gripping the card.

"Now catch it."

Falcon waited for a few seconds; then, without warning, he let go of the card. Webster's thumb and fingers closed on empty air.

"I'll do it again, just to show there's no deception. You see?"

Once again, the falling card slipped through Webster's fingers.

"Now you try it on me."

This time, Webster grasped the card and dropped it without warning. It had scarcely moved before Falcon had caught it; Webster almost imagined he could hear a click, so swift was the other's reaction.

"When they put me together again," Falcon remarked in an expressionless voice, "the surgeons made some improvements. This is one of them—and there are others. I want to make the most of them. Jupiter is the place where I can do it."

Webster stared for long seconds at the fallen card, absorbing the improbable colors of the Trivium Charontis Escarpment. Then he said quietly, "I understand. How long do you think it will take?"

"With your help, plus the bureau plus all the science foundations we can drag in—oh, three years. Then a year for trials—we'll have to send in at least two test models. So with luck—five years."

"That's about what I thought. I hope you get your luck; you've earned it. But there's one thing I won't do."

"What's that?"

"Next time you go ballooning, don't expect *me* as passenger."

THE WORLD OF THE GODS

The fall from Jupiter V to Jupiter itself takes only three and a half hours; few men could have slept on so awesome a journey. Sleep was a weakness that Howard Falcon hated, and the little he still required brought dreams that time had not yet been able to exorcise. But he could expect no rest in the three days that lay ahead and must seize what he could during the long fall down into that ocean of clouds, a hundred thousand kilometers below.

As soon as Kon-Tiki had entered her transfer orbit and all the computer checks were satisfactory, he prepared for the last sleep he might ever know. It seemed appropriate that at almost the same moment Jupiter eclipsed the bright and tiny Sun, he swept into the monstrous shadow of the planet. For a few minutes a strange, golden twilight enveloped the ship; then a quarter of the sky became an utterly black hole in space, while the rest was a blaze of stars. No matter how far one traveled across the Solar System, *they* never changed; these same constellations now shone on Earth, half a billion kilometers away. The only novelties here were the small, pale crescents of Callisto and Ganymede; doubtless there were a dozen other moons up there in the sky, but they were all much too tiny and too distant for the unaided eye to pick them out.

"Closing down for two hours," he reported to the mother ship, hanging a thousand kilometers above the desolate rocks of Jupiter V, in the radiation shadow of the tiny satellite. If it never served any other useful pupose, Jupiter V was a cosmetic bulldozer perpetually sweeping up the charged particles that made it unhealthy to linger close to Jupiter. Its wake was almost free of radiation, and here a ship could park in perfect safety while death sleeted invisibly all around.

Falcon switched on the sleep inducer and consciousness faded swiftly out as the electric pulses surged gently through his brain. While Kon-Tiki fell toward Jupiter, gaining speed second by second in that enormous gravitational field, he slept without dreams. They always came when he awoke; and he had brought his nightmares with him from Earth.

Yet he never dreamed of the crash itself, though he often found himself again face to face with that terrified superchimp, as he descended the spiral stairway between the collapsing gasbags. None of the simps had survived; those that were not killed outright were so badly injured that they had been painlessly euthed. He sometimes wondered why he dreamed only of this doomed creature, which he had never met before the last minutes of its life—and not of the friends and colleagues he had lost aboard the dying Queen.

The dreams he feared most always began with his

first return to consciousness. There had been little physical pain; in fact, there had been no sensation of any kind. He was in darkness and silence and did not even seem to be breathing. And—strangest of all—he could not locate his limbs. He could move neither his hands nor his feet, because he did not know where they were.

The silence had been the first to yield. After hours or days, he had become aware of a faint throbbing and eventually, after long thought, he deduced that this was the beating of his own heart. That was the first of his many mistakes.

Then there had been faint pinpricks, sparkles of light, ghosts of pressures upon still unresponsive limbs. One by one his senses had returned, and pain had come with them. He had had to learn everything anew, recapitulating babyhood and infancy. Though his memory was unaffected and he could understand words that were spoken to him, it was months before he was able to answer except by the flicker of an eyelid. He could still remember the moments of triumph when he had spoken the first word, turned the page of a book—and, finally, learned to move under his own power. *That* was a victory, indeed, and it had taken him almost two years to prepare for it. A hundred times he had envied that dead superchimp, but *he* had been given no choice. The doctors had made their decision—and now, twelve years later, he was where no human being had ever traveled before and moving faster than any man in history.

Kon-Tiki was just emerging from shadow and the Jovian dawn bridged the sky ahead in a titantic bow of light, when the persistent buzz of the alarm dragged Falcon up from sleep. The inevitable nightmares (he had been trying to summon a nurse but did not even have the strength to push the button) swiftly faded from consciousness; the greatest—and perhaps last—adventure of his life was before him.

He called Mission Control, now a hundred thousand kilometers away and falling swiftly below the curve of Jupiter, to report that everything was in order. His velocity had just passed fifty kilometers a second (*that* was one for the books) and in half an hour, Kon-Tiki would hit the outer fringes of the atmosphere, as he started on the most difficult entry in the entire Solar System. Although scores of probes had survived this flaming ordeal, they had been tough, solidly packed masses of instrumentation, able to withstand several hundred gravities of drag. Kon-Tiki would hit peaks of thirty *g* and would average more than ten before she came to rest in the upper reaches of the Jovian atmosphere. Very carefully and thoroughly, Falcon began to attach the elaborate system of restraints that anchored him to the walls of the cabin. When he had finished, he was virtually a part of the ship's structure.

The clock was counting backward; a hundred seconds to entry. For better or worse, he was commited. In a minute and a half, he would graze the Jovian atmosphere and would be caught irrevocably in the grip of the giant.

The countdown was three seconds late—not at all bad, considering the unknowns involved. Beyond the walls of the capsule came a ghostly sighing that rose steadily to a high-pitched, screaming roar. The noise was quite different from that of a re-entry on Earth or Mars; in this thin atmosphere of hydrogen and helium, all sounds were transformed a couple of octaves higher. On Jupiter, even thunder would have falsetto overtones.

With the rising scream came also mounting weight; within seconds, he was completely immobilized. His field of vision contracted until it embraced only the clock and the accelerometer; fifteen *g*, and 480 seconds to go.

He never lost consciousness; but then, he had not

expected to. Kon-Tiki's trail through the Jovian atmosphere must be really spectacular—by this time, thousands of kilometers long. Five hundred seconds after entry, the drag began to taper off: ten *g*, five *g*, two . . . Then weight vanished almost completely; he was falling free, all his enormous orbital velocity destroyed.

There was a sudden jolt as the incandescent remnants of the heat shield were jettisoned. It had done its work and would not be needed again; Jupiter could have it now. He released all but two of the restraining buckles and waited for the automatic sequencer to start the next and most critical series of events.

He did not see the first drogue parachute pop out, but he could feel the slight jerk and the rate of fall diminished immediately. Kon-Tiki had lost all her horizontal speed and was going straight down at a thousand kilometers an hour. Everything depended on the next sixty seconds.

There went the second drogue. He looked up through the overhead window and saw, to his immense relief, that clouds of glittering foil were billowing out behind the falling ship. Like a great flower unfurling, the thousands of cubic meters of the balloon spread out across the sky, scooping up the thin gas until it was fully inflated. Kon-Tiki's rate of fall dropped to a few kilometers an hour and remained constant. Now there was plenty of time; it would take him days to fall all the way down to the surface of Jupiter.

But he would get there eventually, if he did nothing about it; the balloon overhead was merely acting as an efficient parachute. It was providing no lift, nor could it do so while the gas inside and out was the same.

With its characteristic and rather disconcerting crack, the fusion reactor started up, pouring torrents of heat into the envelope overhead. Within five minutes, the rate of fall had become zero; within six, the ship had started to rise. According to the radar altimeter, it had leveled out at 430 kilometers above the surface—or whatever passed for a surface on Jupiter.

Only one kind of balloon will work in an atmosphere of hydrogen, which is the lightest of all gases—and that is a hot-hydrogen balloon. As long as the fusor kept ticking over, Falcon could remain aloft, drifting across a world that could hold a hundred Pacifics. After traveling more than half a billion kilometers, Kon-Tiki had at last begun to justify her name. She was an aerial raft, adrift upon the current of the Jovian atmosphere.

Though a whole new world was lying around him, it was more than an hour before Falcon could examine the view. First he had to check all the capsule's systems and test its response to the controls. He had to learn how much extra heat was necessary to produce a desired rate of ascent and how much gas he must vent in order to descend. Above all, there was the question of stability. He must adjust the length of the cables attaching his capsule to the huge, pear-shaped balloon, to damp out vibrations and get the smoothest possible ride. So far, he was lucky; at this level, the wind was steady and the Doppler reading on the invisible surface gave him a ground speed of 350 kilometers an hour. For Jupiter, that was modest; winds of up to a thousand had been observed. But mere speed, of course, was unimportant; the real danger was turbulence. If he ran into that, only skill and experience and swift reaction could save him—and these were not matters that could yet be programmed into a computer.

Not until he was satisfied that he had got the feel of this strange craft did Falcon pay any attention to Mission Control's pleadings. Then he deployed the booms carrying the instrumentation and the atmospheric samplers; the capsule now resembled a rather untidy Christmas tree but still rode smoothly down the Jovian winds, while it radioed up its torrents of information to the recorders on the ship a hundred thousand kilometers above. And now, at last, he could look around.

His first impression was unexpected and even a little disappointing. As far as the scale of things was concerned, he might have been ballooning over an ordinary cloudscape on Earth. The horizon seemed at a normal distance; there was no feeling at all that he was on a world eleven times the diameter of his own. Then he looked at the infrared radar, sounding the layers of atmosphere beneath him—and knew how badly his eyes had been deceived.

That layer of clouds, apparently five kilometers away, was really sixty kilometers below. And the horizon, whose distance he would have guessed at two hundred, was actually three thousand kilometers from the ship.

The crystalline clarity of the hydro-helium atmosphere and the enormous curvature of the planet had fooled him completely. It was even harder to judge distances here than on the Moon; everything he saw must be multiplied by ten.

It was a simple matter and he should have been prepared for it. Yet somehow it disturbed him profoundly. He did not feel that Jupiter was huge but that *he* had shrunk—to a tenth of his normal size. Perhaps, with time, he would grow accustomed to the inhuman scale of this world; yet as he stared toward that unbelievably distant horizon, he felt as if a wind colder than the atmosphere around him was blowing through his soul. Despite all his arguments, this might never be a place for man. He could well be both the first and the last to descend through the clouds of Jupiter.

The sky above was almost black, except for a few

wisps of ammonia cirrus perhaps twenty kilometers overhead. It was cold up there on the fringes of space, but both pressure and temperature increased rapidly with depth. At the level where Kon-Tiki was drifting now, it was fifty degrees centigrade below zero and the pressure was five atmospheres. A hundred kilometers farther down, it would be as warm as equatorial Earth —and the pressure about the same as at the bottom of one of the shallower seas. Ideal conditions for life.

A quarter of the brief Jovian day had already gone; the Sun was halfway up the sky, but the light on the unbroken cloudscape below had a curious mellow quality. That extra half billion kilometers had robbed the Sun of all its power; though the sky was clear, Falcon found himself continually thinking that it was a heavily overcast day. When night fell, the onset of darkness would be swift, indeed; though it was still morning, there was a sense of autumnal twilight in the air. But autumn, of course, was something that never came to Jupiter. There were no seasons here.

Kon-Tiki had come down in the exact center of the Equatorial Zone—the least colorful part of the planet. The sea of clouds that stretched out to the horizon was tinted a pale salmon; there were none of the yellows and pinks and even reds that banded Jupiter at higher latitudes. The Great Red Spot itself—most spectacular of all the planet's features—lay thousands of kilometers to the south. It had been a temptation to descend there, but the South Tropical Disturbance was unusually active, with currents reaching fifteen hundred kilometers an hour. It would have been asking for trouble to head into that maelstrom of unknown forces. The Great Red Spot and its mysteries would have to wait for future expeditions.

The Sun, moving across the sky twice as swiftly as it did on Earth, was now nearing the zenith and had become eclipsed by the great silver canopy of the balloon. Kon-Tiki was still drifting swiftly, smoothly west-ward at a steady 350, but only the radar gave any indication of this. Was it always as calm here? Falcon asked himself. The scientists who had talked learnedly of the Jovian doldrums and had predicted that the equator would be the quietest place seemed to know what they were talking about, after all. He had been profoundly skeptical of all such forecasts and had agreed with one unusually modest researcher who had told him bluntly, "There are *no* experts on Jupiter." Well, there would be at least one by the end of this day.

If he managed to survive until then.

THE VOICES OF THE DEEP

That first day, the Father of the Gods smiled upon him. It was as calm and peaceful here on Jupiter as it had been, years ago, when he was drifting with Webster across the plains of northern India. Falcon had time to master his new skills, until Kon-Tiki seemed an extension of his own body. Such luck was more than he had dared hope and he began to wonder what price he might have to pay for it.

The five hours of daylight were almost over; the clouds below were full of shadows, which gave them a massive solidity they had not possessed when the Sun was higher. Color was swiftly draining from the sky, except in the west itself, where a band of deepening purple lay along the horizon. Above this band was the thin crescent of a closer moon, pale and bleached against the utter blackness beyond.

With a speed perceptible to the eye, the Sun went straight down over the edge of Jupiter, three thousand kilometers away. The stars came out in their legions—and there was the beautiful evening star of Earth, on the very frontier of twilight, reminding him how far he was from home. It followed the Sun down into the west; man's first night on Jupiter had begun.

With the onset of darkness, Kon-Tiki started to sink. The balloon was no longer heated by the feeble sunlight and was losing a small part of its buoyancy. Falcon did nothing to increase lift; he had expected this and was planning to descend.

The invisible cloud deck was still fifty kilometers below and he would reach it about midnight. It showed up clearly on the infrared radar, which also reported that it contained a vast array of complex carbon compounds, as well as the usual hydrogen, helium and ammonia. The chemists were dying for samples of that fluffy, pinkish stuff; though some atmospheric probes had already gathered a few grams, that had only whetted their appetites. Half the basic molecules of life were here, floating high above the surface of Jupiter. And where there was food, could life be far away? That was the question that, after more than a hundred years, no one had been able to answer.

The infrared was blocked by the clouds, but the microwave radar sliced right through and showed layer after layer, all the way down to the hidden surface more than four hundred kilometers below. That was barred to him by enormous pressures and temperatures; not even robot probes had ever reached it intact. It lay in tantalizing inaccessibility at the bottom of the radar screen, slightly fuzzy and showing a curious granular structure that his equipment could not resolve.

An hour after sunset, he dropped his first probe. It fell swiftly for a hundred kilometers, then began to float in the denser atmosphere, sending back torrents of radio signals, which he relayed up to Mission Control. Then there was nothing else to do until sunrise, except to keep an eye on the rate of descent, monitor the instruments and answer occasional queries. While she was drifting in this steady current, Kon-Tiki could look after herself.

Just before midnight, a woman controller came on watch and introduced herself with the usual pleasantries. Ten minutes later, she called again, her voice at once serious and excited.

"Howard! Listen in on channel forty-six—high gain."

Channel 46? There were so many telemetering circuits that he knew the numbers of only those that were critical; but as soon as he threw the switch, he recognized this one. He was plugged into the microphone on the probe, floating 130 kilometers below him in an atmosphere now almost as dense as water.

At first, there was only a soft hiss of whatever strange winds stirred down in the darkness of that unimaginable world. And then, out of the background noise, there slowly emerged a booming vibration that grew louder and louder, like the beating of a gigantic drum. It was so low that it was felt as much as heard and the beats steadily increased their tempo, though the pitch never changed. Now it was a swift, almost infrasonic throbbing—and then, suddenly, in mid-vibration, it stopped, so abruptly that the mind could not accept the silence, but memory continued to manufacture a ghostly echo in the deepest caverns of the brain.

It was the most extraordinary sound that Falcon had ever heard, even among the multitudinous noises of Earth. He could think of no natural phenomenon that could have caused it, nor was it like the cry of any animal, not even one of the great whales.

It came again, following exactly the same pattern. Now that he was prepared for it, he estimated the length of the sequence; from first faint throb to final crescendo, it lasted just over ten seconds.

And this time, there was a real echo, very faint

and far away. Perhaps it came from one of the many reflecting layers deeper in this stratified atmosphere; perhaps it was another more distant source. Falcon waited for a second echo, but it never came.

Mission Control reacted quickly and asked him to drop another probe at once. With two microphones operating, it would be possible to find the approximate location of the sources. Oddly enough, none of Kon-Tiki's own external mikes could detect anything except wind noises; the boomings, whatever they were, must have been trapped and channeled beneath an atmospheric reflecting layer far below.

They were coming, it was soon discovered, from a cluster of sources about two thousand kilometers away. The distance gave no indication of their power; in Earth's oceans, quite feeble sounds could travel equally far. And as for the obvious assumption that living creatures were responsible, the chief exobiologist quickly ruled that out.

"I'll be very disappointed," said Dr. Brenner, "if there are no microorganisms or plants here. But nothing like animals, because there's no free oxygen. All biochemical reactions on Jupiter must be low-energy ones—there's just no way an active creature could generate enough power to function."

Falcon wondered if this were true; he had heard the argument before and reserved judgment.

"In any case," continued Brenner, "some of those sound waves are a hundred meters long! Even an animal as big as a whale couldn't produce them. They *must* have a natural origin."

Yes, that seemed plausible, and probably the physicists would be able to come up with an explanation. What would a blind alien make, Falcon wondered, of the sounds he might hear when standing beside a stormy sea or a geyser or a volcano or a waterfall? He might well attribute them to some huge beast.

About an hour before sunrise, the voices of the deep died away and Falcon began to busy himself with preparation for the dawn of his second day. Kon-Tiki was now only five kilometers above the nearest cloud layer; the external pressure had risen to ten atmospheres and the temperature was a tropical thirty degrees. A man could be comfortable here with no more equipment than a breathing mask and the right grade of heliox mixture.

"We've some good news for you," Mission Control reported soon after dawn. "The cloud layer's breaking up. You'll have partial clearing in an hour—but watch out for turbulence."

"I've already noticed some," Falcon answered. "How far down will I be able to see?"

"At least twenty kilometers, down to the second thermocline. *That* cloud deck is solid—it never breaks."

And it's out of my reach, Falcon told himself; the temperature down there must be over a hundred degrees. This was the first time that any balloonist had ever had to worry not about his ceiling but about his— basement?

Ten minutes later, he could see what Mission Control had already observed from its superior vantage point. There was a change in color near the horizon and the cloud layer had become ragged and humpy, as if something had torn it open. He turned up his little nuclear furnace and gave Kon-Tiki another five kilometers of altitude so that he could get a better view.

The sky below was clearing rapidly—completely, as if something was dissolving away the solid overcast. An abyss was opening up before his eyes; a moment later, he sailed out over the edge of a cloud canyon twenty kilometers deep and a thousand kilometers wide.

A new world lay spread beneath him; Jupiter had stripped away one of its many veils. The second layer of clouds, unattainably far below, was much darker in color than the first. It was almost salmon pink and curiously mottled with little islands of brick red. They were all oval-shaped, with their long axes pointing east-west, in the direction of the prevailing wind. There were hundreds of them, all about the same size, and they reminded Falcon of puffy little cumulus clouds in the terrestrial sky.

He reduced buoyancy and Kon-Tiki began to drop down the face of the dissolving cliff. It was then that he noticed the snow.

White flakes were forming in the air and drifting slowly downward. Yet it was much too warm for snow—and, in any event, there was scarcely a trace of water at this altitude. Moreover, there was no glitter nor sparkle about these flakes as they went cascading down into the depths; when, presently, a few landed on an instrument boom outside the main viewing port, he saw that they were a dull, opaque white—not crystalline at all—and quite large, several centimeters across. They looked like wax and Falcon guessed that this was precisely what they were. Some chemical reaction was taking place in the atmosphere around him, condensing out the hydrocarbons floating in the Jovian air.

A hundred kilometers ahead, a disturbance was taking place in the cloud layer. The little red ovals were being jostled around and were beginning to form a spiral—the familiar cyclonic pattern so common in the meteorology of Earth. The vortex was emerging with astonishing speed; if that was a storm ahead, Falcon told himself, he was in big trouble.

And then his concern changed to wonder—and to fear. For what was developing in his line of flight was not a storm at all. Something enormous—something scores of kilometers across—was rising through the clouds.

The reassuring thought that it, too, might be a cloud—a thunderhead boiling up from the lower levels of the atmosphere—lasted only a few seconds. No; this was *solid*. It shouldered its way through the pink-and-salmon overcast like an iceberg rising from the deeps.

An *iceberg*, floating on hydrogen? That was impossible, of course; but perhaps it was not too remote an analogy. As soon as he focused the telescope upon the enigma, Falcon saw that it was a whitish mass, threaded with streaks of red and brown. It must be, he decided, the same stuff as the "snowflakes" falling around him—a mountain range of wax. And it was not, he soon realized, as solid as he had thought; around the edges, it was continually crumbling and re-forming.

"I know what it is," he radioed Mission Control, which for the past few minutes had been asking anxious questions. "It's a mass of bubbles—some kind of foam. Hydrocarbon froth. Get the chemists working on—*just a minute!*"

"What is it?" called Mission Control. "What is it?"

He ignored the frantic pleas from space and concentrated all his mind upon the image in the telescope field. He had to be sure; if he made a mistake, he would be the laughingstock of the Solar System.

Then he relaxed, glanced at the clock and switched off the nagging voice from Jupiter V.

"Hello, Mission Control," he said very formally. "This is Howard Falcon aboard Kon-Tiki, Ephemeris Time Nineteen Hours Twenty One Minutes Fifteen Seconds. Latitude Zero Degrees Five Minutes North. Longitude One Hundred Five Degrees Forty Two Minutes, System One.

"Tell Dr. Brenner that there is life on Jupiter. And it's *big*."

THE WHEELS OF POSEIDON

"I'm very happy to be proved wrong," Dr. Brenner radioed back cheerfully. "Nature always has something up her sleeve. Keep the long-focus camera on target and give us the steadiest pictures you can."

The things moving up and down those waxen slopes were still too far away for Falcon to make out many details, and they must have been very large to be visible at all at such a distance. Almost black and shaped like arrowheads, they maneuvered by slow undulations of their entire bodies, so that they looked rather like giant manta rays swimming above some tropical reef.

Perhaps they were sky-borne cattle browsing on the cloud pastures of Jupiter, for they seemed to be feeding along the dark, red-brown streaks that ran like dried-up river beds down the flanks of the floating cliffs. Occasionally, one of them would dive headlong into the mountain of foam and disappear completely from sight.

Kon-Tiki was moving only slowly with respect to the cloud layer below; it would be at least three hours before she was above those ephemeral hills. She was in a race with the Sun; Falcon hoped that darkness would not fall before he could get a good view of the mantas, as he had christened them, as well as the fragile landscape over which they flapped their way.

It was a long three hours; during the whole time, he kept the external microphones on full gain, wondering if here was the source of that booming in the night. The mantas were certainly large enough to have produced it; when he could get an accurate measurement, he discovered that they were almost a hundred meters across the wings. That was three times the length of the largest whale—though he doubted if they could weigh more than a few tons.

Half an hour before sunset, Kon-Tiki was almost above the "mountains."

"No," said Falcon, answering Mission Control's repeated questions about the mantas. "They're still showing no reaction to me. I don't think they're intelligent—they look like harmless vegetarians. And even if they try to chase me—I'm sure they can't reach my altitude."

Yet he was a little disappointed when the mantas showed not the slightest interest in him as he sailed high above their feeding ground. Perhaps they had no way of detecting his presence; when he examined and photographed them through the telescope, he could see no signs of any sense organs. The creatures were merely huge black deltas rippling over hills and valleys that, in reality, were little more substantial than the clouds of Earth. Though they looked so solid, Falcon knew that anyone who stepped on those white mountains would go crashing through them as if they were made of tissue paper.

At close quarters, he could see the myriads of cellules or bubbles from which they were formed. Some of these were quite large—a meter or so in diameter—and Falcon wondered in what witch's caldron of hydrocarbons they had been brewed. There must be enough petrochemicals deep down in the atmosphere of Jupiter to supply all Earth's needs for a million years.

The short day had almost gone when he passed over the crest of the waxen hills and the light was fading rapidly along their lower slopes. There were no mantas on this western side and for some reason, the topography was very different. The foam was sculpted into long, level terraces, like the interior of a lunar crater. He could almost imagine that they were gigantic steps leading down to the hidden surface of the planet.

And on the lowest of those steps, just clear of the swirling clouds that the mountain had displaced when it came surging skyward, was a roughly oval mass two or three kilometers across. It was difficult to see, being only a little darker than the gray-white foam on which it rested. Falcon's first reaction was that he was looking at a forest of pallid trees, like giant mushrooms that had never seen the Sun.

Yes, it must be a forest—he could see hundreds of thin trunks springing from the white, waxy froth in which they were rooted. But the trees were packed astonishingly close together; there was scarcely any space between them. Perhaps it was not a forest after all but a single enormous tree—like one of the giant, multiple-trunked banyans of the East. He had once seen, in Java, a banyan tree two hundred meters across; this monster was at least ten times that size.

The light had almost gone; the cloudscape had turned purple with refracted sunlight and in a few seconds that, too, would have vanished. In the very last light of his second day on Jupiter, Howard Falcon saw—or thought he saw—something that cast the very gravest doubts on his interpretation of the white oval.

Unless the dim light had totally deceived him, those hundreds of thin trunks were beating back and forth, in perfect synchronism, like fronds of kelp rocking in the surge.

And the tree was no longer in the place where he had first seen it.

"Sorry about this," said Mission Control soon after sunset, "but we think Source Beta is going to blow within the next hour. Probability seventy percent."

Falcon glanced quickly at the chart. Beta—Jupiter latitude 140 degrees—was thirty thousand kilometers away and well below his horizon. Even though major eruptions ran as high as ten megatons, he was much too far away for the shock wave to be a serious danger. The radio storm that it would trigger was, however, quite a different matter.

The decameter outbursts that sometimes made Jupiter the most powerful radio source in the whole sky had been discovered back in the 1950s, to the utter astonishment of the astronomers. Now, more than a century later, their real cause was still a mystery. Only the symptoms were understood; the explanation was completely unknown.

The "volcano" theory had best stood the test of time—although no one imagined that this word had the same meaning on Jupiter as on Earth. At frequent intervals—often several times a day—titanic eruptions occurred in the lower depths of the atmosphere, probably on the hidden surface of the planet itself. A great column of gas, more than a thousand kilometers high, would start boiling upward, as if determined to escape into space.

Against the most powerful gravitational field of all the planets, it had no chance. Yet some traces—a mere few million tons—usually managed to reach the Jovian ionosphere; and when they did, all hell broke loose.

The radiation belts surrounding Jupiter completely dwarf the feeble Van Allen belts of Earth. When they are short-circuited by an ascending column of gas, the result is an electrical discharge millions of times more powerful than any terrestrial flash of lightning; it sends a colossal thunderclap of radio noise flooding across the entire Solar System—and on out to the stars.

It had been discovered that these radio outbursts came from four main areas of the planet; perhaps there were weaknesses here that allowed the fires of the interior to break out from time to time. The scientists on Ganymede, largest of Jupiter's many moons, now thought that they could predict the onset of a decameter storm; their accuracy was about as good as a weather forecaster's of the early 1900s.

Falcon did not know whether to welcome or to fear a radio storm; it would certainly add to the value of the mission—if he survived it. His course had been planned to keep as far as possible from the main centers of disturbance, especially the most active one, Source Alpha. As luck would have it, the threatening Beta was the closest to him; he hoped that thirty thousand kilometers—almost the circumference of Earth—was a safe enough distance.

"Probability ninety percent," said Mission Control with a distinct note of urgency. "And forget that hour. Ganymede says it may be any moment."

The radio had scarcely fallen silent when the reading on the magnetic-field-strength meter started to shoot upward. Before it could go off-scale, it reversed and began to drop as rapidly as it had risen. Far away and thousands of kilometers below, something had given the planet's molten core a titanic jolt.

"There she blows!" called Mission Control.

"Thanks—I already know. When will the storm hit me?"

"You can expect onset in five minutes. Peak in ten."

Far round the curve of Jupiter, a funnel of gas as wide as the Pacific Ocean was climbing spaceward at thousands of kilometers an hour. Already, the thunderstorms of the lower atmosphere would be raging around it—but they were as nothing to the fury that would explode when the radition belt was reached and it began dumping its surplus electrons onto the planet. Falcon began to retract all the instrument booms that were extended out from the capsule; there were no other precautions he could take. It would be four hours before the atmospheric shock wave reached him—but the radio blast, traveling at the speed of light, would be here in a tenth of a second once the discharge had been triggered.

The radio monitor, scanning back and forth across the spectrum, still showed nothing unusual—just the normal mush of background static. Then Falcon noticed that the noise level was slowly creeping upward. The explosion was gathering its strength.

At such a distance, he had never expected to *see* anything. But suddenly a flicker as of far-off heat lightning danced along the eastern horizon. Simultaneously, half the circuit breakers jumped out of the main switchboard, the lights failed and all communications channels went dead.

He tried to move but was completely unable to do so. The paralysis that gripped him was not merely psychological; he seemed to have lost all control of his limbs and could feel a painful tingling sensation over his entire body. It was impossible that the electric field could have penetrated into this shielded cabin—yet there was a flickering glow over the instrument board and he could hear the unmistakable crackle of a brush discharge.

With a series of sharp bangs, the emergency systems operated and the overloads reset themselves. The lights flickered on again and Falcon's paralysis disappeared as swiftly as it had come. After glancing at the board to make sure that all circuits were back to normal, he moved quickly to the viewing ports.

There was no need to switch on the inspection lamps —the cables supporting the capsule seemed to be on fire. Lines of light, glowing an electric blue against the darkness, stretched upward from the main lift ring to the equator of the giant balloon; and rolling slowly along several of them were dazzling balls of fire.

The sight was so strange and so beautiful that it was hard to read any menace in it. Few people, Falcon knew, had ever seen ball lightning from such close quarters—and certainly none had survived if they were riding a hydrogen-filled balloon back in the atmosphere of Earth. He remembered the flaming death of the Hindenburg, destroyed by a stray spark when she docked at Lakehurst in 1937; as it had done so often in the past, the horrifying old newsreel film flashed through his mind. But at least that could not happen here, though there was more hydrogen above his head than had ever filled the last of the zeppelins. It would be a few billion years yet before anyone could light a fire in the atmosphere of Jupiter.

With a sound like briskly frying bacon, the speech circuit came back to life.

"Hello, Kon-Tiki—are you receiving? Are you receiving?"

The words were chopped and badly distorted but intelligible. Falcon's spirits lifted; he had resumed contact with the world of men.

"I receive you," he said. "Quite an electrical display, but no damage—so far."

"Thanks—thought we'd lost you. Please check telemetry channels three, seven, twenty-six. Also gain on camera two. And we don't quite believe the readings on the external ionization probes."

Reluctantly, Falcon tore his gaze away from the fascinating pyrotechnic display around Kon-Tiki, though from time to time he kept glancing out the windows. The ball lightning disappeared first, the fiery globes slowly expanding until they reached a critical size, at which they vanished in a gentle explosion. But for an hour later, there were still faint glows around all the exposed metal on the outside of the capsule; and the radio circuits remained noisy until well after midnight.

The remaining hours of darkness were completely uneventful—until just before dawn. Because it came from the east, Falcon assumed that he was seeing the first faint hint of sunrise. Then he realized that it was still twenty minutes too early for it—and the glow that had appeared along the horizon was moving toward him even as he watched. It swiftly detached itself from the arch of stars that marked the invisible edge of the planet and he saw that it was a relatively narrow band, quite sharply defined. The beam of an enormous searchlight appeared to be swinging beneath the clouds.

Perhaps a hundred kilometers behind the first racing bar of light came another, parallel to it and moving at the same speed. And beyond that another, and another—until all the sky flickered with alternating sheets of light and darkness.

By this time, Falcon thought, he had been inured to wonders and it seemed impossible that this display of pure, soundless luminosity could present the slightest danger. But it was so astonishing and so inexplicable that he felt cold naked fear gnawing at his self-control. No man could look upon such a sight without feeling a helpless pygmy, in the presence of forces beyond his comprehension. Was it possible that, after all, Jupiter carried not only life but intelligence? And, perhaps, an intelligence that only now was beginning to react to his alien presence.

"Yes, we see it," said Mission Control in a voice that echoed his own awe. "We've no idea what it is. Stand by—we're calling Ganymede."

The display was slowly fading; the bands racing in from the far horizon were much fainter, as if the energies that powered them were becoming exhausted. In five minutes, it was all over; the last faint pulse of light flickered along the western sky and then was gone. Its passing left Falcon with an overwhelming sense of relief. The sight was so hypnotic and so disturbing that it was not good for any man's peace of mind to contemplate it too long.

He was more shaken than he cared to admit. The

electrical storm was something that he could understand, but *this* was totally incomprehensible.

Mission Control was still silent. Falcon knew that the information banks up on Ganymede were now being searched while men and computers turned their minds to the problem. If no answer could be found there, it would be necessary to call Earth; that would mean a delay of almost an hour. The possibility that even Earth might be unable to help was one that Falcon did not care to contemplate.

He had never before been so glad to hear the voice of Mission Control as when Dr. Brenner finally came on the circuit. The biologist sounded relieved—yet subdued, like a man who had just come through some great intellectual crisis.

"Hello, Kon-Tiki. We've solved your problem, but we can still hardly believe it.

"What you've been seeing is bioluminescence—very similar to that produced by micoorganisms in the tropical seas of Earth. Here they're in the atmosphere, not the ocean, but the principle is the same."

"But the pattern," protested Falcon. "It was so regular—so *artificial*. And it was hundreds of kilometers across!"

"It was even larger than you imagine—you observed only a small part of it. The whole pattern was five thousand kilometers wide and looked like a revolving wheel. You merely saw the spokes, sweeping past you at about a kilometer a second—"

"A *second*," Falcon could not help interjecting. "No animals could move that fast!"

"Of course not—let me explain. What you saw was triggered by the shock wave from Source Beta, moving at the speed of sound."

"But what about the pattern?" Falcon insisted.

"That's the surprising part. It's a very rare phenomenon, but identical wheels of light—except that they're a thousand times smaller—have been observed in the Persian Gulf and the Indian Ocean. Listen to this: British India Company's Patna, Persian Gulf, May 1880, eleven-thirty P.M.—'An enormous luminous wheel, whirling round, the spokes of which appeared to brush the ship along. The spokes were two hundred or three hundred yards long . . . each wheel contained about sixteen spokes. . . .' And here's one from the Gulf of Oman, dated 23 May, 1906: 'The intensely bright luminescence approached us rapidly, shooting sharply defined light rays to the west in rapid succession, like the beam from the searchlight of a warship. . . . To the left of us, a gigantic fiery wheel formed itself, with spokes that reached as far as one could see. The whole wheel whirled around for two or three minutes.' The archive computer on Ganymede dug up about five hundred cases—it would have printed out the lot if we hadn't stopped it in time."

"I'm convinced—but still baffled."

"I don't blame you; the full explanation wasn't worked out until late in the twentieth century. It seems that these luminous wheels are the results of submarine earthquakes and always occur in shallow waters, where the shock waves can be reflected and cause standard wave patterns. Sometimes bars—sometimes rotating wheels—the 'Wheels of Poseidon,' they've been called. The theory was finally proved by making underwater explosions and photographing the results from a satellite. No wonder sailors used to be superstitious. Who would have believed a thing like *this*?"

So that was it, Falcon told himself. When Source Beta blew its top, it must have sent shock waves in all directions—through the compressed gas of the lower atmosphere, through the solid body of Jupiter itself. Meeting and crisscrossing, those waves must have canceled here, reinforced there; the whole planet must have rung like a bell.

Yet the explanation did not destroy the sense of wonder and awe; he would never be able to forget those flickering bands of light racing through the unattainable depths of the Jovian atmosphere. He felt that he was not merely on a strange planet but in some magical realm between myth and reality.

This was a world where absolutely *anything* could happen and no man could possibly guess what the future would bring.

And he still had a whole day to go.

MEDUSA

When the true dawn finally arrived, it brought a sudden change of weather. Kon-Tiki was moving through a blizzard; waxen snowflakes were falling so thickly that visibility was reduced to zero. Falcon began to worry about the weight that might be accumulating on the envelope; then he noticed that any flakes settling outside the windows quickly disappeared. Kon-Tiki's continuous outpouring of heat was evaporating them as swiftly as they arrived.

If he had been ballooning on Earth, he would also have worried about the possibility of collision. That, at least, was no danger here; any Jovian mountains were several hundred kilometers below him. And as for the floating islands of foam, hitting them would probably be like plowing into slightly hardened soap bubbles.

Nevertheless, he switched on the horizontal radar, which until now had been completely useless; only the vertical beam, giving his distance from the invisible surface, so far had been of any value. And then he had another surprise.

Scattered across a huge sector of the sky ahead were dozens of large and brilliant echoes. They were completely isolated from one another and hung apparently unsupported in space. Falcon suddenly remembered a phrase that earliest aviators had used to describe one of the hazards of their profession—"clouds stuffed with rocks." That was a perfect description of what seemed to lie in the track of Kon-Tiki.

It was a disconcerting sight; then Falcon again reminded himself that nothing *really* solid could possibly hover in this atmosphere. Perhaps it was some strange meteorological phenomenon—and, in any case, the nearest echo was over two hundred kilometers away.

He reported to Mission Control, which could provide no explantion. But it gave the welcome news that he would be clear of the blizzard in another thirty minutes.

It did not warn him, however, of the violent cross wind that abruptly grabbed Kon-Tiki and swept it almost at right angles to its previous track. Falcon needed all his skill and the maximum use of what little control he had over his ungainly vehicle to prevent it from being capsized. Within minutes, he was racing northward at five hundred kilometers an hour; then, as suddenly as it had started, the turbulence ceased; he was still moving at high speed but in smooth air. He wondered if he had been caught in the Jovian equivalent of a jet stream.

Then the snowstorm suddenly dissolved and he saw what Jupiter had been preparing for him.

Kon-Tiki had entered the funnel of a gigantic whirlpool, at least three hundred kilometers across. The balloon was being swept along a curving wall of cloud; overhead, the Sun was shining in a clear sky, but far beneath, this great hole in the atmosphere drilled down to unknown depths, until it reached a misty floor where lightning flickered almost continuously.

Though the vessel was being dragged downward so slowly that it was in no immediate danger, Falcon increased the flow of heat into the envelope, until

Kon-Tiki hovered at a constant altitude. Not until then did he abandon the fantastic spectacle outside and consider again the problem of the radar.

The nearest echo was now only forty kilometers away —and all of them, he quickly realized, were distributed along the wall of the vortex; they were moving with it, apparently caught in the whirlpool like Kon-Tiki itself. He aimed the telescope along the radar bearing and found himself looking at a curious mottled cloud that almost filled the field of view.

It was not easy to see, being only little darker than the whirling wall of mist that formed its background. Not until he had been staring for several minutes did Falcon realize that he had met it once before.

The first time, it had been crawling across the drifting mountains of foam and he had mistaken it for a giant, many-trunked tree. Now at last he could appreciate its real size and complexity and he could give it a better name to fix its image in his mind. It did not resemble a tree at all but a jellyfish—a medusa, such as might be met trailing its tentacles as it drifted along the warm eddies of the Gulf Stream.

This medusa was two kilometers across and its scores of dangling tentacles were hundreds of meters long. They swayed slowly back and forth in perfect unison, taking more than a minute for each complete undulation—almost as if the creature were clumsily rowing itself through the sky.

The other echoes were more distant medusae; Falcon turned the telescope on half a dozen and could see no variations in shape or size. They all seemed to be of the same species and he wondered just why they were drifting lazily around in this thousand-kilometer orbit. Perhaps they were feeding upon the aerial plankton sucked in by the whirlpool—as Kon-Tiki itself had been.

"Do you realize, Howard," said Dr. Brenner when he had recovered from his initial astonishment, "that this thing is about a hundred thousand times as large as the biggest whale? And even if it's only a gasbag, it must still weigh a million tons! I can't even guess at its metabolism; it must generate megawatts of heat to maintain its buoyancy."

"But if it's just a gasbag, why is it such a damn good radar reflector?"

"I haven't the faintest idea. Can you get any closer?"

Brenner's question was not an idle one; if Falcon changed altitude to take advantage of the differing wind velocities, he could approach the medusa as closely as he wished. At the moment, he preferred his present forty kilometers and said so, firmly.

"I see what you mean," Brenner answered a little reluctantly. "Let's stay where we are for the present." That "we" gave Falcon a certain wry amusement; an extra hundred thousand kilometers made a considerable difference to one's point of view.

For the next two hours, Kon-Tiki drifted uneventfully in the gyre of the great whirlpool, while Falcon experimented with filters and camera contrast, trying to get a clear view of the medusa. He began to wonder if its elusive coloration were some kind of camouflage; perhaps, like many animals of Earth, it was trying to lose itself against its background. That was a trick used both by hunters and by the hunted.

In which category was the medusa? That was a question he could hardly expect to have answered in the short time that was left to him. Yet just before noon, without the slightest warning, the answer came.

Like a squadron of antique jet fighters, five mantas came sweeping through the wall of mist that formed the funnel of the vortex. They were flying in a V formation, directly toward the pallid gray cloud of the medusa—and there was no doubt, in Falcon's mind, that they were on the attack. He had been quite wrong to assume that they were harmless vegetarians.

Yet everything happened at such a leisurely pace that it was like watching a slow-motion film. The mantas undulated along at perhaps fifty kilometers an hour; it seemed ages before they reached the medusa, which continued to paddle imperturbably along at an even slower speed. Huge though they were, the mantas looked tiny beside the monster they were approaching; when they flapped down onto its back, they appeared about as large as birds landing on a whale.

Could the medusa defend itself? Falcon wondered. As long as they avoided those huge, clumsy tentacles, he did not see how the attacking mantas could be in any danger. And perhaps their host was not even aware of them; they could be insignificant parasites, as tolerated as fleas upon a dog.

But now it was obvious that the medusa was in distress. With agonizing slowness, it began to tip over, like a capsizing ship. After ten minutes, it had tilted forty-five degrees; it was also rapidly losing altitude. It was impossible not to feel a sense of pity for the beleaguered monster, and to Howard Falcon the sight brought bitter memories. In a grotesque way, the fall of the medusa was almost a parody of the dying Queen's last moments.

Yet he knew that his sympathies were on the wrong side. High intelligence could only develop among predators—not among the drifting browsers of either sea or air. The mantas were far closer to him than was this monstrous bag of gas; and anyway, who could *really* sympathize with a creature a hundred thousand times larger than a whale?

Then he noticed that the medusa's tactics seemed to be having some effect. The mantas had been disturbed by its slow roll and were flapping heavily away from its back—like gorged vultures interrupted at mealtime. But they did not move very far, continuing to hover a few meters from the still capsizing monster.

There was a sudden, blinding flash of light, synchronized with a crash of static over the radio. One of the mantas, slowly twisting end over end, was plummeting straight downward. As it fell, it trailed behind it a smoky black plume. Though there could be no fire, the resemblance to an aircraft going down in flames was quiet uncanny.

In unison, the remaining mantas dived steeply away from the medusa, gaining speed by losing altitude. Within minutes, they had vanished back into the wall of cloud from which they had emerged. And the medusa, no longer falling, began to roll back toward the horizontal. Soon it was sailing along once more on an even keel, as if nothing had happened.

"Beautiful!" said Dr. Brenner after a moment of stunned silence. "It's developed electric defenses—like some of our eels and rays. But that must have been about a million volts! Can you see any organs that might produce the discharge? Anything looking like electrodes?"

"No," Falcon answered, after switching to the highest power of the telescope. "But here's something odd. Do you see this pattern? Check back on the earlier images—I'm sure it wasn't there before."

A broad, mottled band had appeared along the side of the medusa. It formed a startlingly regular checkerboard, each square of which was itself speckled in a complex subpattern of short horizontal lines. They were spaced equal distances apart, in a geometrically perfect array of rows and columns.

"You're right," said Dr. Brenner, and now there was something very much like awe in his voice. "That's just appeared. And I'm afraid to tell you what I think it is."

"Well, I have no reputation to lose—at least as a biologist. Shall I give my guess?"

"Go ahead."

"That's a large meter-band radio array. The sort of

thing they used back at the beginning of the twentieth century."

"I was afraid you'd say that. Now we know why it gave such a massive echo."

"But why has it just appeared?"

"Probably an aftereffect of the discharge."

"I've just had another thought," said Falcon rather slowly. "Do you suppose it's *listening* to us?"

"On this frequency? I doubt it. Those are meter— no, *decameter* antennas, judging by their size. Hmm . . . that's an idea!"

Dr. Brenner fell silent, obviously contemplating some new line of thought. Presently, he continued: "I bet they're tuned to the radio outbursts! That's something nature never got around to doing on Earth. We have animals with sonar and even electric senses, but nothing ever developed a radio sense. Why bother, where there was so much light?

"But it's different here. Jupiter is *drenched* with radio energy. It's worth while using it—maybe even tapping it. That thing could be a floating power plant!"

A new voice cut into the conversation.

"Mission Commander here. This is all very interesting—but there's a much more important matter to settle. *Is it intelligent?* If so, we've got to consider the First Contact directives."

"Until I came here," said Dr. Brenner somewhat ruefully, "I would have sworn that anything that can make a shortwave antenna system *must* be intelligent. Now I'm not sure. This could have evolved naturally. I suppose it's no more fantastic than the human eye."

"Then we have to play safe and assume intelligence. For the present, therefore, this expedition comes under all the clauses of the Prime Directive."

There was a long silence while everyone on the radio circuit absorbed the implications of this. For the first time in the history of space flight, the rules that had been established through more than a century of argument might have to be applied. Man had—it was hoped—profited from his mistakes on Earth. Not only moral considerations but his own self-interest demanded that he should not repeat them among the planets. It could be disastrous to treat a superior intelligence as the American settlers had treated the red Indians or as almost everyone had treated the Africans.

The first rule was: Keep your distance—make no attempt to approach nor even to communicate until "they" have had plenty of time to study you. Exactly what was meant by plenty of time no one had ever been able to decide; it was left to the discretion of the man on the spot.

A responsibility of which he had never dreamed had descended upon Howard Falcon. In the few hours that remained to him on Jupiter, he might become the first ambassador of the human race.

And *that* was an irony so delicious that he almost wished the surgeons had restored to him the power of laughter.

PRIME DIRECTIVE

It was growing darker, but Falcon scarcely noticed as he strained his eyes toward that living cloud in the field of the telescope. The wind that was still sweeping Kon-Tiki steadily around the funnel of the great whirlpool had now brought him within twenty kilometers of the creature; if he got much closer than ten, he would take evasive action. Though he felt certain that the medusa's electric weapons were short-ranged, he did not wish to put the matter to the test. That would be a problem for future explorers, and he wished them luck.

Now it was quite dark in the capsule—and that was strange, because sunset was still hours away. Automatically, he glanced at the horizontally scanning radar, as he had done every few minutes. Apart from the medusa he was studying, there was no other object within a hundred kilometers of him.

Suddenly, with startling power, he heard the sound that had come booming out of the Jovian night—the throbbing beat that grew more and more rapid, then stopped mid-crescendo. The whole capsule vibrated with it, like a pea in a kettledrum.

Howard Falcon realized two things almost simultaneously, during the sudden, aching silence. *This* time, the sound was not coming from thousands of kilometers away, over a radio circuit. It was in the very atmosphere around him.

The second thought was even more disturbing. He had quite forgotten—it was inexcusable, but there had been other apparently more important things on his mind —that most of the sky above him was completely blanked out by Kon-Tiki's gasbag. Being lightly silvered to conserve its heat, the great balloon was an effective shield both to radar and to vision.

He had known this, of course; it had been a minor defect of the design, tolerated because it did not appear important. It seemed very important to Howard Falcon now—as he saw that fence of gigantic tentacles, thicker than the trunks of any tree, descending all around the capsule.

He heard Brenner yelling: "Remember the Prime Directive! Don't alarm it!" Before he could make an appropriate answer, that overwhelming drumbeat started again and drowned all other sounds.

The sign of a really skilled test pilot is how he reacts not to foreseeable emergencies but to ones that nobody could have anticipated. Falcon did not hesitate for more than a second to analyze the situation; then, in a lightning-swift movement, he pulled the rip cord.

That word was an archaic survival from the days of the first hydrogen balloons; on Kon-Tiki, the rip cord did not tear open the gasbag but merely operated a set of louvers round the upper curve of the envelope. At once, the hot gas started to rush out; Kon-Tiki, deprived of her lift, began to fall swiftly in this gravity field two and a half times as strong at Earth's.

Falcon had a momentary glimpse of great tentacles whipping upward and away; he had just time to note that they were studded with large bladders or sacs, presumably to give them buoyancy, and that they ended in multitudes of thin feelers like the roots of a plant. He half expected a bolt of lightning, but nothing happened.

His precipitous rate of descent was slackening as the atmosphere thickened and the deflated envelope acted as a parachute. Kon-Tiki had dropped more than three kilometers; it should be safe to close the louvers again. By the time he had restored buoyancy and was in equilibrium once more, he had lost another two kilometers of altitude and was getting dangerously near his safety limit.

He peered anxiously through the overhead windows, though he did not expect to see anything except the obscuring bulk of the balloon. But he had side-slipped during his descent and part of the medusa was just visible a couple of kilometers above him. It was much closer than he expected—and it was still coming down, faster than he would have believed possible.

Mission Control was calling anxiously; he shouted, "I'm OK—but it's still coming after me. I can't go any deeper."

That was not quite true. He could go a lot deeper— about 300 kilometers. But it would be a one-way trip and most of the journey would be of little interest to him.

Then, to his great relief, he saw that the medusa was leveling off about a kilometer above him. Perhaps it had decided to approach this strange intruder with caution—or perhaps it, too, found this deeper layer uncomfortably hot. The temperature was over fifty degrees and Falcon wondered how much longer his life-support system could handle matters.

Dr. Brenner was back on the circuit, still worrying about the Prime Directive.

"Remember—it may only be inquisitive!" he cried without much conviction. "Try not to frighten it!"

Falcon was getting rather tired of this advice and recalled a TV discussion he had once seen between a space lawyer and an astronaut. After the full implications of the Prime Directive had been carefully spelled out, the incredulous spacer had exclaimed: "So if there were no alternative, I must sit still and let myself be eaten?" The lawyer had not even cracked a smile when he answered: "That's an *excellent* summing up."

It had seemed funny at the time; it was not at all amusing now.

And then Falcon saw something that made him even more unhappy. The medusa was still hovering a kilometer above him—but one of its tentacles was becoming incredibly elongated and was stretching down toward Kon-Tiki, thinning out at the same time. As a boy, he had once seen the funnel of a tornado descending from a storm cloud over the Kansas plains; the thing coming toward him now evoked vivid memories of that black, twisting snake in the sky.

"I'm rapidly running out of options," he reported to Mission Control. "I now have only a choice between frightening it and giving it a bad stomach-ache. I don't think it will find Kon-Tiki very digestible, if that's what it has in mind."

He waited for comments from Brenner, but the biologist remained silent.

"Very well—it's twenty-seven minutes ahead of time, but I'm starting the ignition sequencer. I hope I'll have enough reserve to correct my orbit later."

He could no longer see the medusa; it was directly

overhead once more. But he knew that the descending tentacle must now be very close to the balloon. It would take almost five minutes to bring the reactor up to full thrust.

The fusor was primed. The orbit computer had not rejected the situation as wholly impossible. The air scoops were open, ready to gulp in tons of the surrounding hydrohelium on demand. Even under optimum conditions, this would have been the moment of truth—for there had been no way of testing how a nuclear ram jet would *really* work in the strange atmosphere of Jupiter.

Very gently, something rocked Kon-Tiki. Falcon tried to ignore it.

Ignition had been planned ten kilometers higher than this, in an atmosphere of less than a quarter of the density—and 30 degrees cooler. Too bad.

What was the shallowest dive he could get away with for the air scoops to work? When the ram ignited, he'd be heading *toward* Jupiter, with two and a half *g* to help him get there. Could he possibly pull out in time?

A large, heavy hand patted the balloon. The whole vessel bobbed up and down, like one of the yo-yos that had just become the craze back on Earth.

Of course, Brenner *might* be perfectly right. Perhaps it was just trying to be friendly. Maybe he should try to talk to it over the radio. Which should it be: "Pretty pussy"? "Down, Fido!"? or "Take me to your leader"?

The tritium-deuterium ratio was correct. He was ready to light the candle, with a hundred-million-degree match.

The thin tip of the tentacle came slithering round the edge of the balloon, only twenty meters away. It was about the size of an elephant's trunk and by the delicate way it was moving, appeared to be almost as sensitive. There were little palps at its very end, like questing mouths. He was sure that Dr. Brenner would be fascinated.

This seemed about as good a time as any. He gave a swift scan of the entire control board, started the final four-second ignition count, broke the safety seal and pressed the JETTISON switch.

There was a sharp explosion and an instant loss of weight. Kon-Tiki was falling freely, nose down. Overhead, the discarded balloon was racing upward, dragging the inquisitive tentacle with it. Falcon had no time to see if the gasbag actually hit the medusa, because at that moment the ram jet fired and he had other matters to think about.

A roaring column of hot hydrohelium was pouring out of the reactor nozzles, swiftly building up thrust—but *toward* Jupiter, not away from it. He could not pull out yet, for vector control was too sluggish. Unless he could gain complete control and achieve horizontal flight within the next five seconds, the vehicle would dive too deeply into the atmosphere and would be destroyed.

With agonizing slowness—those five seconds seemed like fifty—he managed to flatten out, then pull the nose upward. He glanced back only once and caught a final glimpse of the medusa many kilometers away. Kon-Tiki's discarded gasbag had apparently escaped from its grasp, for he could see no sign of it.

Now he was master once more—no longer drifting helplessly on the winds of Jupiter but riding his own column of atomic fire back to the stars. The ram jet would steadily give him velocity and altitude, until he had reached near orbital speed at the fringes of the atmosphere. Then, with a brief burst of pure rocket power, he would regain the freedom of space.

Halfway to orbit, he looked south and saw the tremendous enigma of the Great Red Spot—that floating island twice the size of Earth—coming up over the horizon. He stared into its mysterious beauty until the computer warned him that conversion to rocket thrust was only sixty seconds ahead, then tore his gaze reluctantly away.

"Some other time," he murmured.

"What's that?" said Mission Control. "What did you say?"

"It doesn't matter," he replied.

BETWEEN TWO WORLDS

"You're a hero now, Howard," said Webster, "not just a celebrity. You've given them something to think about—injected some excitement into their lives. Not one in a million will actually travel to the Outer Giants —but the whole human race will go in imagination. And that's what counts."

"I'm glad to have made your job a little easier."

Webster was too old a friend to take offense at the note of irony. Yet it surprised him; this was not the first change in Howard that he had noticed since the return from Jupiter.

The administrator pointed to the famous sign on his desk, borrowed from an impresario of an earlier age: ASTONISH ME!

"I'm not ashamed of my job. New knowledge, new resources—they're all very well. But men also need novelty and excitement. Space travel has become routine; you've made it a great adventure once more. It will be a long, long time before we get Jupiter pigeonholed. And maybe longer still before we understand those medusae. I still think that one *knew* where your blind spot was. Anyway, have you decided on your next move? Saturn, Uranus, Neptune—you name it."

"I don't know. I've thought about Saturn, but I'm not really needed there. It's only one gravity, not two and a half like Jupiter. So men can handle it."

Men, thought Webster. He said men. He's never done that before. And when did I last hear him use the word we? He's changing—slipping away from us.

"Well," he said aloud, rising from his chair to conceal his slight uneasiness. "Let's get the conference started. The cameras are all set up and everyone's waiting. You'll meet a lot of old friends."

He stressed the last word, but Howard showed no response; the leathery mask of his face was becoming more and more difficult to read. Instead, he rolled back from the administrator's desk, unlocked his undercarriage so that it no longer formed a chair and rose on his hydraulics to his full seven feet of height. It had been good psychology on the part of the surgeons to give him that extra twelve inches as some compensation for all else that he had lost when the Queen had crashed.

He waited until Webster had opened the door, then pivoted neatly on his balloon tires and headed for it at a smooth and silent thirty kilometers an hour. The display of speed and precision was not flaunted arrogantly; already, it was quite unconscious.

Howard Falcon, who had once been a man and could still pass for one over a voice circuit, felt a calm sense of achievement—and, for the first time in years, something like peace of mind. Since his return from Jupiter, the nightmares had ceased. He had found his role at last.

He knew now why he had dreamed about that superchimp aboard the doomed Queen Elizabeth. Neither man nor beast, it was between two worlds; and so was he.

He alone could travel unprotected on the lunar surface; the life-support system inside the metal cylinder that had replaced his fragile body functioned equally well in space or under water. Gravity fields ten times that of Earth were an inconvenience but nothing more. And no gravity was best of all.

The human race was becoming more remote from him, the ties of kinship more tenuous. Perhaps these air-breathing, radiation-sensitive bundles of unstable carbon compounds had no right beyond the atmosphere; they should stick to their natural homes—Earth, Moon, Mars.

Some day, the real masters of space would be machines, not men—and he was neither. Already conscious of his destiny, he took somber pride in his unique loneliness—the first immortal, midway between two orders of creation.

He would, after all, be an ambassador; between the old and the new—between the creatures of carbon and the creatures of metal who must one day supersede them.

Both would have need of him in the troubled centuries that lay ahead.

1971

SELECTIONS FROM THE PUBLISHER OF THE BEST SCIENCE FICTION IN THE WORLD

———◆———

GODS AND GOLEMS	Lester del Rey
THE NEUTRAL STARS	Dan Morgan & John Kippax
BLOODHYPE	Alan Dean Foster
ARRIVE AT EASTERWINE	R. A. Lafferty
THE CLOUD WALKER	Edmund Cooper
THE ALIEN CONDITION	edited by Stephen Goldin
DAVY	Edgar Pangborn
A WORLD OF TROUBLE	Robert E. Toomey, Jr.
TRULLION—Alastor: 2262	Jack Vance
THE END BRINGERS	Douglas R. Mason
RIGHT-HANDED WILDERNESS	Robert Wells
THE BEST SCIENCE FICTION OF THE YEAR, #2	edited by Terry Carr
TO RIDE PEGASUS	Anne McCaffrey
TRANSFER TO YESTERDAY	Isidore Haiblum
THE PROTECTOR	Larry Niven
THE FLIGHT OF THE HORSE	Larry Niven
DYING INSIDE	Robert Silverberg
ALPHA 4	edited by Robert Silverberg
TRAITOR TO THE LIVING	Philip José Farmer

THE CHRONICLES
OF COUNTER-EARTH

John Norman

TARNSMAN OF GOR
OUTLAW OF GOR
PRIEST-KINGS OF GOR
NOMADS OF GOR
ASSASSIN OF GOR
RAIDERS OF GOR
CAPTIVE OF GOR

Here is the magnificent world of Gor, known also as Counter-Earth, a planet as strangely populated, as threatening, as beautiful as any you are likely to encounter in the great works of fiction. Here too is Tarl Cabot—the one picked out of millions to be trained and schooled and disciplined by the best teachers, swordsmen, bowmen on Gor . . . Toward what end, what mission, what purpose?

Only Gor holds the answer